When the old man died

Richard Patton's first murder case as a Detective Inspector was straightforward, and resulted in a conviction. Now, ten years later, that conviction is quashed on a technicality involving unsafe evidence. This Richard naturally finds very disturbing, but even more so when Julian Caine, released from prison, pays him a visit.

It is not enough, claims Caine, to be released on such grounds. He wants Richard to prove his positive innocence. As this can be done only by discovering another, and true, murderer, Richard is reluctant to tackle it after so long a lapse of time.

But gradually he realizes that his original efforts were far from satisfactory. His self-esteem is now at stake. And always haunting him is the grandfather clock. Was it stopped deliberately in order to provide a faked alibi? Or did it stop at the moment Eric Prost died?

It is only after an illegal midnight 'court' and a shoot-out in the dark that Richard finds himself with an answer.

WHEN
THE OLD MAN
DIED

Roger Ormerod

Constable · London

First published in Great Britain 1991
by Constable & Company Ltd
3 The Lanchesters, 162 Fulham Palace Road
London W6 9ER
Copyright © 1991 by Roger Ormerod
The right of Roger Ormerod to be
identified as the author of this Work
has been asserted by him in accordance
with the Copyright, Designs and Patents Act 1988
ISBN 0 09 470540 2
Set in Linotron 10pt Palatino by
CentraCet, Cambridge
Printed in Great Britain by
St Edmundsbury Press Limited
Bury St Edmunds, Suffolk

A CIP catalogue record for this book
is available from the British Library

This book is dedicated to my friend, Peter Everall, for once more helping so much in the preparation. I would also like to thank Frank Spittle for his assistance on weaponry.

R.O.

My grandfather's clock was too large for the shelf
So it stood ninety years on the floor.
It was taller by half than the old man himself,
And it weighed not a pennyweight more.

It was bought on the morn of the day that he was born,
And 'twas always his pleasure and pride,
But it stopped, short, never to go again
When the old man died.

Extract from a song by Henry Clay Work (1832–1884)

1

I was at least given prior warning, though it was fortunate that Amelia was out shopping with Mary, otherwise there would perhaps have been what she calls 'strong words'. But really, the criticism was only implied, and I could persuade myself that it was, indeed, no more than a hint of things to come.

He introduced himself in the front porch as Chief Superintendent Wainwright. 'May I have a few words with you, Mr Patton?' he asked. Without the introduction I might have taken him for a farmer or a retired wrestler. Bulky, tough, inflexible, that was Wainwright, his voice surprisingly soft and low pitched, his face . . . well, a face, all chunks as though it'd been thrown together casually, not enough room having been left to accommodate his teeth, which seemed to be trying to escape.

'You *are* Inspector Richard Patton?' he asked, raising bushy eyebrows in interrogation.

'I am. Retired.' As he would very well know. 'Come in. I'm alone at the moment.' That was a hint that he didn't need to be reticent. Had he come to tell me they'd doubled my pension? More likely that they'd cancelled it, I thought morosely. I'd been in opposition to the police, if not in actual conflict, a number of times since my retirement. But if that had been the problem I'd have been called to face a board.

'In here,' I said. 'There's a fire. Rather chilly for the time of the year, don't you think? Perhaps you'd care for a drink?'

'Thank you, no.' He nodded to indicate he recognized my pose of bland confidence.

That he had come alone indicated something unusual. An officer of his rank would, in any event, rarely move from his desk, and if he did venture into the great outdoors he would do so only if accompanied by, say, a chief inspector and probably a sergeant, if only to display his dignity and authority. But he was alone, not even with somebody to take notes. I was intrigued, minimally concerned, but not vastly impressed.

He stood in our living-room, undisguisedly staring round to take it all in. We had finished redecorating it only recently. To me, there seemed to be more light in it than before, though he wouldn't know that. It was certainly more welcoming, having acquired a companionable clutter. I gestured him to one of the wing-back easy chairs. He hitched his trousers, perched one ankle on the other knee, and relaxed. He was wearing short socks. His feet were huge.

'Nice place you've got.'

'Yes. More correctly, it's my wife's.' I frowned to myself, reaching for my pipe. Damn him, he'd got me on the defensive already, as though I needed to explain a source of wealth not expected of a retired inspector. But he merely nodded, apparently not in any way interested.

'How's your memory, Mr Patton?' he asked.

'Memory? Depends. Better visual than with figures or dates. And names! I'm hopeless on names.'

He stared for a moment at his knee, as though nonplussed by such an admission, but when he looked up there were crinkles about his eyes, as though he too had the same trouble, and sympathized. But after all, he'd have people to remember figures and dates for him.

'What if I mention Eric Prost?' An eyebrow was cocked, his teeth gleamed. 'And Julian Caine?' Another pause. 'Arthur Pierce?'

'Wait a minute.' I snapped my fingers, drew on my pipe, and got it. 'That'd be nine or ten years ago. My first big case as an inspector, that was. Yes. My first murder. Eric Prost was shot. Julian Caine got life for it. But . . . Arthur Pierce . . . I'm not certain.'

My mind was now racing. I'd been having a quiet afternoon nap on that wet and chilly May afternoon, vaguely wondering how Amelia and Mary were coping with the shops in Worcester.

8

So I'd been a little fuzzy when woken abruptly by the doorbell. Not now. I'd detected the direction of his interest.

'You'd perhaps remember Pierce better as Detective Constable Pierce,' he suggested.

'Of course! Just transferred from the uniformed branch. Ah yes! Smart, brisk. Little moustache. Eager and helpful, but kept his thoughts to himself.'

'You'd have preferred suggestions and ideas? Perhaps he was nervous.'

'Perhaps.' I was watching him, trying to appear casual. But every word he said probably had a meaning. He wasted nothing.

'But you thought he was sharp enough to have ideas of his own?' he persisted gently.

'He wasn't with us for long, as I remember it. Not really long enough to get to know him. He wasn't the sort of person to lay himself open. Not chummy, if you see what I mean. But he did his job, didn't argue, went by the book.' Which, I thought, should please a senior officer.

He smiled. It wasn't a splendid thing to observe. 'For your information, he was Chief Superintendent Pierce.' He paused. 'At the end.'

'End?'

'He died. A month ago. It was a car accident, way up north somewhere.' He left it at that, then changed his mind. 'He was only forty.'

I didn't know what he expected from me in answer to that. I could feel no grief, no sense of loss. I'd not really known Pierce. Yet there'd been mention of the Eric Prost case. What the hell was this all about?

'I'm sorry,' I murmured.

'Yes. A wheel came off.' His tone hadn't changed. Steadily he plodded on. 'Stupid. The steering-wheel, it was.'

'Came off?'

'Apparently. In his hands. He was travelling fast.'

There was another short silence. An officer of his authority would give away nothing of himself. Yet there'd been a hint of dry and sardonic humour. I couldn't guess how he would be with a genuine suspect. They all have their personal techniques.

I couldn't decide whether he was driving and forceful, or very subtle and patient. In the end I ventured, 'But the car would continue in a straight line, surely.'

'Yes, so it would. But he was going round a bend at the time. Unfortunately.'

'Why're you telling me this, Mr Wainwright?' I asked. 'Are you saying there was foul play? Why would I be interested?'

He put down one leg, then lifted the other into place. Spreading the load. He grabbed hold of an ankle and drew himself forward. 'Just putting you in the picture, Mr Patton. That's all. This is supposed to be a friendly chat. So I'll tell you my guess is foul play, but it's not my concern, not my region. The word is that he was very much hated, a lot of villains feared him, and he'd tramped on a lot of toes and heads and fingers to get where he was. But a top-class officer. Make no mistake. His record shows that. What he did was always tight and correct in every detail. Now he's dead. Mind you, he didn't die at once. No. In hospital, he had time to make a deposition. There was one tiny error in his whole career, and it'd been haunting him. Apparently, he didn't want to take it with him, where he was going. Guess what it was. Go on. Have a guess.'

'How can I possibly . . . oh, hell, you're talking about the Eric Prost killing, aren't you?'

He leaned back and slapped his bulging thigh. 'Got it in one go. And his mistake? He put a dustbin lid back on. Now isn't that marvellous . . . really splendid? How many of us go through our careers with only one piddling error to haunt us? A dustbin lid! Whatever next!'

He had come to tell me about a dustbin lid? No, he hadn't. There had to be a bit more behind it than that.

'What about the dustbin lid?' I asked, keeping things moving.

He seemed to be enjoying himself, reaching up to run his fingers through a tight mass of hair that I'd thought to be a wig, but surely couldn't be, then rubbing his hands all over his face to rearrange its more unfortunate chunks into perhaps a less unacceptable pattern.

'It was your case,' he said. 'You've got a right to know. Another couple of days on it and you'd have had a super from DHQ taking it over. But you cleared it in . . . how long?'

'A week. It was straightforward. One day on the site, six for reports and statements. That's how long.'

'Hmm!' Fingertips together, tapping his lips, his eyes bright above them. 'Tell me how straightforward.'

'You'll have read the file.'

'All the same – as you remember it, please. Anything that slips your memory, then I might be able to help you. Just as you remember it.'

It was all coming back, and quite clearly, that dreary and unkempt house in its large patch of scruffy ground, part weeds and overgrowth, part mud, the outbuildings nearly collapsing and the fences untended. Eric Prost had lived there alone, with his clocks hectically ticking his life away. Eric Prost, grouchy and anti-social, suspected of writing scurrilous letters to all and sundry – what they used to call poison pen. But in our modern society very little is sufficiently reprehensible to bring about any shivers of apprehension, certainly not to spark a murderous assault. Yet it's impossible to prove such a thing, and there'd been no reports of abusive letters. Nevertheless, he'd apparently been writing one, of a threatening nature, at the time of his death.

It was the milkman who'd phoned in. He'd been late on his rounds that morning, ten o'clock when he reached Winter Haven, as Prost called it. And there were no empty bottles on the step. So he'd gone round the side of the house, and a desk lamp was still switched on in the study, or whatever Prost called it. Office, perhaps. Ten o'clock on a bright morning in late September. Yes – it would be getting on for ten years ago. Prost was head down, facing away from the window with his cheek resting on the desk surface. The milkman shouted through the hole in the window pane, that critically important hole in one corner of a pane, clearly done years before, and no attempt made to replace it. It was four inches across, enough to shout through. The milkman had shouted, but got no response. Sensibly he'd withdrawn and phoned the police. We'd got there at ten-thirty, myself a crisply new detective inspector, Sergeant Ken Latchett, and DCs Burton, Thomas . . . and Pierce.

'Yes,' I said. 'It's all coming back now. I got in easily. The doors were locked, but there were no chains. All the windows

11

were latched, upstairs and downstairs, some of the latches rusted solid. But the side door was so floppy in its frame that I could slip the latch easily.'

'No need to break anything.'

'Exactly. Anyway, I walked into that study place, glass crunching under my feet – I remember that, because of the question of access to the room. It was all over the floor behind the door. It swept an arc in it. I was thinking of access in and out, of course. We didn't know, at that stage, exactly how Prost had died.'

'Glass from where?'

'The face of the grandfather clock standing by the side of the door into the room.'

'Long-case,' he said.

'Pardon?'

'Long-case clocks, they're called. Not grandfather. That name was given to them because of an old song.'

'Thank you. I'll treasure that. So . . . Eric Prost was head down on one of his letters, half written. I couldn't see how he'd died, as there wasn't much blood. At that time there was no suggestion of foul play, though the glass was suggestive. But the ME turned up a few minutes later. It was a bullet. Small calibre. Twenty-two, as it turned out, from a target-pistol. There's a vulnerable point just at the nape of the neck . . .'

'Yes, yes.' He was impatient.

To hell with him. I went on steadily. 'While the ME was looking at him, I went out and set the others on a general search. The usual. Footprints . . . ha, the milkman had ruined whatever there might've been beneath the window, but that was where we found the two cartridge cases, and the pistol itself was in a dustbin . . .'

'Now hold it right there,' he said, breathing heavily on the words. 'You've got to the dustbin. Think now before you speak. Try to recall it exactly.'

'It was nearly ten years ago.'

'All the same – try.'

I took a little time refilling my pipe. Think before you speak? I said evenly, 'I'd gone back inside. Now that the ME had said a bullet killed him, I looked again at the clock. The long-case clock. It'd stopped at eight-ten, and I could see a bullet had done that too. Shattered the glass front to the face, and stopped it. The second bullet.'

'Second?' Very gently, that was said.

'If it'd been the first shot that shattered the clock-face, then Eric Prost would've reacted. Lifted his head or something. Jumped out of his skin, more likely. The bullet in the base of his skull, the ME said, must've penetrated at an upwards angle, so his head must have been bent. Writing. All right?'

He considered me for a few moments, then his lips twitched and he nodded. I went on.

'The clock, as I said, had stopped at eight-ten.'

'Which meant nothing.'

'I've read detective stories, Chief Super. Smashed watches, smashed clocks, all apparently linked in time to the killing! Who's going to fall for that, these days? So I assumed it meant nothing, except a possibly faked alibi, and as it turned out the obvious suspect could've faked it easily. And probably nobody else. But eight-ten did fit as the time of the shootings. In a way.'

He held up a finger to stop me. His voice was casual. 'What kind of way?'

I'd been about to explain that. He was prodding now, trying to force words from me before I'd considered them and marshalled them into their correct order. Deliberately, I was speaking slower, and with more precision, striving to frame sentences that couldn't be misinterpreted.

'This was a Tuesday, I recall. Tuesday morning. The previous evening there'd been a bit of a downpour, from about eight until nine. Enough to leave the surface muddy in places. The two shell cases we found beneath the window had been tramped into the mud by the milkman. But while I was inside, talking to the ME – that was old Dr Blessingham, very reliable – anyway, along came DC Pierce, and he said he'd found the weapon. I went out with him, and there it was.'

'Where?'

'I was about to tell you,' I said gently. 'There was a dustbin, round the back of the house and near a corner of one of the outbuildings. It was full of what looked like hedge clippings, and this pistol was lying there on the top, just waiting to be found.'

He swung his leg down, leaning foward far enough to tap my knee with a hard finger. Every word, now, seemed to be critically important. 'He hadn't touched the weapon?'

'Of course not.'

'You asked him?'

'No. He just lifted the lid, and there it was.'

'Ah!' He slumped back. 'Lifted the lid off. And that lid was . . . where? When he got to the dustbin, where had the lid been? Did he say?'

It annoyed me that I couldn't see what was worrying him. All this fuss! 'On the ground. Beside the dustbin.'

'Did he tell you that?'

'No. He didn't have to. There was a circular area that was dry, on the ground beside the dustbin. He lifted the lid off the dustbin, said something like, "there it is," and dropped the lid down on the dry patch.'

'Handle up?'

'What?'

'Did he drop it with the handle upwards?'

'Well . . . yes. Surely that's natural.'

'And you noticed nothing strange about it?'

'About the lid, d'you mean? No – nothing. I was looking at the pistol.'

'Yes. You would be,' he conceded.

'A twenty-two target-pistol, it turned out to be. A semi-automatic. One of those with a specially shaped handgrip.'

'And?'

'And what? What else *is* there? When I checked with our office, I found it was licensed to a Mr Julian Caine. Two shots had been fired from a full load. The fatal bullet was later shown to have been fired from it. The one that hit the clock-face was distorted, but the weight of metal matched. Caine was at his pistol club that evening from eight to ten, which checked out, and would've had to drive very close to Eric Prost's place. It all tied in. No fingermarks on the weapon, of course.'

'And the pistol? Anything about it that told you something relating to the timing? You suggested there was.'

14

I played with the cold pipe in my fingers. Carefully now. I'd realized my voice had become rather too crisp, too challenging. 'It was wet, if that's what you mean.' I watched his head incline minimally, a reaction he'd been unable to repress. His eyes gleamed, his teeth showed themselves in a brief grimace of pleasure. 'It'd rained. The previous evening,' I reminded him, as though he might be a little slow on the uptake.

No flicker of expression crossed his face. 'And that, you assumed, meant that the pistol had been lying there, open to the sky, since some time before the rain stopped, which had been nine the previous evening?'

I hesitated a moment. His voice had warned me that this was the critical question. 'That was the obvious conclusion, the gun being wet.'

'Open to the sky, you said.'

'Yes. The dry patch on the ground indicated that.'

'The dry patch and the wet dustbin lid?' he prodded.

I sighed. 'What're you getting at, Chief Super? I'm tired of all this fencing.'

'Pierce's deposition. He states that when he reached that dustbin the lid was lying upside-down on the ground. Handle down. He made a mistake – a kind of instinct he claimed – by putting on the lid, to sort of protect the weapon from any outside contamination, while he went to find you. And it'd been upside-down, so that rain-water had collected in it, and before he realized what he was doing water had slopped out of it into the dustbin.' He gave me a thin smile. '*Now do you see?*'

'I see. Oh yes, I see. You're saying the weapon could've been dry when he found it. Did he mention, in this deposition of his, that it *was* dry?'

'He states that he didn't notice.'

We sat silent, staring at each other. It was good of him to give me time to assimilate it. In the end, it was I who broke the tension, and tension it was. 'You're saying that I ought to have noticed the top of the dustbin lid was dry. Right. I'll concede that. But my attention was naturally on the pistol . . .' I stopped. I was fumbling for excuses, but I didn't have to express them aloud. He was smiling, having at last jolted me into a positive reaction.

15

'It means', he said ponderously, 'that your case wasn't sound. That's what we've decided. The evidence, as presented to the court, wasn't safe, because there was no mention of the dustbin lid incident. Not your fault . . . perhaps. But the fact is that the weapon *could* have been dry, when found. It could therefore have been discarded at a later time than your estimate. Not *before* nine o'clock, but possibly after the rain had stopped on that Monday evening.'

He put his hands on the chair arms and levered himself to his feet. I was a second or so behind him; he'd moved abruptly. My voice was challenging, my intention being to retain him a little longer. It was all very well for him to make bland statements on evidence – it was his job, and he was paid for that sort of thing. But now he'd touched on the legal aspects of it, and I couldn't see why he should assume I was completely ignorant.

'You know damn well the time issue wasn't important,' I told him decisively. 'We'd got no positive time of death, no time the shots were fired, which needn't have been the same. The only fixed time was the one shown on that clock-face, and *that* could've been faked. Now you're talking about the time the pistol was dumped. What the hell does that matter? On his way to his club, or on his way back! It's just a load of bull, and you know it. I could've presented just as good a case if the gun'd been dry when Pierce found it. I assumed it'd been wet. Either way – what's all the sweat about? If you've read the file with any care, you'll know what I mean. I'd got just as good a case.'

Heading for the door, he paused, glancing at me, just a hint of a smile lurking at the corners of his mouth. 'But it wouldn't have been the same case as the one presented to the jury. That's the legal point.'

'Specious!' I said. 'Piffling.'

'Ah yes. But you know how it is, these days. They're nervous, way up the top there. Any little point – anything – and they start wondering. Has justice been done? Seen to have been done. They're like old maids dithering over an embroidery pattern. We've got to live with it, Patton.'

Outside in the hall our boxer, Sheba, was waiting. She'd heard voices and had sensed the mood. There was a gentle, warning grumble deep in her throat. I put a hand on her head and held open the front door for Wainwright.

'And now?' I asked.

'The report'll move up the ladder. Maybe the DPP or the Home Secretary will take it to the Appeal Court themselves, if they're not happy. I don't know. We're still working on it. They might want a statement from you, but I think not. We'll let you know, if necessary.'

'Right.'

I watched him go, being careful not to close the front door until he'd turned his car and driven away. Subtle, I decided, that was what he'd been. No hectoring, no crisp questions, he'd simply stated the facts, dangling a bait and teasing out a distant memory. And he'd gone away with the response he'd wanted. What was it all about, anyway? A dustbin lid that'd been dry on the top, and I hadn't noticed. If I had, it probably wouldn't have meant anything. The ground would've remained wet when a metal lid could quite well have dried. As could the weapon itself, come to think of it. Nothing, that was what it all meant. But I knew I was simply indulging in self-justification, because that wasn't the real point. DC Pierce had wrongly replaced the lid, and I'd been aware of that fact. I should have rapped his knuckles for that and produced the basic fact; that he'd slopped water on the weapon in a murder case.

I didn't need Wainwright to ram that down my throat. I knew it. I blamed myself. A man had gone to prison, and not because Pierce had made a mistake, but because I hadn't spotted it.

Suddenly I realized that the Chief Superintendent's attitude had warped my thinking. There I was, pondering the technicalities of evidence presentation and its psychological effect on a jury, and I was completely ignoring the vital issue. Was Caine or was he not guilty? That was what mattered. And I recalled distinctly that I'd been convinced he was as guilty as hell.

Considerably cheered, I took Sheba for a walk. But she was not her usual happy self. She sensed my underlying mood of self-reproach. The walk did neither of us any good.

I had to decide whether I needed to tell Amelia. It is just the sort of thing that always annoys her, and she would instantly leap to my defence, as though I'd done something marginally

17

criminal. And I would feel obliged to justify Wainwright's thinking on it, and thus irritate her even more.

But it's tricky, keeping these minor secrets from your wife. I might never hear another thing about it, but if I did I'd have a hell of a job justifying my silence. Besides, I would be uneasy, keeping anything at all from her, so, by the time she returned home, I'd decided to tell her.

But it was very much later that I got round to it, as she and Mary were still mentally embroiled in their trip, still uncertain their choices had been wise, still regretting rejections of this, that and the other. But the appropriate occasion eventually arose.

'How ridiculous!' my wife predictably stated. 'As though it matters.' Thus she dismissed my twenty-minute exposition.

Justice, rightness, the truth! None of these could I present to her. She has always denigrated what she calls playing with words, when, to her, as it had been to me, the basic important fact is: did he do it or did he not? If he did, then what could it matter what exact words were spoken in court?

'Did he?' she demanded.

'Yes. Clearly.'

'Well then . . .'

'The jury were possibly misled.'

'You see! Playing with words. You men!'

'The barrister for the defence, I recall, was a woman.'

'That's no excuse.'

As there was no answer to that I grinned at her, and we dropped the subject. Forgot it. She did, anyway, and I very nearly managed to, because nothing happened for four months, not even a hint from my former superiors or an item from the news media. Nothing, until he came in person. Julian Caine. There he was, in the front porch, and I knew him at once. In a second. Perhaps, subconsciously, he'd been on my mind, and I'd been carrying around the mental image.

'I've been expecting you,' I said. A lie does no harm, when all I intended was to relax him. He was a quivering mass of tension, clearly believing I would simply throw him out, which wouldn't have been difficult as I must have been twice his size. I'd been putting on weight; the prison had been stripping it

18

from him. Not that he'd ever been physically impressive, small and slim and naturally neat, but the sort of person you see and forget. I hoped he'd managed to preserve his hands. These were his major physical attribute. Julian Caine, murderer of Eric Prost, was an expert on antique firearms and antique clocks, a repairer and restorer. Had been. I didn't know what he was now.

'You wouldn't guess the trouble I've had finding you,' he said, trying to disguise his uncertainty.

I took him through to the living-room, where both Amelia and Sheba eyed him suspiciously. I introduced him. Amelia was still suspicious, but Sheba waved the undocked stump of her tail tentatively. I settled him in a chair, and Sheba moved over. Without hesitation, Caine fondled an ear, then looked up quickly.

'A pleasure that's been denied me for ten years,' he explained. Sheba crooned deep in her throat. Caine glanced at Amelia apologetically, and she grimaced, not quite a smile.

'What's happened?' I asked.

'My conviction's been quashed. I've been released. Big deal, as they say inside. I was due for parole, anyway.'

'It's the same as a not-guilty verdict,' I assured him, not really believing that myself.

'No it's not. Nobody believes I didn't do it. I've got off on a technicality, that's all it is. Got off. Tcha! It's as bad as that Scottish thing: not proven.'

I was considering him more carefully now. There were changes, as of course there would be. Prison had hit him hard. That wide, intellectual brow was furrowed, the hair receding now, but thicker at the neck. And his eyes, so bright and mellow they'd been, were sunken and defensive, never quite meeting mine. He seemed to stare steadfastly at my left ear. The cheeks, too, were sunken, lending prominence to his cheek-bones and stretching his mouth, which now had a sour line to it. His chin I couldn't comment on, as he'd previously worn a trim beard and was now clean-shaven. It seemed to jut, a stubborn, unresponsive thrust at life and its problems.

He touched his chin, having noticed my attention. 'I shaved it off. It was turning grey. At my age!'

19

What would he be? Fifty? Probably. I didn't want to argue with him about hair changes or about legal complexities, but that was clearly why he'd come.

'But you're free now,' I said quietly. 'Your business . . . you'll surely have that to return to. Your antiques . . .'

He shrugged. 'I can drop back into it. If people will let me.'

I nodded. Whatever the law said, he would still be considered guilty in his own community.

'You've come to me . . .' I began.

'It was your case,' he pointed out tentatively, then he waited.

'And?'

'And your evidence.'

I said nothing, glancing at Amelia. Slowly, she was shaking her head. No. Whatever it was – no.

'Don't tell me I'm free of it now,' he went on. 'It's not true. All around me, . . . damn it, your people won't even renew my pistol licence.'

I stared at him. No, they wouldn't.

'I can't shoot, can't buy new pistols. Oh, I don't blame them for confiscating my two target-pistols, but they won't give me a licence to buy new ones,' he cried from a deep frustration.

There didn't seem to be anything I could say. Amelia, recognizing my uneasiness, rescued me.

'What is it you want from my husband, Mr Caine?'

Still staring at my ear, he burst out, 'To prove I didn't do it.'

'Mr Caine . . .' I cleared my throat, my voice not sounding quite right. 'You had the motive, you had the opportunity, and it was your pistol.'

'Oh yes,' he said, jerking a hand in the air, as though something there irritated him. 'Yes, I could've killed him. I was certainly mad enough about his stupid complaints. I might have shot *him*. But that clock! I'm supposed to have put a shot into the clock-face. That was a Tompion, Mr Patton. A treasure. I could never, never have brought myself to harm it. Prost yes, the clock no. Of course it wasn't me.'

Then, disconcertingly, he clamped one hand over his mouth and began silently to weep.

Sheba went and hid behind the settee. There was nowhere for me to hide.

2

I assured Amelia she would like the trip, trying not to press the issue because I didn't want to stiffen the opposition.

'A small country town,' I told her. 'Intriguing shops, though I must admit they seem to specialize in antiques around there. But you'd like that, and the old bridge is very attractive.'

'Thank you, Richard,' she said, 'but no, I think not. You know very well that I don't approve, but I'm not going to try to dissuade you, if you want to go there.'

But it wouldn't be the same. I was used to having her at my shoulder, noticing the tiny details I might miss, offering advice and suggestions.

'It's only thirty miles.'

'Then it'll be a pleasant run for you, across country. I'm sure you'll enjoy yourself,' she told me.

Enjoy myself? I didn't expect to. The case was now exactly ten years old, and there was little I could expect to extract that would be new to me. Well . . . this one trip . . . I'd call it a memory prodder. Nothing more. But, as I'd pointed out to Caine, it was impossible to prove a negative. What he wanted, what he made almost a demand as of right, was that I should prove his innocence. How? That was what I'd demanded. Nothing had changed.

'By proving who really did do it,' he had said, which, after a gap of ten years, would be almost impossible, even if I could bring myself to accept that it hadn't been him.

Yet, at the back of my mind, there was an awareness that I myself had changed in that length of time. It was almost with embarrassment that I remembered that younger Richard Patton,

21

the new inspector who'd been determined to get everything exactly correct. The procedures, the evidence, the presentation of the case, all those had to be precise and beyond reproach. Facts, facts, that was what I'd aimed for. Black was black and white was white. How very pragmatic I'd been at that time!

Now I'd changed. It was not so much a softening of attitude as a broadening, which had begun from the time I first met Amelia. It had been her fault, her influence. Now, because I'd become very suspicious of blacks that were impenetrable and whites that were too brilliant, there was even a touch of healthy cynicism creeping in, truth consisting of so many shades of grey. Facts, I was beginning to realize, when they involved people, could still be laid down on paper, as solid and indisputable as they'd always been, but now I could pick up that sheet of paper and move it around. Turn it on edge, and those facts became so thin that they melted away. Turn it over and hold it to a strong, harsh light of scrutiny, and they reversed themselves, left to right, backwards to forwards. The same facts.

There seemed to be no harm, therefore, in examining the facts all over again, with a more open mind, in so far as I could drag them from the past. No harm at all.

So I journeyed to the town of Markham Prior without Amelia to appeal to, when she was really the only one who would understand such an appeal. Part of me was missing.

The small town lies in a bend of the river Penk, a tributary of the Severn, so that there are two bridges, one as you come in from the Bridgnorth road, sweeping down the flank of Markham Hill and emerging from the trees that clothe the slope so that the town is spread out in one tight grouping, like a child's conglomeration of building blocks, compact and contained in the bend of the river, but now visibly edging outwards into the surrounding countryside. There's a motorway lurking just ten miles the other side of Markham Prior. Commuters are discovering the town, and the thin line of the Borough Surveyor's map that marks the edge of the Green Belt is gradually being moved a little this way, a little that, to accommodate new construction.

The bridge to which I was heading was the old one, a double-arch constructed when the stones were shaped to hold themselves together with their own weight. *Limit – 5 tons*, the sign stated. The other bridge, the far side of town, is modern, utility, stressed concrete. Very practical.

I drifted the Stag along the high street. It wasn't very wide. They'd originally planned on the width of two horse-drawn coaches. The congestion was already reaching stopping point. But they had a large car-park just off to the right, behind which there'd been a genuine park at one time, a walk-through park with flowers and grass and a pool with geese on. All gone. One flat stretch of concrete, it was now, and four brick walls.

I parked, bought myself a ticket and stuck it inside my window, and walked out into High Street. Very little had changed since I saw it last, the town having developed naturally from its original country market centre, so that its trend was towards arts and crafts. Everywhere there were leather goods made on the premises, or ceramics, costume jewellery, wood carvings. All handed down, father to son or to daughter. Second-hand bookshops lurked mustily down side passages, and here and there tiny cafés managed still to provide their home-made cakes and scones and muffins. You could smell them baking. So it was a prosperous and bustling little town, attracting visitors who sought to buy what they couldn't get elsewhere.

Caine Antiques was still there, occupying a prominent corner opposite the old horse trough. (Cromwell's horses quenched their thirst here.) And opposite the shop was what pretended to be a town square, but was no more than a negligible widening to accommodate the market stalls. Every Wednesday, market-day, don't expect to get through on anything wider than a pedal cycle.

I stood outside the shop and gazed through the glass, multi-paned in bow-windows. Dim inside. Not much was displayed: a bracket clock dated 1750, and a short-case clock of 1800 by someone called Knibb, in one window; and in the other, round the corner, there were two pistols, a beautifully chased French pin-fire revolver, and an Allen & Wheelock revolver of around 1850, also beautifully worked.

The interior seemed dark. I saw no movement inside.

Procrastinating, I went to have a cup of tea and a toasted teacake, came out and bought a brooch for Amelia, a green

23

stone to match her eyes, set in a filligree of cast white alloy that they'd probably perfected in a room at the back. I wouldn't have been surprised if they'd hacked out the stone themselves, from some alien hillside, and cut and polished it.

Then I made up my mind and went back to Caine's, and walked confidently in through the door. I felt I was taking an irrevocable step forward.

Inside, it wasn't so very dim. It was simply that the lighting was subdued. After all, these were antiques that they were displaying, originally expected to be viewed in the light of oil-lamps or candles, some old enough to have opened their eyes to rushes burning in sconces. And in their present ambience, they glowed.

Here, I knew, Caine displayed principally his clocks. In the rear he had a workshop, where he repaired and renovated the movements and cases where necessary. All this required lathes and craftsmen's tools, and a hell of a lot of experience. If a tooth was missing from a gear in a clock from 1650, he'd have to make another gear with exactly the same tooth profile. Or so he'd told me. His antique firearms collection had been kept at his house, where he had a specially secure room. He would take customers there, to see the display, and any pistol renovation work was done at the house. It was there, too, in that room, that he'd kept his matched pair of Hammerli model 211 target-pistols. What could be safer, he'd said, than that room? Yet, if he was to be believed, one of them had been stolen from there.

Now I came to think about it, I recalled that it was the presence of so much weaponry that had caused his wife to leave him. So he'd claimed.

The sales area was by no means confined to clocks, though I soon realized that the furniture was there to display the clocks. A delicate round table, plain and dignified, perfectly set off an ornate bracket clock. A splendid, maturely glowing Welsh dresser displayed on its shelves another pair of bracket clocks, and negligently laid down, as though left there after a journey, was a flintlock pistol, chased in brass and silver, and a pair of leather gauntlets. Around a corner, the shop being partitioned like a maze so that you always anticipated new and exciting experiences, I found myself faced by a long-case clock, proud

24

and confident and placidly ticking. Beside it there was a squat, black chest, on which were lying four delicately chased pistols, there purely as a decorative contrast.

It seemed to me, at first, that it was strange to match pistols with clocks, in some way anomalous, the clocks signifying the continuity of life, some of those displayed having justified their purpose through ten or fifteen generations, and the pistols signifying sudden death. Yet, come to think of it, there was something chilling in the way a clock ticked away life after life, each second being one less in a personal existence. Callous and cynical. Whereas the pistol's very reason for its existence was the purpose of terminating life abruptly. It could be argued as to which was the more desirable.

But I knew one instance when clocks had marched to the pace of a life, stopping and not continuing at the owner's death.

I was aware, during my gentle ambulations, that a shadowy personage was hovering on the outer edge of my vision. There are degrees to hovering. One doesn't care to be pounced on, yet there are times when a helpful word would be welcome. I turned quickly. It was a woman, whom I marginally recognized. A smile hovered, as she did. She'd understood my reaction.

'If you need any help, I'm here,' she murmured.

'Thank you, but I'm not a genuine customer.'

'We're pleased if people do no more than admire.' It seemed to be a prepared speech.

'I'm absolutely packed with admiration,' I assured her.

She was a trim and slim woman in her forties, dressed simply in a dark, straight dress, with a belt at the waist. Her only jewellery was what I thought at first to be a gold brooch pinned to the breast, but which, I realized, was in fact an antique dress-watch. Everything this side of the entrance fitted into a pattern. She stood now with her head on one side, hair dark but with grey tinges here and there, eyes large, and mouth and chin small.

'I think we've met,' she said softly, her voice even and unstressed, a husky undertone to it.

I'd been thinking the same, though I couldn't place where. Then I could. She was Julian Caine's wife, and I'd seen her at the trial.

'My name is Patton. If it'll help you to remember, it was Inspector Patton . . .'

'Of course!' She bit off the words, cutting me short. 'Julian said he'd been to see you.' She frowned. 'Foolish, of course. What could you expect to do after all this time? Why should you be expected to do anything?'

'I don't know,' I said. 'To both questions.'

'Marie, I . . .' The words came from behind me. She seemed to jerk, a flicker of the nerves, then she was smiling. 'Julian's here now,' she told me. 'He's come, after all, Julian.'

There was a hint in there that she'd expected it, but he not. I turned to face him. Already there were changes in him. No more the almost manic light in his eyes; they were softer and steadier, as had been the tone in his voice when he'd used her name. He was growing his beard again. As he'd said, it was going to be grey, but with a dark streak down the front of his chin.

'So you've come,' he said.

'It doesn't mean anything.'

'Come into my office,' he suggested. 'Marie, you could lock the door for a while if you'd like to hear . . .'

'No, no. I'll stay on duty.' She wrinkled her nose at me. 'But try to remember', she told him, 'every word that's said.' Then she nodded to me and turned away.

'First,' I said to him, 'there's something I want you to show me.' He had his hand on the office door.

'Oh? You're interested in clocks?'

'In craftsmanship, yes. It's the long-case clock.'

He protruded his lips. 'Of course it is.' Which seemed a strange remark to make.

He knew short-cuts back through his maze. Within half a dozen yards we were standing, shoulder to shoulder, staring at it.

I wouldn't consider myself an emotional person, but any aspect of perfection in performance and construction always touches something inside me. I stood and looked at that beauty with a lump in my throat, and perhaps Caine recognized this, applauded it, because when he spoke it was with a laugh in his voice, a joy.

26

'You couldn't afford it, I assure you.'

Oh, he knew I coveted it! 'It depends.'

As with all dealers, he slid from the question of price while he praised the goods. 'It's a Tompion, numbered 481. We know that that places it at 1709, because he kept careful records. He died a few years after that. Burr-walnut case, and the movement is in perfect condition. I know that, because I did some work on it before . . .' He broke off.

'Before the killing?' I asked quietly. 'It looks very like the one at Eric Prost's.'

'It *is* the one.'

I turned and stared at him. 'But it can't be!'

He nodded, a gleam of something in his eyes. 'Yes it is. And it's mine.'

'Could you explain that?'

'Come into my office.' That was because we couldn't know who might be the other side of that partition.

I followed him, needing those few moments in which to think. That clock had belonged to Eric Prost. It had stood in the room where he'd died. His inheritors would have acquired it. Had Julian Caine bought it, through intermediaries, while in prison?

Then we were inside what he called his office. After the mellow, relaxing lighting in the shop, this was a brilliant white, with strip tubes everywhere, so that you'd have had difficulty casting a shadow; might be disturbed to discover you no longer did. A desk in the corner justified the title of office. The rest, the important portion, was his workshop. Whatever equipment Tompion had used, Julian Caine had it, with the addition of a small lathe, vertical millers, and even a forge with crucibles.

'Sometimes', he said, noticing my eyes on it, 'I have to cast my own brass sheet in order to match the original. Their brass was a different formula from the modern stuff, and looks yellower.'

'You do the woodwork, too?' I gestured to the lengths of walnut, oak and mahogany against one wall.

'Where necessary. It has to match. To tell you the truth, Mr Patton, I find the carpentry more difficult than the metalwork.'

'Hmm!' I wandered round. What a life he led; what a

splendid, satisfying life! Out of which he'd lost ten years. 'The clock,' I prompted. 'The Tompion.'

'Yes. It's the one that used to stand beside Eric's door, you'll remember. Facing the window. The one that some wretched vandal put a shot into.'

I cast my mind back. Whatever happened, I was caught in this now, and my mental recall was all I had to work with. The window at Prost's house, through which I'd first peered, had had a hole in the corner of one pane. The door into the passageway beyond the facing wall was a yard from the corner on the right. In that space the clock had been placed, which explained why the shattered glass from its face had been all over the floor, where the door opened into it. Eric Prost had his desk against the right-hand wall, his back to the window. Perhaps he liked to be able to stare at his clock. Seated, as he was, the clock-face would have appeared about two feet above his head to anyone staring through that hole in the window. As I'd explained to Wainwright, the shot at the clock-face had not been a wildly inaccurate one, intended for Prost's head, but must have been the second shot, so apparently intended to stop the clock.

It *had* stopped, indicating eight-ten. The shot that had killed Eric Prost must have been precise and exact, requiring the ability, from that hole in the window, of a marksman. Therefore it was reasonable to assume that the second shot had been intended for exactly what it hit. The clock-face. We'd been looking for a marksman.

I'd checked this at Caine's pistol club. Some of those people, with a twenty-two target-pistol, could pick a pencil from your fingers at twenty-five yards. I didn't check this, though they offered to lend me a pencil. The distance from outside the window, through the hole and aimed at Prost's head, would have been about five yeards. At that range a marksman could have taken the lead from the pencil. Not so an amateur.

They'd lent me a twenty-two target-revolver. In six shots I managed to hit the target only once, the circles not at all. The darned thing, however hard I tried, kept wavering around. And that vital target, that small and vulnerable spot in the nape of

28

Prost's neck, had been very small indeed. Yes, it would've needed a marksman, even at five yards.

I was aware that Caine was staring at me, waiting for my comment on the vandal who'd put a shot into the Tompion. I smiled at him. He'd been such a marksman.

'I remember the clock-face,' I said. 'Tell me why you claim it to be your clock.'

He positively grinned, a fiendish kind of triumphant grin, as though he'd won a point, or was about to. 'You never really dug into it,' he claimed. 'All you found out was that he'd been making public claims that I'd cheated him. He wasn't really sane, you know, not all the time. Otherwise he wouldn't have said the things he did, we being friends.' He smiled at my expression. 'Oh yes we were. Over years. We both loved clocks.'

'And guns?' I asked gently.

'No.' He shook his head. 'We shared only the clocks. He had eleven in all, the Tompion being the prize one. I kept them all in working order for him, and I used to call in to wind them and check them. Every Sunday.'

I held up a hand, cutting into the flow. 'You did tell me that. But I assumed you meant you'd been doing that, but surely hadn't continued to do so, after you'd fallen out . . .'

'Fallen out! He was accusing me of cheating him. Yes, we had rows, yes, we shouted at each other – but I couldn't let him mess with those clocks of his himself. Ham-fisted, that was Eric. So I'd still call every Sunday evening to wind the clocks. All of them were eight-day clocks, including the Tompion. I'd go round the house, checking and winding, while he stood behind me and called me a crook. We were friends, Patton. You don't let a bit of shouting stop you – not with a friend.'

'You didn't tell me this.'

'Why should I? You thought you had a motive – the fact that he was publicly ruining my reputation, because he didn't confine it to me, you know. But why should I have helped you with it?'

I picked up a curved needle-file and stared at it. Even his tools had a delicate grace. 'The prosecution doesn't have to

29

prove a motive, though it helps. We had one, and it was good enough. Now you claim you were friends.'

'I told you.' A hint of impatience entered his voice. 'He went strange after his wife died, over a year before. So I had to allow for that. About a couple of months before he was shot, he was talking about a shortage of cash. Went on and on about it, so I suggested he ought to sell one of the clocks, one of the other ten, and he brooded over it for a while. It'd mean delay, you see, finding and choosing the best auction sale. Then one day I went along and he told me a smart young woman had called and looked at his clocks and made him an offer for the Tompion. From London, he said, driving a Mercedes. Which of course made her a top authority. Unlike me. In comparison, I knew nothing. No man is a prophet in his own country, as they say. You'll never guess how much she'd offered.'

'Tell me.'

'Two thousand.'

'Well now.' It meant nothing to me.

'I was absolutely furious with him. He was set on it, wanted to get it over with, feel the cash in his fingers. I could've killed him.'

'I can understand that.' I cocked my head at him. 'And you did?'

'Don't treat this as a joke, for God's sake!' he burst out.

I blinked. 'Sorry. Carry on.' It was as though he'd slapped me.

'I'd got a few days to do something about it. Then this female wonder would be back. I raised cash from the bank, cash on insurance policies. In the end, I got together three thousand pounds, in cash. I knew I had to work fast, because any smart alec from London was going to be able to better that. I had to persuade Eric, and I was two hours shouting at him. In the end, he agreed. He gave me a receipt and a bill of sale. It was mine!'

'Good for you. And then he found out you'd cheated him?'

'That was how he put it. They came again, two of them this time, with a van. They obviously expected to take it away with them, and you can imagine how furious they'd be when they heard it was sold. Wish I'd been there. But they were annoyed enough to tell him the Tompion's real worth.'

'Which was?'

'Even ten years ago it would've fetched forty thousand at auction. Now . . .' He shrugged. 'Fifty? Sixty?'

I turned away, wandered to his work-bench and ran a finger over its surface. Clean. No dust or swarf. I picked up a brass gear he'd cut, and a steel pinion, meshed them together and held them to the light. A perfect fit. I said quietly, 'You ask me to prove your innocence, and now you build up your motive even stronger than it was before. He would be furious with you. No wonder he went round claiming you were a crook.'

'Well, yes. He really was upset. That's why I left the clock with him, as a kind of insurance. I haven't finished telling you. Listen. You'll have to try to believe this. I intended to put it up for auction, or arrange a private sale. That sort of thing takes time, though, putting feelers out here and there. But I intended to sell it at its genuine value, and pay it over to him. Less the three thousand, and less my commission, of course. You can believe that or not. I don't care. But that was what I intended.'

'And you told him that?'

'I did. He called me a liar and a cheat. Said if I came to collect it he'd take a shotgun to me.'

I looked at him for a long while, searching for truth, but he met my eyes calmly. He'd handed me the perfect motive, and *he* was the sort of marksman who could've fired the killing shot through the hole in that window.

'And now you have the clock?'

'Yes. It's mine.' Again that quiet, proud possessiveness.

I sighed. 'I don't suppose it's worth ten years of your life, though.'

'You don't believe me, do you?'

'What does it matter what I . . . hell, of course it matters. I believe you, yes, but simply because you didn't need to tell me. Your intentions at that time were excellent and honest. That's all very fine. But the shot that killed Prost was from your pistol, and you could've fired it, and because of his death you've acquired the Tompion. On the cheap.'

'I don't see why I should pay his relatives. I've done ten years for it. Put it like that.'

'And the clock gave you an alibi, sort of. You could have put

31

the shot into the face of the clock, which just happened to be showing ten minutes past eight . . .'

'No.'

'No you didn't, or no it wasn't?'

'No to both. I didn't fire a shot at the clock-face, and in any event I was at the club by eight-ten.'

I sighed. 'It was too obvious, Mr Caine. Nobody believed the shot was fired at eight-ten. Nobody on the prosecution side, anyway. Look at it. You tell me you went round every Sunday to wind and check his clocks, however grumpy and inhospitable Eric Prost might've been. *That* Sunday, the day before he died, we reckoned you could have been planning to kill him.'

'I'd never . . .'

'Leave it,' I said sharply. 'I'm talking about that clock and about an alibi. Say you went there that Sunday . . .'

'I didn't. The previous Sunday, but not *that* one.'

'. . . and when you wound the Tompion you put it forward an hour. Would he have noticed? With another ten clocks in the house, would he notice the time shown by the Tompion, or care if he *did* notice? Damn it all, he was wearing a quartz digital watch. He probably never looked at his clocks.'

'I *did* protest. I mean . . . a quartz digital!' It offended him.

'So,' I continued, refusing to be diverted, 'that Tompion of yours could've been showing eight-ten on Monday evening when the time was actually seven-ten, which would be convenient for you on your way to the club. Could have been!' I said sharply, seeing he was about to interrupt again. 'So it would then have been so simple for you to create for yourself an alibi, simply by putting a shot into the clock-face.'

He gave a short bark of laughter. 'Is this a joke? No?' Then his mood switched, and suddenly his voice was crisp, challenging. '*If* I'd gone there that Sunday, it would've been to prepare an alibi? Prepare. That's the word. And if I'd prepared one, why didn't my barrister use it? If you remember, she said nothing about alibis. Nor did your lot.' He seemed proud of that claim, lifting his chin.

'It's not for the prosecution to produce alibis. Your barrister knew the facts. Wisely, she didn't mention an alibi, because she knew we could destroy it.'

32

'You really believe all this?' he asked, contempt in his voice.

'I'm telling you why you were the obvious suspect. It was so easy for you to stop that clock with a bullet in its face.'

For a moment he stared at me blankly, then he tossed his head. 'You believe that?' he repeated. 'You actually believe the bullet stopped the clock? That's nonsense. A twenty-two bullet from a target-pistol would barely jolt the mechanism, certainly not enough to stop it. And it couldn't have penetrated the face-plate and reach the movement. In fact, it didn't. They had to cast their face-plates in those days, I'll have you know. There was no such thing as sheet brass. And they cast them thick. In practice, the bullet made no more than a dent in the face.'

'What the hell d'you think you're playing at?' I demanded with some heat. He was deliberately leading me on, playing on my ignorance, pointing mockingly to all the details I'd failed to probe. 'Your only hope was that clock and the time it showed. At eight-ten you were at your club – proved and checked. Your barrister could've flogged that point, could have said Eric Prost would surely have noticed the clock was wrong – *if* it was wrong – and set it right himself. The jury might have accepted that. Just might. Now you're telling me the bullet couldn't have stopped the clock – and that you knew it couldn't.'

'Exactly.' He was complacent about it. 'So why would I try to fake an alibi that I knew couldn't work?'

'Then what *did* stop the clock?' I demanded impatiently.

He shrugged. 'I don't know. All I'm saying is that the bullet didn't. Just that. Take it or leave it.' He was clearly losing any confidence he might have had in my ability to help him, or my intention to.

I allowed a silence to build up. Out in the shop the chimers were striking the three-quarters. Warily, I considered carrying on the conversation to its logical conclusion, but the conclusion I had to reveal was in no way logical.

I had told nobody. It hadn't even gone down in my report. They would have said I was becoming fanciful, the pragmatic and unimaginative Richard Patton getting strange ideas. But it was the feeling of it I'd been unable to express . . . the facts were positive and unshakable. As I'd walked through that house, after the team and the forensic squad and the body had all gone, I'd been aware of a chill in the air. It was September, and there'd been no fire on for nearly twenty-four hours. Yet it wasn't that kind of a chill. The building held a vacant quality, an atmosphere of evil glee, waiting and watching for my reaction. I do not believe in good and evil, one positive and one negative. To me, they are all on the same plane, all neutral, simply aspects of character, when sometimes one could be mistaken for the other, so closely could they lie together. But these were things of character, of people, and in no way possessed by bricks and mortar. Yet the house had it, as though hatred and fear lurked there. I recalled that I'd been conscious of it, but not aware of its source.

Then I'd noticed the first of the clocks, then another, and eventually accepted the background if not the basis of my uneasiness. It hadn't helped, knowing why. I'd still been glad to get out of the house.

I looked at Caine consideringly, wondering whether I might trust him with it. But he'd trusted me. I spoke therefore abruptly, perhaps with a touch of anger.

'What you don't know, Mr Caine, is that the actual time of death was not necessarily the same time as the shot that killed him. It was in the pathologist's report, and your lawyer would've had a copy of it. No . . . please let me finish. This was a twenty-two target-pistol. Not a killing weapon. Its power wasn't enough to kill outright, as with a larger calibre, unless a sensitive spot was hit. Such as where he *was* shot. It's the reason we knew the murderer had to be a marksman. But the bullet was *in* the brain, two inches . . . I won't go into unpleasant details. The opinion was that Prost could have remained unconscious for some time, perhaps an hour, two even, before actual death took place. You're following me?'

His face stiff and expressionless, he nodded.

'So the clock, even if stopped by the bullet, was not relevant to damn all. We'd got a vague time of death – it's always like that – and a vague time for the shots, and now you tell me the bullet didn't stop the clock! For heaven's sake . . .'

He muttered something. It sounded like, 'It did not.'

I sighed. I'd have loved to light my pipe, but this was his work-room. I desisted, shrugging. 'We're right back to where we were at the trial. The alibi didn't mean anything unless we assumed it was faked. I could see just one way you could've faked it, and now you've shattered that into little bits.'

He just nodded, waiting. He knew I hadn't finished.

'But what you don't know, Mr Caine,' I said heavily, 'and what I didn't put into my report, is something that might – only might – tell us the time he actually died. When I went round that house, every clock, the whole collection, had stopped at eight-ten. Not only the Tompion.'

For several seconds he said nothing, then he raised his chin. There was a strange light in his eyes.

'When the old man died,' he said softly.

'Exactly. And if he *did* die at eight-ten, and the actual death was delayed by, say, an hour, you could still have shot him at seven-ten. So tell me . . . for heaven's sake, and before I decide I've gone crazy . . . how else could the clocks have stopped?'

For a moment he stared at me, then he turned on his heel and went back into the shop, leaving me to follow.

3

'For heaven's sake, Richard,' Amelia said, 'do stop walking round. Take Sheba for a walk, or something.'

'I've done that.'

'I'm trying to watch this programme.'

'Interesting, is it?' I asked. I hadn't even noticed the telly was switched on.

'No. It's boring. Put it off, if you like, then tell me what's worrying you.'

What was really worrying me was that she hadn't earlier indicated any interest, but nevertheless had allowed her disapproval to drift between us like a heavy and dark cloud. I didn't say that, simply dropped myself into my chair and spread my hands.

'The man's had his conviction quashed over a technicality. It really produces nothing that would've helped him at his trial, because it affects the time the pistol was left there, not the time it was fired.' I flapped my palms on my knees in exasperation. 'Anybody else would've been pleased to be released, legally free. But not him. Oh no.'

'Why don't you tell me all about it,' she suggested gently.

Why hadn't she asked before? 'You didn't seem interested.'

'I wasn't pleased he'd involved you, if you must know. Why did he have to rake it all up again, when he's free? Legally, too.'

'Ah, but it's not quite the same,' I explained. 'He wants to be exonerated. Proved positively innocent, not negatively.'

Then I plunged in and told her all about the killing at the house, and the shots through the hole in the window, the clock stopped at eight-ten, the pistol, the lot. No, not quite the lot. I

36

didn't tell her about the other clocks that'd also stopped at eight-ten. That bit was weird.

'So nothing's changed,' she said, nodding.

'Nothing's changed.' I shook my head in exasperation. 'But I went along there and met him again. Not expecting to, you see. Just nosing around. And what did he do? He didn't produce a great load of rubbish. Not him. In less than half an hour he gave me details of an even tighter motive than we produced in court.'

'Tighter?'

I explained. 'Not only had he more reason than I appreciated to be mad at Eric Prost, but arising from Prost's death he became the legal owner of a long-case clock worth probably fifty thousand.'

I expanded on this. She dropped sharply on the weakness of my argument.

'But he was already the owner.'

'Ah yes, but his intention was to sell it for Prost's gain – and I believe him in that. It was too magnanimous a gesture to be claimed, unless it was true. So Prost's death released him from the compulsion to sell it. All right?'

'What is he, a saint?'

'I don't know what he is. You try to understand, and tell me if you do, because he also, in the next few minutes, completely destroyed any sort of alibi, faked or not, that the shot gave him when it hit the clock-face. In half an hour he lifted his motive to the status of overwhelming, and also proved the time of eight-ten wasn't related to the time of the shot – or to anything else, if it comes to it. So he could well have done that.' I stared at Sheba gloomily. She came across to see what ailed me. 'I've now got a better case against him than I had at the time.'

'A very perverse man.' She pouted at me.

'Or a very innocent one.'

'But why . . . tell me this, Richard, why would he have left the gun in the dustbin? Surely that was very foolish.'

I shrugged. 'He's a pistol expert. He'd know all about rifling and the marks it makes on a bullet. He'd have known we'd be looking for a target-pistol, and that we'd find out from our records that the owner of this one lived only a mile away. Hell, he'd have had two hours at the club to think it over – if he'd done it – and that would be *all* he could do. Leave the pistol and pretend it'd been stolen, and hope.'

'And could it have been?'

'His pistols were kept in a room almost as secure as a bank vault.'

She smiled her delightful smile, her eyes gleaming. 'Well then, Richard, he clearly must have done it. Why d'you think I didn't want you to get involved? It's because you'd start getting yourself upset over nothing. And you *are* upset. Yes you are, don't shake your head. It's unsettled you.'

'And that's why he came to me – to unsettle me?'

'Really, you're so naïve, Richard. He wants to be able to claim he's had the police there, at his own request, and the very same policeman who dealt with the shooting originally, and *you* can't find anything.'

'Anything what?' I was puzzled. What could she mean?

'Anything to level against him now. He's after honour in his own territory, his friends drinking again with him at the pubs, calling in and chatting. As men do.'

'He wants to be proved innocent,' I muttered.

'And you can do that?'

'I don't think so.'

'Well then . . .' And she stared meaningfully at the blank TV screen. Not that she goes much for television, but that evening her apparent fascination with it had been purposeful; to dismiss from our lives this annoying intervention.

'It's those damned clocks,' I burst out.

'Clocks? What clocks?'

So I had to tell her, after all, about the other ten clocks. It affected her as it had done me at the time. I could see the blood draining from her cheeks, her eyes widen. I ended up: 'I can understand that Caine might have returned to that house after ten that night, entered it – it was easy to get in – and stopped that Tompion to show eight-ten, then have gone out and shot at the face with the pistol through the hole in the window. That at least would make *some* sense, though he's intelligent enough to realize it really meant nothing. But to stop the others . . . there would be absolutely no point in that. None at all. It did nothing. Yet, if he didn't . . . well, what then? Are we to accept that something – unearthly if you like – stopped those eleven clocks at eight-ten, the moment the last breath of life drifted from Eric Prost? Are we?'

'Now, Richard . . .'

'I will *not* accept that something supernatural stopped those clocks. There had to be a reason for it, something logical. Caine piles facts on me, and at least I can rationalize them, but those blasted clocks . . . no, it makes no sense. And you expect me to walk away from it?'

'Not until you *can* explain it. Oh yes, I know you, Richard. But – such a paltry thing! Is that your only reason for wanting to go on with it? If so, I'd advise you to drop it. This very minute.'

'Yet I can't, my love. You see, I'm now quite certain he didn't do it.'

Then there was silence for a long, long while. Sheba walked over and put her head in Amelia's lap. Absent-mindedly she fondled her ears. In the end I suggested softly, 'I'd prefer not to be alone in this.'

'No!' she said, with surprising violence. 'No,' she repeated, more softly. 'I'm sorry, Richard. I really am sorry, but I couldn't. Just couldn't.'

I ought to have realized. She is much more imaginative than me, more sensitive to mood and atmosphere. At a noisy party, she can sense, the other side of the room, a solitary discordant note. She would laugh at any suggestion of ghosts, wraiths, spirits, but leave her in a supposedly haunted room for five minutes and she'd be a screaming wreck. No, I couldn't ask her to go near that house, and I would certainly have to go there again. Yet if I left her alone here – heavens, would she watch our own antique case-clock for every second, fearing for my safety, waiting for its tick to stop?

Lordy me, I was catching it now!

When she abruptly began to speak, it was as though she was listening to herself. The words, for me, seemed to come from a long way away, something I didn't wish to contemplate.

'Promise me this, Richard,' she murmured. 'Only that you'll

tell me everything. Please. Then it'll be as though I was with you all the time.'

'Of course.'

'Then that's settled.' She tried to smile.

Oh no it wasn't. I was left with the compulsion to go on with it, but now with my own personal misery, knowing it was causing her distress.

With this shade of reluctant encouragement urging me onwards, it's not surprising that I found myself able to draw back and hesitate. Fortunately, I was encouraged into our terraced garden by a short spell of late September summer, and I could believe I was merely marshalling my thoughts, deciding how I might tackle the affair. There was even the possiblity that if I allowed the matter to slip from conscious thought it might melt away altogether. But always I could hear those blasted clocks not ticking away.

On the third of such days I returned to the house for lunch, and found Amelia about to come and call me.

'The phone, Richard. It's *him*.'

I glanced at my filthy hands, then went through and picked up the phone.

'Mr Caine?'

'It's started,' he burst out. 'I knew it would.'

'What's started?'

'Some obscene campaign. A brick through my window last night . . .'

'The shop?'

'No, no. The house. And threats being stuck through my letter-box.'

'Ah!' I hesitated. This was not part of what you might call my brief; it did no more than hint at an urgency. 'It's a police matter. Have you called them?'

'And a lot of good *that* did. Oh . . . somebody came. He didn't say anything direct, I'll grant you that, but it was there in his voice.'

'What was?'

'And in his attitude. What could I expect, coming back here? That sort of thing.'

'It might have been better . . .'

'D'you want me to run away, all conscience and guilt?'

I thought about it. Clearly, I had to go and see him, at the very least. I took too long for him.

'Are you still there, Mr Patton?'

'Thinking,' I told him. 'I'll have a bite of lunch and be right along. The shop . . .'

'I've put the guard mesh at the windows and closed it. For now. He advised that.'

'I'll see you soon, at the house.'

I hung up thoughtfully. The local police officer hadn't been very tactful. He would know, as well as I did, that Caine was legally exonerated, but he was no doubt a local man, and to him Caine was still guilty, but had 'got away with it'.

'I'm not having you hurrying over your lunch,' Amelia said.

'Don't worry, my love, I'm not exactly anxious to get there.'

Caine hadn't asked whether I remembered how to find his house, and I wasn't sure that I did. But it was this side of Markham Prior, up along Markham Hill. That much I recalled. He would therefore, ten years before, have had to drive through the town in order to reach his pistol club, and would in that way have had to pass very close to Eric Prost's house, and call in there on the way or back – or both. If he'd wished.

As most of the development in recent years had taken place on the far side of the river, there had been no change to the right-hand turn-off that I remembered near the top of Markham Hill. My impression was that Prior Close (it ran away to nothing further along) was narrower than I recalled, but this was no doubt due to ten years of growth to the trees lining each side.

He called his house Markham View, for the driveway was steep, curving only at the top in front of the entrance, and as the trees had been cleared, apart from larches each side of the drive, he had a splendid view over the town and river below. The house was a sturdy stone construction, with mullioned windows and tall chimneys adding grace. I drew up, climbed out of my Triumph Stag, and stood for a moment admiring the vista. It would be quite a trip from town for someone with no other purpose but to hurl a stone through the window and thrust threatening messages through the letter-box – in the opposite order, no doubt.

41

'You've come, then,' he said from behind me.

I turned. 'I said I would. It's a fine view.'

'Indeed.'

I followed him into the house. There was no sign, at this time, of his wife. I recalled that we were heading towards his pistol den, and I was correct. The door stood open.

Once again, as at his shop, it would have been difficult to put a name to his room. On one wall, arranged most carefully, was his collection of weaponry, not entirely made up of antique pistols. A pair of pikes gave a little decorative length to the display, and a pair of inlaid wheel-lock rifles added dignity. The total effect was breath-taking, if one could forget that everything on that wall was intended to maim or to kill. And yet, the makers had, in all cases, applied loving skill to them, as though their beauty might mask their deadly intent. It was quite clear that Caine would not be interested in the purely practical, the brutally blunt statement of death. Each was decorated exquisitely.

That was one wall. He brought his customers here, where they could fondle them at the large oak table in the middle of the floor, take their time, absorb the mystic aura of history expressed in them.

At one end of the room was his work-bench. No doubt very little work would be needed on his pistols, or perhaps one might say only very delicate work. Nothing large was visible in the way of tools, not that I could see.

He had the offending stone on the table. Nothing special about that, either. Why had he kept it? Had he thought I'd wish to weigh it in my hand and draw clues from it?

'A front window,' he said, his voice quite calm and flat. 'No damage inside the house. And two messages. This through the letter-box here, the other one at the shop.'

They were not the same hand, I saw, and in no way matched. One was blunt and precise, poorly printed on a piece of cardboard. This was the one left at the shop: WE DON'T WANT MURDERERS ROUND HERE.

The other was in an envelope, on good-quality paper and neatly handwritten. No stamp, so delivered by hand.

I am surprised that you should return to the scene of your enormous sin. One trusts that this is temporary, as no one will feel safe until you have gone.

This had been delivered to the house. It didn't seem to me that it in any way related to the violence implied by the stone. So . . . three visitors, three enemies.

'It might be the best thing to do,' I told him quietly.

'What would?' He was suspicious.

'The suggestion. Leave the district and set up somewhere else.'

'I told you . . .' It began violently, then he sighed, his shoulders straightened, and he made a gesture of rueful defeat. 'You're right, of course. But antiques aren't the same as other commodities. Part of the business is getting known, and I mean internationally. There are clients – friends – who know what I deal in, how I deal, and whether I can be trusted. They travel here. They expect me to be here. If I moved, I'd have to advertise all over the world: Caine Antiques is now at Bishop's Stortford, or wherever. No. It'd be change. Antiques and change don't go together. I'd lose a lot of trust and good-will that've taken years to build up.'

'Umm!' I said. It was all quite logical. 'Very well. Let's start all over again from scratch. You went regularly to this pistol club of yours?'

'You know all this.'

'Pretend it's ten years ago and we've never met before. The club . . .'

'It's ten miles away. Most of the others live close. Every Monday evening I did the trip.'

'Which fact could be known?'

'What? I suppose so. I didn't make any secret of it.'

'And you always took your matched pair of Hammerli twenty-two target-pistols?' I asked blandly.

'Catch questions, Mr Patton?' He lifted his eyebrows, his eyes twinkling with humour. 'No, I took only one. Alternating.'

'Then why own two?' That was a new thought.

'Sometimes you get jamming. Rarely, with a top-class pistol like that. You need two. Competition work. You can't afford to mess about with unjamming . . .'

43

'I get it, I get it. But for a casual evening, one is quite enough?'
'Yes.'

'The prosecution case was that you took both that evening. That you used one to kill Eric Prost, and left it behind to be found. When I came here on the Tuesday evening, you seemed surprised to find that one of your pistols was missing.'

'I couldn't believe it. Absolutely flabbergasted, I was.'

'I remember. You could be a good actor, for all I knew. You could've expected the visit and rehearsed your reaction.'

'Say what you like.'

'Thank you. I'll say, then, what you don't seem to have realized. At that time, we thought you'd taken both pistols, with the intention of abandoning one of them. In other words – premeditation. It's why you got life, not a shorter sentence.'

He walked a few yards one way, a few yards the other. 'Nobody told me that,' he said plaintively.

I waited until he'd settled, until he'd lifted a finely chased flintlock from its wall-supports and was balancing it in his hands, drawing some sort of comfort from it.

'So . . .' I went on. 'If you're telling the truth, then a pistol was stolen from here, that pistol was left to be found, and a possibly rigged alibi for the time of eight-ten was left behind, apparently to cover *you*, Mr Caine. All this done by somebody who knew Monday night was club night. You, you, you. There is – or was – somebody who didn't like you. You were very carefully landed right in it.'

He was staring at me, the pistol raised to rest against his shoulder, like a dueller. 'Eric was killed just to get at me?' he breathed, his eyes bright, his lips moist.

'Prost was killed because Prost had to be killed. You were the fallguy. Who didn't like you, Mr Caine?'

He laughed, lowering the pistol to lie beside his leg. 'Multitudes. Every dealer I've ever outbid, you could say.'

'Seriously now,' I warned.

He shrugged. 'I don't know.'

I reached forward and took the pistol from him. It seemed very long in my hand, and heavy. I hadn't liked the ease with which he'd swung it around, the confidence, the way its arc had included me.

44

'Can you make this thing fire?'

His eyes met mine, wickedly naïve, his expression one of pained innocence. 'Yes I could, if you gave me time to get a few things together. But I wouldn't recommend you trying to fire it. The ball was lead, almost five-eighths of an inch in diameter. That'd weight over a pound. The thing'd nearly break your wrist.'

'Is that so? With all this armament around, I don't suppose anybody dared to make an enemy of you. Very well, we'll take it from the other end. Who had access to this room?'

'Only me.'

'Nonsense. Think. A pistol was stolen. Let's not have any more impossiblities. Who?'

He nodded, conceding a fact. 'I'll show you, if you like.'

'Your security? Good. Let's see it again, in case I missed something the first time.' I handed him the pistol and he restored it to its position of decoration. Suddenly, it seemed harmless.

'Windows,' he said. 'Two. Both barred. Nothing was disturbed. Door. Look at it yourself.'

He held it for me. I swung it, feeling it move heavily and sluggishly in my hand.

'Sheet steel, each side,' he told me. 'And set in a reinforced frame. Special lock, unpickable, so they told me.'

'Key?'

'It's here.'

He produced it from his trouser pocket, a peculiar tubular thing with little teeth sticking out from it. I'd seen such a thing before.

'Not exactly unpickable,' I told him. 'But it'd take a top man.'

'All the same . . .' He shrugged.

'You carry it with you?'

'No. I might be tapped on the head one dark night, just in order to get at all this stuff.'

'So where do you keep it?'

'You know where,' he said with some irritation.

'Show me again.'

He took me out into the hall, where he naturally had a long-case clock. It hadn't the weathered patina of an antique, and was clearly modern.

'I made this myself,' he told me. 'The whole thing. I was experimenting with a new escapement, but it hasn't been a complete success. Look.' He opened the door in the trunk and stopped the pendulum, reached behind it with the key in his hand, there was a click, and his hand returned empty.

'I made it to take the key,' he explained. 'There's a magnet. Nobody would think to look there.' He reached behind once more and retrieved the key, then set the pendulum going again.

'Somebody knew. There's no other way.'

He shook his head stubbornly.

'No other way,' I repeated, watching him, noting his agitation, the way his eyes avoided mine. 'Your wife knows,' I told him softly.

His head came up. 'No!'

I shrugged. 'Then somebody else.'

'No. I don't know. It's impossible.'

'It happened. Think now. That night. Monday. You're not likely to forget it, because it was the night before I came here first. I have just watched you. The pendulum was stopped for perhaps ten seconds, then you set it swinging again. Now . . . assume somebody came here, after you'd left for your club. Somebody who could get into the house, who knew about where you kept that key.'

'You are not – I say *not* – to implicate Marie.'

'Somebody,' I plodded on. 'Leave it there. Such a person, intending to use the gun-room key, then grab the pistol you hadn't taken, lock up, replace the key – that person would most likely leave the pendulum lying dead during that time. The clock would be stopped, not for two seconds but for two or three minutes. It would therefore, after restarting, be that amount slow. Now, you're a clock-man. You made the clock, so you'd be interested in its performance. So you'd notice such a thing. Think back . . .'

'Yes!' He snapped his fingers. 'I noticed. I remember. Two minutes slow, it was. I couldn't understand it.'

'Well then.'

He gave me one quick and startled glance, then he walked rapidly, taking short but crisp strides, into his room. I followed more slowly. He was giving himself time to think about it.

'The target-pistols,' I said. 'Where were those left?'

He made a gesture, angry and impatient. I already knew. I went over to the cupboard and opened the door. It was a small, low cupboard in heavy gauge metal, I saw as the door opened, but it wasn't locked. The two gun cases were still there, leather covered, forlorn. I opened them.

The recessed velvet linings revealed the shapes of the missing pistols. The long, narrow cartridge boxes were empty. But the cleaning materials, brush, swabs, oil bottle, were still there.

I straightened. 'No lock,' I said.

He'd recovered. 'It was not necessary. A secure place, the regulations say. This whole room is secure.'

'Sure it is,' I commented. 'Did anybody from the police give it the okay?'

'Oh yes.' He glanced away. 'An officer came. I went through the same performance I've shown you, and I was told it'd do just fine.'

'That's one, then.'

'What?'

'One person who knew where the key was kept,' I told him placidly.

For one second he stared at me blankly, then he laughed out loud. 'Oh yes. Very amusing.'

'You were so sure that nobody knew. Already we've got two.'

'I told you – forget my wife.'

I shrugged. 'Heaven knows how many people you've trusted, and who've watched where you kept the key.' I was remembering that Tuesday evening, when I'd come to the house, having traced the pistol to Julian Caine. Standing there now beside the metal cupbaord, I could distinctly remember him crouching there, opening the door. 'My pistols? They're here.' And his shocked, almost pained expression when he'd lifted the lid of the second case and found it empty. There'd been something there I'd been unable to interpret, some desperate awareness. But mainly it had been bewilderment. Or faked emotion?

Just then, Marie called from the hall. 'I've made some tea, Julian. In the kitchen.'

He turned to me. 'You see! My wife indeed! She won't even enter this room, let alone handle a pistol.'

47

'Yes,' I said, feeling his hand at my elbow as he ushered me out. 'You told me that was why she left you.'

'Did I? Yes, I suppose I did.'

'But she came back?'

'She's been a veritable Godsend. Kept the clock business going . . .'

'But not the pistols?'

'Not', he agreed, 'the pistols.'

4

By the time I left I was getting very close to thumping him. Every time I searched for a way out for him, he produced fresh evidence of his incontestable guilt. First the alibi and the motive, now the access to his pistols. He was almost frantic to prove that nobody else but himself could have done it. In fact, over that cup of tea, Marie sitting quietly and apparently uninvolved, he had happily made it clear that there was nobody else in his pistol club – and thus no other marksman – living within fifteen miles of Eric Prost's place.

And he had cheerfully claimed that he, from the outside of that window, could have pierced Prost's ears for ear-rings, with two quick shots. If they hadn't already been pierced, he'd told me.

'There was gypsy stock there, Mr Patton. Hence the clocks, I suppose.'

'How d'you mean?'

'You can't have pendulum-clocks in a caravan. So it becomes a craving.'

'I never thought of that.'

I could've killed him. He seemed to want to tease me with his apparent guilt, make a fool of me by demonstrating the shallow furrow of my original dig.

It was therefore with Eric Prost's house in mind that I drove away, heading there although the daylight was already failing. For some reason, I assumed the house would be empty, dark and deserted. In fact, by the time I got there it was very dark, because I'd forgotten it was Wednesday and had become embroiled in traffic before I reached the bridge, so that there was no turning back and less than a walking pace driving onwards around the meandering one-way circuit the police had laid out.

The other side of the far bridge the crush began to disperse, and after a further half-mile or so I had no difficulty in turning right into one of those apparently purposeless lanes so common amongst those rolling hills, originally no doubt a worn path trodden by languid farm-hands, unwilling to climb and searching for a level footing. Eric Prost's house, therefore, was secluded in its setting. It lay back, with no apparent reason for its location on that exact spot. Had there been a convenient well, located by a hazel wand and a water-diviner? Doubtless it had been a farm. The sprawl of outbuildings suggested that. There was no specific entrance to it, merely a wide gap in the continuous thorn hedge that side of the lane.

I drove in from the lane, headlights now full on in order to pick a way through the rutted mud, and the house sat there, waiting for me, with not a sign of life from it, darkness and silence when I got out of the car, and a sad, almost threatening gloom seeming to embrace it.

I needed no more than this atmosphere, I told myself. Prost had lived here alone. How *could* he? If the house had been bright and cheerful I could have understood, but it was a place to leave, not to return to.

Slowly, torch in hand now, I walked round it. The dustbin was still there, empty now. The curtains were still there, it seemed the very same ones, almost petrified for eternity in their tattered drapes. The window! This was the same window, but the pane with the hole had been replaced. Inside the room, my torchlight reaching through, there was the same desk. No Tompion was there now, of course; it was in Caine's showroom. But no other had replaced it. I moved on round. Here was the side door, ten years older than when I'd seen it last and even more loose in its frame, not resisting at all the urging of my credit card, which I edged through to the tongue of the cylinder lock.

I was facing a short hall. I stood, head cocked, hand still on the door. There was a rustling sound, as of scuttling rats, but it was not that. No. I concentrated, and it was with shocked realization that I suddenly identified the sound. It was clocks, clocks ticking and tocking, not quite in unison, not at the same measured interval, with their divergent pendulums. I was listening to the susurration of overlapping and interlocking ticks, fluttering away like tiny urgent hands, thrusting elements of time into the past.

It meant I was in an occupied house, that I'd broken into and entered enclosed premises. With a sigh of expelled breath I backed out and drew the door shut behind me with a delicate click from the lock, and torchlight suddenly bathed me, freezing me in the glare. It was the light from three separate torches, two of them further back so that the person holding the nearest one was caught, half in silhouette, half in illumination. At the same time I realized – so desperately had I been concentrating on that infernal susurration – that there was a powerful roaring and snarling sound in the air from the far side of the house, a sound alien to that remote setting. Powerful diesel engines!

The leader of that stolid triangle, one person and two glaring orbs of light, I was now able to identify as a woman. Not from the hair, which was short, nor from the features, which had a gaunt and masculine cast to them, nor from the clothes, which were neutral in their sex, jeans and a leather jacket and rubber boots, but from the stance, from a certain lissom poise. When she spoke, though the voice was deep, it was definitely feminine.

'Who the hell are you, and what d'you think you're doing here?'

I didn't know what was behind the other two torches, possibly two somethings, heavy and male. I played safe. 'I was in the district. I've got an interest in this house.'

'It's not for sale,' she said briskly.

'I didn't think it was. My name's Patton. I was the investigating officer in a crime here, ten years ago.'

'A murder. Say it. Murder.'

'A murder, then.'

'And it was ten years and one week.'

'I suppose it was.'

The torch was lowered and switched off, her other hand resting on a very feminine hip. I'd by that time decided she was

51

around forty-five. The noise the other side of the house was becoming louder, more frenetic.

'You was the one as put him away,' she stated, cocking her head, viewing me with distrust. 'That Julian Caine.'

'I was.'

'And now you've bloody well let him off.'

'Not me exactly.'

'All the same . . . you did a bloody rotten job on it, in the first place.'

I grinned at her. 'I'm coming to that conclusion myself.'

She in no way relaxed, continuing to eye me sourly. Then abruptly she lifted her head. 'That soddin' idiot Daley's takin' his Dennis to the south fence! Christ! I warned him, Juno. Go'n roust him out. The north fence, Juno, the north!'

One of the torches swung away and Juno, now at last visible as a very large man with bowed legs, galloped away. 'Daley!' I heard him shouting. 'Daley, you damned fool, it's soft there . . .'

Now only one torch was levelled at me, and that was lowered to my feet. I felt the tension had relaxed, at least the part of it that was aimed at me. She clearly had an urge to be round at the front, involved in what was going on there.

'I did really believe the house was empty,' I told her. 'There was something . . . I don't know. I just wanted to look at it again.'

'I live here!' she snapped, sensing some sort of criticism in what I'd said. 'Damn it, I can't talk to you now. I'll see you later.'

With that, she abruptly swung around, said something to her companion, whom she called Patch, and who was a younger woman, and then she stalked away round the house, her smaller companion striding beside her. A teenager, I would have guessed. Maybe twenty. Perhaps I'd been talking to a family.

There had been something I couldn't understand in her final remarks. There had been the suggestion of a command. She would see me later, as though I would have no choice. Slowly I followed them, deciding simply to climb into the Stag and drive away. Then I saw the background to her confidence. Nobody was going to drive away from there inside an hour or two . . . or more.

Light streamed in beaded procession along the approach lane, as far as my eyes would reach, engines throbbed into the night, and to my right I saw, with something of a shock, what she had meant by the Dennis. It was a high and huge diesel ten-wheeled tractor vehicle, its massive square nose high above the ground, its exhaust puffing out smoke and fumes above and behind the cab. It was towing a square, canvas-covered four-wheel trailer, wide, longer than a double-decker bus and nearly as tall, and behind that a living caravan. It was headed towards the south fence, where, one guessed, the surface would be too soft for it. Juno was explaining in words of one syllable and mainly four letters that the driver had better get the bleedin' thing over the far side. As it would be impossible to back it, with a double trail, they were discussing, even above the roar of the engine, how it was to be achieved.

Immediately behind was waiting a venerable and carefully preserved Fowler steam-tractor. I could smell its distinctive odour even from where I was. Lights, from vehicles behind it, at that moment caught it and held it for my admiration, its flywheel flickering as it spun, the whole equipage finished in green and brown and yellow, as perfect as when it had been made. It had a dynamo on the platform in front of the high funnel, the whole covered by the bowed canopy, supported on twisted brass rods. Along the side of the canopy were the words: MIGHTY IN STRENGTH AND ENDURANCE. How true, how true! Oh, how I yearned to sit at the rear, spinning that steering wheel!

Then it was all obvious. This – these – were the elements of a travelling fair, of more than one perhaps, and the lights behind and angling in through the opening were those of other wagons and their tractor vehicles, all bearing the broken-down portions of roundabouts, coconut shies, rifle ranges, swings, side-shows, big dippers, perhaps, and little dippers, everything of any possible entertainment value. This place was their winter quarters. They would settle in, and, weather permitting, would refurbish and repair their attractions, paint and dandify the

53

side-shows, grease the rails and oil the wheels. They would be there all winter.

It began to look as though I would be there all winter, too. There was no way I could get my car out into that lane, and no way I could drive along it if I did. Not until they were all settled inside.

Anxiously, I moved around, watching how it worked, how it was organized. Oh, but it was neat! I'd have to admit that. Point to a spot and they edged into it, parked, set-to, and in very little time became settled entities. But oh dear me, it was going to take a hell of a long while, and still they came, in from the shires and the counties, from north and south.

I found her, legs straddled, shouting instructions, whistling shrilly with two fingers and pointing, gesticulating. She danced those ponderous vehicles on the end of a string, and slotted them in like bits of jigsaw.

I tugged at her elbow. She glanced round. 'You still here?'

'How could I be anywhere else?'

'Serves you right. Shouldn't come nosing.'

We were shouting at each other to a background of roaring engines, in a kaleidoscope of moving headlights, running shadows, bellowed greetings, waving torches.

'How long?' I roared.

'Oh . . . hours.'

'I've got to get to a phone. My wife. She'll want to know where I am.'

She jerked a thumb. 'My Range Rover. Behind yours. Use my phone.'

I ran to it. The door was open and I clambered inside. I got through, once I got the hang of the radio phone.

'It's Richard, love.'

'Where *are* you?'

'You're not going to believe this,' I told her.

'Try me,' she said. 'Perhaps I will.'

So I told her. By this time I'd begun to feel amused at the situation in which I found myself, caught up too in the bustle and excitement on the site. Perhaps I didn't sound as concerned as I ought to have been, because at the end (she'd been so silent

54

I'd had to check, from time to time, that she was still there) she made her suggestion without hesitation.

'Can you get out on foot?'

'To the main road, yes.'

'Then it could be quicker if I bring the Granada and pick you up. Then we'll drive back tomorrow for your Stag.'

Without hesitation, that was, when she hates driving at night.

'If you'll do that,' I said, 'it'd certainly be best. Otherwise I'll be stuck here until midnight.'

'Then tell me how to get there, Richard, and what to look for.'

I told her. 'You won't be able to go wrong once you've got Markham Prior ahead of you. There's so much light around here it'll show up like a beacon. I'll be the solitary, miserable pedestrian at the roadside.'

Then I hunted out Patch, she being the first I met, and told her I'd be back in the morning for my car.

She was a pert little thing, all big eyes and a wide grin. 'Should have this lot settled in by morning,' she told me.

I plodded back towards the main road, past the parked and patiently waiting wagons along the lane, small ones, medium, large, all with their personal caravans hitched on behind. They stood and chatted together. 'Couldn't make Newcastle this year.' 'Nottingham was a wet un.' 'How they doing, friend?' This last to me.

'A bit of a tangle.'

'Then that's all right.'

They all, I noted, kept their engines running, their lights on full beam. Ready to roll.

Even stopping to chat here and there, I was out on the main road a good half-hour before Amelia could be expected. I'd discovered that these people comprised the elements of five travelling fairs, all under the control of Juno Ritter. There would be more arriving in the morning, those from much more distant patches. Even now, with wagons still approaching from both directions on the main road, I couldn't see how they were going to be squeezed in. But perhaps there was land I hadn't seen.

Musing in this way, I strolled up and down the main road, at first paying no attention to a small blue car that was parked, well out of the way, on the grass verge. It didn't seem that it belonged to the fairground people, but there was no reason why some of them shouldn't use ordinary motor vehicles. Someone was sitting inside, behind the wheel. From time to time I saw the red glow of a cigarette, the flare of a lighter; she was a heavy, nervous smoker. In the flare I'd seen it was a woman. I walked back and forth, past it, until I found myself walking towards it at the time when one of the fair wagons splashed me with light, on its way in.

The door opened and she got out, clearly having been waiting to get a good look at me. I marched towards her, maintaining a steady pace and leaving any initiative to her.

'You're Mr Patton, aren't you?' she asked, stepping sideways in front of me.

I stopped. 'Yes. That's me.'

'I remember you, but you probably never noticed me. My husband was talking to you, but we never actually met.'

'Ah,' I said. 'Yes.'

'Veronica Pierce.' She let it hang there between us, giving me time to connect. There'd been no emphasis in her voice.

'You mean Arthur Pierce's . . .'

'Widow. Yes.'

'I'm sorry. I heard how he died. Shocking.'

'It was,' she agreed flatly. She threw away her cigarette. There was anger in the gesture, but it hadn't been in her voice. I couldn't see her face, shaded as it was. 'It was so damned simple for somebody, they told me. There's a cap that comes off the centre of the steering-wheel. There's a big nut underneath, and all they did was remove it. I bet you never knew about that. He wouldn't have noticed, they told me. It's on splines. Wouldn't notice till it lifted off . . .' A flip of the hand. 'He died in hospital.'

I was finding the lack of emotion in her voice difficult to understand. 'I know,' I said encouragingly.

'Yes. It's why you're here, too, isn't it? This is Eric Prost's place. It's why you're here.'

It was at this point that another of the fairground vehicles came along, a flat-backed lorry with something huge and cumbersome under its canvas, and a long caravan behind. Its

56

headlights for one second flicked over her, revealing my first real glimpse of her face. I stood, unable to speak.

'Isn't it?' she insisted.

Fair hair and a wide brow, the eyes deep and blue – I couldn't see this, but I recognized the intensity of their glow – the proud, high cheeks, the full lips, the commanding chin . . . and now the tiny hint of impatience because I hadn't answered at once. I was looking at and standing before and almost stammering at my first wife, Vera, whom I'd lost in a traffic accident one snowy morning. Instantly, the dreadful loss of that time flooded up, almost choking me. I turned away, and she touched my arm in protest. Just a touch. As Vera had so often done.

'Yes,' I said, managing to turn back, managing even to look at her face now that the shadows again cloaked it.

If there was anything I didn't want at that time, with Amelia speeding towards me through the night, it was the image of Vera intruding. No, not intruding; the memory was always welcome. But I'd been able to face the pain of loss and force it into the background only by burying other, more welcome, memories. I had never, therefore, made comparisons between my two wives. I'd loved each in different ways, for different reasons. You just cannot compare. It would be an odious proceeding.

But now it flooded over me, a veritable tide of memory. Vera had urged me forward, but never become involved with my career; Amelia couldn't bear to be left out. Vera had been precise, critical, wildly active in our loving; Amelia was at times vague, always encouraging, and soft, gentle, warm and responsive.

You can't compare; you must not compare.

She said, 'I heard you were here, around the town.'

Had she? Briefly, I wondered how. 'You did?' I asked. 'I was naturally interested in the man's release. Julian Caine's.'

'You would be, of course.' She nodded.

I began to fill my pipe, anything to keep my hand occupied. I'd had the impulse to reach out and brush the breeze-blown hair from her eyes, as I'd done for Vera, the urge to touch her hand in emphasis, when it would have been too personal a gesture. We found ourselves strolling along, side by side. I wondered whether she might take my arm, dreaded it.

'The whole case is taking on a new light,' I told her. 'I'm seeing it differently.'

'And all from what Arthur put in his statement?' There was a hint of amusement in her voice, of disbelief. 'It seemed such a small point to me – a splash of rainwater on the pistol.'

'Yes, quite minor. But I've heard he was a very precise man. It clearly worried him.'

'Arthur', she stated, 'had a mania for correctness. He had no time for poor workmanship, wouldn't listen to excuses, and he was always furious over mistakes. Everything had to be *right*. And in all of it, it was himself he was most critical with. He simply hated his own mistakes.'

'He made mistakes, then?'

'Who doesn't! But to Arthur – any little error on his part made him absolutely furious. He'd brood for hours.'

I glanced sideways at her. She'd said this with a fondness in her voice, as though it was one of his more admirable characteristics. 'And yours?' I asked, managing to get my pipe going.

'Pardon?'

'Your mistakes. Your sins of omission and commission.'

'Oh – those. He took those to himself as though I was a part of himself that'd let him down. I *was* part of him, and he of me I suppose. *We* had made that particular error. It hurt him just as much as if he'd done it himself.'

'Fancy that,' I said, wishing Amelia would arrive and rescue me. People could become tedious over the splendours of their spouses, especially when they were dead. And she was clearly accepting her husband's character as unimpeachable. 'Surely', I suggested casually, 'it would make him very difficult to live with.'

'What? Oh no. Stupid me, I'm giving you entirely the wrong impression. He was fun to live with. No trouble in relaxing. Off duty he was a different man, and the mistakes were few and far between.'

But Chief Supers are never off duty. 'Both lots?' I asked.

'You *do* ask the strangest things, I must say. Both of what?'

58

'He took your errors to himself, under his personal protective wing. So both lots were few and far between.'

She was silent for a few moments, tilting her head to the sky in a thoughtful attitude that caught at my throat. 'I think they call it semantics,' she decided at last. 'This playing about with words. Don't take me so *literally*, please.'

'Very well.'

'Promise.'

As though we would be meeting often! 'I can't promise to change my whole personality.'

'Of course you can't. Do forgive me.'

I didn't reply. She too was playing with something, and I felt it was me. She wanted something from me, and she was leading up to it, priming me into a receptive mood. But there wasn't much time, and I thought silence might force her hand.

In the end it did. There was a tart tang to her voice when she spoke again, and I could just detect the little toss of her head.

'I wouldn't want to think that Arthur's little mistake with the dustbin lid made such a critically important difference.'

'Ah . . . then I can reassure you. It made a difference – and that questionable – to the time the pistol was left there, not to the time of the actual shots. So, you see, not exactly a critical difference.'

I thought that ought to satisfy her. It was the fond memory of her Arthur she wished to preserve.

'But all the same,' she said briskly, 'they let him off.'

'Who? Caine? Yes, his conviction was quashed, if that's what you mean.'

'It's exactly what I mean. That mistake of Arthur's *did* make a difference – it got him off.'

That repeated phrase! 'If you care to look at it like that.'

'It's not right! If Arthur hadn't *done* it, Caine wouldn't have got away with it, the way he has now.' She'd varied it a little. 'You just said – it only affected the time that horrible pistol was left there. It doesn't make the man less guilty. It's just a stupid technicality. I don't want that levelled at Arthur's memory, that fact that for one stupid little error a murderer's gone free!'

Any trace of Vera had now disappeared. My first wife, no

more than the second one, would never have indulged in such tortuous reasoning.

'You're looking at it . . .'

'What're you doing about it?' she demanded.

'Doing nothing. Just looking around.' I raised an eyebrow, but she wouldn't have seen it.

'Then while you're at it, just you make sure you don't miss anything else.'

'I beg your pardon.'

'I'm not going to be happy . . . never again . . . until you've found definite evidence that Julian Caine was guilty. Guilty as hell!'

She tossed up her head, her hair flying now in the freshening breeze, as though seeking up there confirmation of her intent. Damn it all, she had to be neurotic. Possibly she'd caught it from her husband, he with his obsessive drive towards the top. What had he been aiming for, Chief Constable? He could probably have made it by the time he was fifty. Others had. But their success had ridden on sheer ability. Perhaps he was aware that he hadn't that ability. That would explain his passionate response to his own mistakes, as they would make the point for him and prod at his inadequacies.

'Perhaps so,' I murmured comfortingly. 'Maybe Caine was guilty. But you know as well as I do, having been the wife of a chief superintendent, that he couldn't be tried again for the same crime, whatever evidence I found.'

She seemed not to have heard. Her voice became clear as a bell, ringing into that night as though calling worshippers to her feet in order to applaud her philosophy. She did not look at me, as a princess might not look at her dresser when commenting on her awkwardness with a pin.

'What I want you to do is prove he's guilty,' she pronounced. 'I want you to bring me the evidence, all laid out, so that I can broadcast the truth. It might not be possible to force him into court, but I'll have it broadcast in every news media in the land . . .' She stopped, speaking and physically, and abruptly turned to me. 'You're not listening.'

'Oh yes I am. I ought to warn you about the law of libel . . .'

'Pff!' she exclaimed, waving her hand elegantly in the air. 'We'll see about that.'

'Yes. You see about it,' I advised. 'Now, I must be off. My wife's meeting me. Goodnight to you.'

Then I resolutely turned my face towards the town and began to walk, fast, to meet Amelia. What a tender romance their marriage must have been, I thought, what a touching alliance.

5

Amelia spotted me coming, drew to a halt, backed into a farm entrance, and had the car ready for a straight run home by the time I reached her.

'Do you mind if I drive?' I asked.

'You're welcome. You know how I hate . . .' She saw my face more clearly now. 'Why? Are you in flight from something?'

'From somebody, yes. I'd hate to have her follow us home. You wouldn't like her, my love, you definitely would not.'

Then I settled down to a period of rapid and circuitous driving, though in fact I didn't spot any headlights following us. We were driving through a thinly populated area for most of the distance, so the traffic was light. A follower would've been easy to pick out.

'Dinner will be a little late,' she said, mildly reproving my error in getting my car trapped.

'Yes. Sorry about that.'

'It doesn't matter.' A pause. 'Are you going to tell me all about it?'

'Certainly. Now, if you wish.'

She so wished, so I took her through my afternoon's and evening's activities, accompanied by many oohs and ahs and ohs, even including the final interview with Veronica Pierce, though not mentioning her likeness to Vera. Wives have a tendency to become silent and distant at any mention of a former spouse.

'You *are* getting yourself into a mess,' she said at the end, as we ran over the new bridge at Bridgnorth.

'Yes, I am. What with Caine doing his best to underline his

own guilt, and expecting me to prove his innocence, and now Mrs Pierce expecting me to prove his guilt, just to satisfy the glowing memory of her husband's perfection – and heaven knows what'll come from those fairground people tomorrow.'

'You think they're connected?'

'With Eric Prost – certainly. They must be. The clocks are still there, you see.'

I could feel her weight against my arm as she shifted across. 'That horrible house!'

'You haven't seen it yet. But I've got an idea it'll seem different to you, with all those people around.' No harm in being reassuring.

'To me! I don't want . . .'

'But of course you must come. Who else will drive this car home when I collect mine? Or do I take the Granada to collect the Stag, then the Stag to collect the Granada . . . *ad infinitum*?'

'Idiot. No, it's me. Foolish me. I'll have to put up with it, I supose.'

We ate late, certainly, with Mary, in the kitchen. She is not our housekeeper, as people seem to think, but a friend who lives with us, a close enough friend to be included in the discussion over the meal and afterwards. She does not approve of my indulgences in ongoing crime, and severely disapproves of Amelia becoming involved.

'She'll have to come, if only to drive the Granada back,' I told her, 'unless you'd like to do it, Mary.'

'Oh no! No, no! All those fairground people!'

I laughed at that. 'Do you think they'll steal Amelia from me, hide her, and force her to work the dodgems under the influence of some secret and exotic drug?'

I'd intended to laugh her out of it, and she looked embarrassed, but all the same she wasn't certain of our safety. It was true that these people, who had to strip down and re-erect their attractions every week in the season, and operate them during the days between, would need to be tough and strong, and that we would be heavily outnumbered there, but I'd detected nothing but casual friendliness, apart from the small disagreement with the woman and her apparent family. All the same, joke or not, Amelia was clearly lacking in enthusiasm. She was remembering those damned clocks.

Fortunately, it was a fine day when we set off next morning. I say fortunately, because the site would indeed have been depressing had it been raining heavily. There was no difficulty in driving in, I discovered to my surprise, my anticipation being coloured by childhood memories of operating fairs. I'd envisaged having to weave around and between all the equipment. But no. All was parcelled away neatly around the perimeter of the site, caravans parked beside the transport, and a few of the shows already being unloaded, piece by piece, for careful inspection and repair, as required. The spread, I saw, extended along both sides of the site, and round at the rear.

The romance of it had been destroyed completely. Quite apart from the fact that the shows, in their stripped-down state, were almost impossible to identify, they all seemed to be so pitifully small. The Tunnel of Fear – I recognized that by the rails and the cars for them – was not a tunnel at all. They had the basic bed of it laid out, without the canvas necessary to close it into darkness, and the rails simply curved and wound back on themselves, almost touching in places. Not a tunnel at all. The skeleton, the ghost, the terror mask, all these were flimsy and innocuous, robbed of the darkness and the abrupt, brief flash of light. The Tunnel of Love was completely stripped of passion in a similar way. Even their modest version of the big dipper wasn't really big when reduced to piles of steel tubing, rails, and coaches that were too small, it seemed, to contain anything but midgets.

We parked beside my Stag. I hadn't even locked it, and it hadn't been touched. Before we went along to the house, whose name of Winter Haven now made sense, we walked back to take a look at the activity. It was Amelia who insisted, suddenly caught up in it, as I'd been, fascinated by a life-style and a special expertise that was so new to her. It was she, too, who seemed so suddenly chatty with these show-people, pausing to ask questions, drawing a smile here and there – at our ignorance, no doubt – and an almost eager desire to satisfy her every request. Even to the extent of our being invited to visit one of the caravans.

They were not all modern touring caravans. Oh no. Several had definitely been constructed under a gypsy influence, lavishly decorated with fretted surrounds to windows and doors, brightly painted and gilded, things of pride and joy. Amelia was so poor at disguising her interest that we were asked to go inside one of them by a woman with a Black Country accent thicker than mine.

She had cause to be proud. It was a travelling home, fully-supplied, you could say, with much-treasured personal items. There were many shelves, on which a large collection of porcelain was displayed. Valuable stuff, I'd have thought. They packed all that away for the travelling, unpacked it on arrival. There were also the modern necessities, without which one might not be said to be alive. Plugged into mains electricity, they were not to be robbed of their hi-fis and tellies. If the power went off, that Fowler with its dynamo could probably supply the whole community.

We were there, around and about, for considerably longer than I'd anticipated, Amelia having encountered more friendliness than she'd expected. It took me some time to realize the background to this. The whole group was an entity in itself; that was the point. It was separated by its occupation from the rest of society. Who ever glances at the attendant of a coconut shy? Who speaks to the operator of the dodgems? They are there only as the background to the fun and the noise and the excitement. So they were interested in anybody who showed interest. I was fascinated, Amelia absorbed. Another half an hour of it and she'd have suggested we buy an outfit and join them on tour.

It was Patch who broke it up, this morning all bright and cheerful in her habitual jeans and a vivid T-shirt, her hair flying around all over the place.

'This is my wife,' I said. 'This is Patch, my love.'

'Patch?' she said. 'Hello. Why Patch?'

'It's Pat really, but I'm a spare part, fitting in if somebody's poorly. Kind of patching up, see.'

'I get it,' I said. 'Patch Ritter, is it?'

'Yes. That was my ma and pa you saw last night.'

'I've come for my car.'

'It's super, isn't it?'

'I think so.'

'Ma said she wanted to see you before you go away. She's got the kettle on.' Then she turned and marched away, a confident and competent young lady, not even looking back to check we'd obeyed the summons.

We glanced at each other. Amelia had, after all, to enter the house, but now it was daylight, and the interior, as far as they'd got in their settling in, was cheerful. One thing I'd noticed about the rest of the community was the use of colour. Of course, their equipment had to be show-pieces, in a literal sense, and bright colours were the norm. It entered their souls. They worshipped colour – and so it was in the house. I'd seen the place only when Eric Prost lived there. Died there. Then it had been drab and miserable. But Mrs Ritter had suggested she lived there permanently, and the feminine and show business aspects blended together to make the house bright and full of life and vigour. The curtains were crisply fresh.

It just goes to show. The previous night I'd seen them as dusty and tattered. Strange how your imagination can be so dominant in these matters. What I'd expected to see, I had seen.

Amelia went off happily on a guided tour of the dreaded clocks, me tailing along. I didn't know much about clocks. I'd thought I did, until I met Julian Caine. But I knew these were collector's items and all valuable, bracket clocks, shelf-clocks, skeleton clocks, each and every one of them pendulum controlled.

I turned to Juno Ritter, who was plodding at my shoulder, apparently morose and certainly silent. In daylight he looked a different man, strong and inflexible, certainly, with a bluff face that'd seen a lot of weather, and huge scarred hands. But there was a twinkle in his eyes. His mouth was very flexible, I discovered, able to change from morose to cheerful to pensive in a flash.

'You don't leave the place empty with this lot here, surely,' I said.

'No, no. Certainly not. My wife – it's Emily – she lives here. Somebody's got to organize it all. Me, I'm just the roustabout,

66

on the spot you'd say, where the action is. Patch travels the fairs with me. But there's six complete fairs out there, or five or seven, dependin'. Sometimes one big un. It all takes a lot of organizing, who goes where and when – and how, sometimes. With some o' the stuff the routes have gotta be worked out, and the police tipped off. Emily does all that from here, with a phone. We're all in touch. If necessary, she goes out with the Range Rover. If there's roadwork or the like. It ain't casual, you gotta understand. It don't do itself.'

'No. I see that. I hadn't thought about it, frankly. Must be complicated.'

'Emily's a genius at it. I can tell you . . .' He lowered his voice. '. . . I'd never be able to manage it.'

There was now, I noticed, none of the command that Emily had displayed the previous evening. Then, she'd ordered Juno around and dealt with me curtly. Tired then, I assumed, probably having been out all day with the Range Rover, gathering them in like flocks of sheep. We were in the kitchen at the time, and Emily was chatting amiably enough with Amelia about household matters, apparently. But no, I heard Amelia say, 'You can drive *anything*?'

'Have to,' Emily told her. 'Anything they've got out there. Somebody's got to be able to, in case of sickness.'

'The Fowler steam-tractor?' I put in.

She turned to me, her face warm and soft with what seemed to be excitement. 'I *could*. Don't you just love it! But that old devil Eustace Hobbs won't let me touch it. I'm just waiting for him to go down with something awful. But the damn thing was born the same year as him, apparently. Daren't lay a hand on it.'

I grinned at her. She'd answered a question I hadn't asked. Clearly, that old devil Hobbs wasn't going to let me have a go with it, which I'd been intending to ask.

'But it does mean', I said, returning to Juno and the subject I'd been pursuing, 'that the house *is* left empty.' I was recalling how easily I'd been able to slip that lock. 'If only for the odd day or so.'

'Oh yes.' He beamed. 'But there's Daisy, you see.'

'Daisy?'

67

He raised his head and used his special fairground voice. 'Dai . . . sy!'

There was a thump upstairs, the crash of a door bouncing from a wall, a thunder down the stairs like the big dipper in full flight, and a huge Rottweiler burst into the kitchen, one mass of black and brown muscle and slavering jaws.

'This is Daisy,' said Juno, effecting the introductions.

There'd been a lot of talk lately about Rottweilers, savage attacks and the like. I'd said nothing. Our Sheba is a quite powerful boxer, but as soft as a puddin', as Mary puts it. It's the owners, not the dogs, I reckon, which I suppose makes me as soft as a puddin'. Train 'em from pups as savage guard dogs, and that's what you'll get. But this amount of Rottweiler, launched on us so abruptly, was more than a little disconcerting, particularly as she pounced up with paws on my shoulders and panted into my face.

'Down Daisy,' said Patch severely, just before I went over backwards, and she downed.

Amelia crouched to be slobbered all over, looking back at me with a laugh. 'Your face, Richard! I'll never forget it.'

'She's as soft as a mop,' said Juno, 'but who's going to enter this house and risk it? She sleeps on Patch's bed, and she's not always so excitable. But we're all here now, you see. She loves it when she can wander the grounds and visit all her friends.'

'Tell me,' I said quietly. 'Was she in the house yesterday evening?'

'Oh yes,' he told me. 'Good job you didn't break in, ain't it.'

I felt my cheeks tighten as the blood ran from them. 'Wasn't it!'

'How about a cup of tea?' said Emily, catching my eye. She'd seen me closing that door behind me, I realized.

We sat around the kitchen table, drinking tea. Daisy had been let out to roam where she wished. Emily tapped a spoon against her cup, calling the meeting to order.

'Now then,' she said. 'You were snooping around last night. Don't deny it. You were. Kindly explain yourself.'

'As I told you, I was the investigating officer at the time Eric Prost, your . . .' I hesitated, looking from one face to the other.

'My brother,' she told me. 'Elder brother. It was him as was shot.'

'Yes. Your brother. I see. So, I take it – seeing that you're here now, organizing things – he used to do the same job at that time.'

'You take it right, friend. And where does it get you? Us, rather. Nowhere. Juno – you listenin' to this?'

'Listenin', Emmie. Don't get yourself all worked up.'

She slapped a palm on the table. 'Let him say it. What's your interest now, mister . . . what was the name?'

'Richard Patton. My wife . . .'

'I know. Amelia. So what's goin' on, Mr Patton?'

I took a deep breath. 'You probably know that Julian Caine was recently released from prison. His conviction was quashed.'

'He was guilty as hell. Go on.'

I thought it best not to mention that he'd been doing his best to convince me of that. 'I seem to be hearing the same thing all over the place. And you're giving me the impression that he's not liked around here.'

'Not surprisin', is it?'

'But legally he's been pronounced as innocent.'

'Who'll believe that!'

'Exactly. So he's asked me to try to find definite proof of his innocence.'

'Hah!' She leaned back. 'That's a good un, ain't it, Juno?'

He scratched his head. 'Too deep for me, Emmie.'

'You!' she said. 'Thank heaven Patch takes after me.'

Patch grinned at her father, who made a funny face at her.

Emily said to me, 'A bit late for that, ain't it?'

'To prove him not guilty? Yes. Probably too late.'

'Gettin' anywhere?'

'Not really.'

'There! Y'see! Y'ought to have done a proper job on it in the first place.'

I admitted ruefully that I might have missed one or two points.

'So that was what you were pokin' around for, last night,' Emily decided. 'What did y'expect to find, peerin' in through windows and suchlike? Tell me that.'

'I was simply wondering if the clocks were still here,' I told her quietly, but watching for her reaction. Beside me, I could feel that Amelia was uneasy. I was allowing Emily to overbear me; I was being hectored and interrogated. But this was a woman who'd been running the whole show, and could have done so only by being authoritative. She wouldn't dare to allow argument if a change of plan caused annoyance. The aggression was now part of her personality and not to be confused with her immediate intent.

'Clocks?' she asked. 'What about the damned clocks?'

'It was only . . . well, you know the Tompion long-case clock was apparently stopped by a bullet. At eight-ten.'

She snorted, looked first at Juno, then at Patch, then back to me. '*That* clock! Oh, I'll get it off him, you see if I don't. Got it there in his showroom, he has, proud as punch, and him as oughta be inside right now. I never oughto've let it go. Never. But I was upset, in a right tizz here with Eric's funeral just over and the show on the road, and due here any day. Didn't think. And that wife of his . . . what's her name?'

'Marie.'

'Yeah, that's it. Brazen as y'like, there she was, demanding the clock. Wavin' a bleedin' receipt at me. Well – I didn't have time to think. "Take the damn thing," I said, laughing sort of, you know, like as if she could put it under her arm an' walk away with it – "take it if you want to". I mean, them old things! Antiques. Can't stand 'em meself. But she'd brought a van and a feller to help her. They was gone before you could say knife, and poor Eric hardly in his grave. You couldn't expect me . . . Juno, you couldn't expect me to be thinkin' about things like clocks! Now, could yer?'

'No Emmie,' he said solemnly. 'Got you hands full, you had, my girl.'

'An' how was I to know how much it was worth?' cried Emily. 'An' I let it go! I could kick myself. Over thirty thousan', they tell me. An' I let it go!' she wailed, appealing now to Patch, who didn't seem to be able to make up her mind as to whether she was in the midst of comedy or high tragedy, and was alternately blushing and paling.

70

'You had no choice, Emily,' I said soothingly. 'Caine had paid for it – it was his. Legally, it was.'

'Cheated him! Took advantage of poor Eric, and him half unhinged over his wife's death. Took advantage.'

'I don't think it was like that,' I said, still softly, trying to calm her so that I could find out more about Eric's wife's death.

'Don't y' then! Don't you just! Then how was it?'

'Your brother would have parted with it to somebody else for only two thousand. Caine scratched around and got together three, and bought it for that . . .'

'There y'are then, that was cheating.'

'No, no. Let me finish. Caine intended to get a genuine client for it at a proper price, then he'd have let your brother have the difference.'

She leaned forward across the table. 'An' you believe that? You must be weak in the head.'

'I believe it,' I assured her simply. 'They were friends.'

'Friends! Friends? Oh . . . fine friends they were, always shoutin' and arguing over somethin' or other. On at each other all the time, they were. I've heard 'em. Religion, politics, chess, the news, clocks . . . clocks . . . clocks. On about clocks all the time. Never stopped fightin', they didn't. Ain't that right, Juno? You've heard 'em at it.'

'Yeah, they argued.' He pulled an ear lobe. 'Who don't!'

'They were friends, ma,' said Patch, patting her mother's arm. Patch, who'd been . . . what? . . . ten or eleven then, oh, she'd have sensed friendship behind the discord.

But Emily was nodding, as though they'd both supported her. People *would* agree with her; it would lead to a quieter life. 'At each other's throats,' she insisted. 'Like I said.'

'Tell me,' I continued, after a little silence had built up, 'was all this squabbling before or after the death of Eric's wife?'

Her eyes dropped. It was the first time since we'd begun talking. She would be able to stare out a mad bull. 'After,' she murmured. 'It shook him up rotten. Thought he'd brood himself into a decline, I did.'

'Hmm!' I said. 'Then don't you suppose this arguing and discussing and disputing might've been *because* of that?' Wasn't it Caine who'd told me that Eric Prost had gone strange?

71

'Y'r sayin' Eric'd gone crazy?' she cried, and I half expected a fist to follow the words across the table.

'If that'd been the case, Caine would've stopped calling on him, I'm sure. Hardly a welcome, was it, to have to face aggression?'

'Huh!' said Emily, not willing to venture into psychological conjecture.

I grabbed hold of the slight advantage, and pursued it. 'Maybe we ought to give Caine credit for seeing that arguing with your brother might take his mind off his distress.'

'I'm sure you're right, Richard,' put in Amelia, obviously convinced I wasn't making much of an impression.

Encouraged, I enlarged on it. 'It'd give Eric something to air his fury on, instead of fate, or destiny, or whatever you care to call it.'

'Oh, fancy words now!' said Emily with scorn. 'He's got at you. I can see that now. That Caine – the crafty bastard. All sweetness and light, I'll bet.'

'On the contrary,' I assured her. 'He seems to be doing his best to prove he did it.'

'What!'

'When of course it's quite obvious he didn't.'

'Ohoh!' she said, looking round for approval. 'What've we got here, then? Persuaded you, has he? Clever bugger. Always was.'

'It's you who's persuaded me, you know. All this talk about the two of them fighting! If that'd been so, and taken seriously by Caine, then why did he leave the Tompion in the house, when he held a receipt and a bill of sale? He left it as a reassurance to his friend.'

Emily stared at me for a moment or two, then she bounced to her feet. 'I'll brew up a fresh pot. That tea'll be stewed by now.'

'I'll do it, ma.' Patch was on her feet.

'No!'

Patch looked hurt, but resumed her seat. Amelia murmured something to her. The girl wasn't used to seeing her mother discomposed.

'Y're wrong, you know,' said Juno abruptly. He'd not spoken for so long that I'd assumed he had no thoughts on the matter.

72

He seemed placidly confident, not concerned about Emily's attitude. 'Y're wrong if you think all that fighting was nothin'. To Eric, it was real enough. He'd gone queer-like. No denying that. It'd been coming on for a year or more, ever since Cara died. That was his wife – Cara. He told me . . . he didn't reckon he'd sold that clock. An instalment, he thought, that three thou' was. He reckoned he oughto get the rest. Said Caine had cheated him. Oh yes, he thought Caine was gonna take the clock away from him. In the end, I think, he hated Caine. Hated him.'

Emily had allowed this to go on, busying herself with the kettle and pot and swilling out the mugs. She was allowing Juno to build it up for her, and now he'd brought it to the right pitch. She spoke to her daughter without turning.

'Fetch the letter, Patch.'

'I've got it right here.'

Patch said this with a rueful little smile at me, taking me into her confidence in what might have been a trifling advantage she'd taken over her mother, anticipating her wishes. And she did indeed have it under her hand on the table, the mystery being from where she'd produced it. There surely couldn't have been room beneath or around those jeans, so very tight as they were and tighter still when sat in, and I could swear there was absolutely nothing beneath the T-shirt but skin. But there it was – a letter.

I stared at it, with an uneasy feeling that it was going to be important, and an even more uneasy conviction that I ought to have seen it ten years before.

It could well have been Eric Prost's last letter.

6

Emily returned to the table and distributed fresh supplies of tea. Amelia moved uncomfortably. My eyes were on the letter. Emily reached over and took Patch's wrist in two fingers, lifted her hand, and slid the letter free. There was something delicately precise about the movement. Patch pouted. Emily thrust it at me and I stared down at it on the table surface, an old and almost forgotten instinct ridiculously forbidding me from touching it.

It was addressed to a box number at Newcastle Central Post Office. Mr and Mrs J. Ritter. The cancellation date was undecipherable.

'That came', explained Emily, 'in August, just a week and a half before . . . before the end of the season. A week before he died.' She nodded, distress in her eyes now we'd approached so close to the event. 'We wasn't half as organized then. Since Cara died, poor Eric went all to pieces. But I've said that. A year she'd been dead by then, and he was just gettin' worse. Yes, he was, Juno. He was!' She hated to have to admit it.

As though Juno had said something, she moved her hand sideways to restrain him. He caught it and held it. She bit her lip, unable to go on, so Juno took it up.

'Cara and Eric used to organize things this end, in those days, but we hadn't got a car phone then, so it all hadda be from here, from his office with his phone. We'd call in if there was trouble. Then they'd drive out. Got a Triumph Dolomite, they had. But Eric didn't drive, which made it a dead loss when Cara died. Sorry – I'm gettin' this all out of order.'

'No, no,' I assured him. 'Take it from the beginning, when Cara died.' I had a feeling that this *was* the beginning.

'Yeah,' he said, rubbing his face with his free hand. 'We'd had some trouble – can't remember what – and they drove out to see the police. Routing, I'd expect. Worked things out with 'em. This was Nottingham-way, weren't it, Emmie?'

'Northampton. What's it matter?' But it was a feeble protest. She didn't want to remember any of it.

'Anyways up,' went on Juno, 'they was drivin' in from the Markham Hill direction. It was late – raining – yeah, raining. Said he got soaked. Oh hell, what's it matter! Cara was drivin' fast. Stupid, if you ask me. She'd had a big day of it, I'd reckon. Must've bin tired out. So – rushin' to get home, when it'd've been best to go slow . . .'

'For God's sake, get *on* with it!' Emily burst out.

'Doin' just that,' he said calmly. 'I was goin' to say, there's a turn-off up there, Markham Hill way. Big houses along there. Prior Close, they call it.'

'I know it,' I said softly.

'An' this car – a woman drivin' – it came shootin' outa there, Eric said, and Cara turned away from it into a ditch and into a tree. Eric got throwed out – broke an arm, he did – but Cara was trapped inside, an' that woman . . . oh, she stopped right enough, ran back and stared. Stared, Eric told me. Stared into the car, an' then she goes and turns round and runs to her car and drives away. Away, Eric said, an' there was a phone-box only a hundred yards down the hill, but she went right past it and to hell gone.'

He stopped. Emily recovered her hand and pressed two fingers to the bridge of her nose, and Patch protested, 'Ma!'

Yet when I glanced at her I saw she was more distressed than her mother, though in a tight and repressed way, her face white and her eyes huge and moist.

Her mother noticed this. She caught Juno's eye and nodded towards Patch, who was now staring at the table. He cleared his throat.

'I'll keep it short,' he said. 'Eric got to that phone-box. There was summat wrong with his leg, he could hardly move. But he got there and dialled 999, an' while he was there he saw the car go up in flames. He was still sittin' there, in the box, when they got to him.'

I looked down at the letter again. 'I suppose I need to know that before I look at the letter?'

'You do.' He was definite about that. 'Or it don't make no sense.'

Emily jerked herself from her silence. 'He remembered, see. Eric did. Said he'd never forget it, that woman starin'.'

'And this letter came around a year after that episode?' I was aware that a year can see many changes.

'Somethin' like that,' said Juno. 'We hadda set up post-office boxes an' phone 'em in to Eric. Go on. Read it. It won't bite.'

I slid out a sheet of bluish writing paper. Eric's hand had been uncertain. His meaning wasn't.

> Dear Emm and Juno,
>
> I think I've got him, good and proper. He'll never wriggle out of this one. I'll get my money now, or know the reason why. You'll see. Or let me keep the clock.
>
> I was in town, last Tuesday evening. Went for a few drinks and it was after closing-time, so it was getting late. And I saw her. Was pretty sure it was her, but the hair was different. You know. Almost walked into me, coming out of that alley-way by the side of Caine's shop. I'll swear it was her.
>
> Don't tell me I was seeing things, 'cause I wasn't. And she knew me, the way she rushed away. Me, I was a bit far gone, so I couldn't run after her, but I seen her, and it means she's around here somewhere, and who could she have been with but Julian?
>
> Oh, won't he be pleased when I spring it on him, after the scene Marie made over the last one. Lovely, isn't it? And the woman before. She said she was leaving him, last time. Remember? Now what's he going to do, when I can tell her he's got another woman? 'Specially <u>this</u> one.
>
> Have a few drinks on me to celebrate.
>
> > Love,
> > Eric

Amelia had been leaning against my arm as I read this. I heard her give a little moan, realizing I suppose how much more deeply this would involve me. Thoughtfully, playing for time in which to arrange my reactions, I slowly folded the letter, slid it back in the envelope, and put it on the table under Emily's eyes. But she seemed not to notice.

'You heard nothing more about it from him?' I asked. I was thinking that there was nothing in this letter, in its tone, to link the woman he'd seen in town with the woman responsible for Cara Prost's death. I'd have expected some expression of loathing for her. 'No other letter? Surely there would be phone calls or messages from him.'

Juno shook his head. 'We was comin' up to the end of the season, see. Things get kind of rough. People tired out an' wantin' to get back here for the break. You'll guess. Busy, we was, me'n Emily. Phone calls to Eric, o' course, there was plenty of *them*. But he never said anythin' else about it. Then it got to be a coupla days before we packed in. Phoned Eric a half dozen times, I did, an' got no answer. We was worried, you can bet. Then we got back here an' found a ruddy great padlock on the side door, an' somethin' in an envelope about phonin' the police. Your lot. A fine home-comin', that was.'

'Sorry about that. I did try, though. Eric's notebook, I remember I couldn't make head nor tail of it, and there was no address anywhere of any next of kin or solicitor. Nothing.'

'*He* knew!' snapped Emily. 'Caine knew all about it. The whole set-up.'

'I'm afraid, at that time, he was far too occupied to think about anything but himself. We had him in custody.'

'All the same . . .'

'The fact is, we couldn't trace anybody. And of course, with valuable stuff in the house we had to seal it up. I sent an officer to seal it, and to leave a note.'

'Nice welcome home!' said Emily bitterly. 'Empty house, and couldn't even get in.'

'I'm sorry.'

'Y' couldn't help it,' said Juno reasonably.

'I could perhaps have investigated the background more deeply,' I said. But I'd had a murder on my hands. It was no damned excuse, I told myself. 'But surely – and you don't seem to have thought of this – surely your brother, Emily, was rather

77

jumping to conclusions. He'd seen and recognized a woman, yes, and we'll accept it wasn't a mistake. But she'd only been coming out of an alley-way alongside Caine's premises. It needn't have been *the* woman, and that alley-way probably leads to other places. It's a bit much of a conclusion to jump to on that evidence, linking her with Caine. Don't you think?'

'He's got a room over that shop,' said Juno. 'All set up. Oh, Marie knew about it, you can bet your life. He's always been a bit over-sexed, has our splendid Julian Caine. So Eric said.'

He'd spoken with his eyebrows raised, just a hint of admiration in his voice.

'Juno!' said Emily sharply, and, 'You hadn't oughto be listening to this, Patch my girl.'

'Oh . . . ma!' Her cheeks flared.

'All the same,' I persisted, 'it'd be a bit of a coincidence, the woman he saw at the time of the car accident being linked with Caine, just because she was coming from that alley-way. If that's what you're suggesting.'

'Coincidence?' Emily was sharp on that. 'No! Nothin' of the sort. She'd been driving outa Prior Close, and Caine lives along there.'

'Of course,' I agreed softly. But so did a lot of other people.

All I'd done was come to collect my car, and now there were all these added complications. Nothing at all I was discovering did anything other than plough Caine in even deeper than he'd been before. And flickering in the back of my conscious mind, attempting to struggle forward into prominent view, was a memory of the letter Eric Prost had been writing at the time of the shot. As near as I could remember, it had been intended for Julian Caine personally, but the contents had been short and vague, as the bullet had cut it off short. I hadn't been certain about it at the time. As there'd been hints as to Prost's mental stability, I'd assumed he'd been writing similar letters to all sorts of people, distributing his bitterness around the district. But perhaps not, after all. It seemed to have been concentrated on one person.

It had been directed to a person he designated as 'J', I remembered, and went something like this, give or take a word or two here and there:

You ought to have known I'd recognize her sooner or later. How much does your better half know, I wonder? And I do mean better, so you . . .'

Half-way through a sentence it'd finished. Abruptly.

Now it began to make sense. He could well have sent similar letters to Caine, and been doing so for some time. In spite of the fact that Caine was still visiting? Well, why not, if Eric Prost was acting strange?

I said, 'We've taken up rather a lot of your time, I'm afraid. We'd better be off.'

Emily nodded. 'It hasn't been a waste of time, if it's shown you what he is.'

'I'm beginning to get something of an idea about that.'

I drew back Amelia's chair as she got to her feet. The usual pleasantries were exchanged, and we went out to our cars. Daisy was out there, and seemed to expect to come riding with us. She'd be used to travelling, no doubt. But when we went to two separate cars it quite confused her.

'Follow me,' I said. 'We'll stop in town and have lunch.'

Amelia looked at me enquiringly and I nodded. She smiled, and we got into our cars, and it was then that I remembered a little point I hadn't mentioned. Juno and Emily were standing there, watching us leave, so I wound down a window and called out, 'It wasn't me who stopped your clocks, in case you're wondering.'

'Clocks?' Juno glanced at Emily, who shook her head. 'What clocks?'

'In the house. They were all stopped when we sealed it up.'

'Nah!' he shouted. 'They were going when we got inside. Right time, too.'

I wound up the window and drove away, Amelia following. My mind wouldn't accept it. Just wouldn't. It took a fair amount of mental effort to drive as far as the car-park in town.

When we'd parked side by side, Amelia walked over quickly. 'Richard, your driving! You went through a pedestrian crossing, and the lights were . . .'

'Didn't you hear what Juno said?'

She clearly hadn't. 'What was that?'

79

'The clocks were all going when they finally managed to get into the house.'

'Oh,' she said.

'Showing the correct time, too.'

'I'm sure they must've made a mistake.' But her frown was of worry.

'Let's go and get some lunch,' I suggested. Then perhaps it'd go away.

It was quite a while, though, before she was ready to eat. This was just the type of shopping-centre she loves to investigate, but I was sure her enthusiasm was at first affected, she not wishing to talk to me face to face and have to discuss the clocks. But very soon the novelty of the town absorbed all her attention and her pleasure became real, so that I was able to have a quiet think about those damned clocks. It had to mean something. Don't tell me we're talking about the supernatural here. I had to cling to the fact that everything that had occurred inside and outside of that house, at that time, had a logical explanation. Or I'd go out of my mind.

Amelia seemed to have shrugged off the thought. She was enjoying herself. The trouble is that she is apt to become over-enthusiastic, and if I hadn't exercised a little judicious restraint her credit card would've become red-hot and melted. As it was, I had to make several trips back to the Granada with bulky packages and bulging plastic carriers before we managed to sit down to eat. We found an upstairs restaurant overlooking the so-called square, and thus facing across to Caine Antiques.

She chattered away happily over the meal, and I listened. The whole aspect of the clocks had disappeared, it seemed. I nodded where necessary, mumbling yes or no as required, my gaze wandering from time to time to the upstairs floor of Caine's premises. There were two small windows. I saw that they had new curtains to them. The suggestion was that these windows were to one, or perhaps two, rooms that were at least usable. But surely . . . fresh curtains suggested a woman's touch, and if Caine did, or had, used the upper floor to entertain women friends, Marie would not have put new curtains to the windows for their delectation. If, of course, they would show any interest at all in the curtains.

80

Amelia had walked past Caine's windows twice during the morning, casually ignoring their display. I knew what she'd been doing; clearing her mind of all the exciting background of a shopping spree, so that she could concentrate in a relaxed frame of mind for the important bit. I realized that she intended to visit Caine's and nose around, just as she knew that it was also my intention.

So, after lunch, I was not surprised when she spent a couple of minutes examining Caine's window-display. It gave me time to slip quickly down the narrow alley-way at the side, only a few yards but enough to locate a nondescript door fitted with a cylinder-lock. Further along, the passage way opened on to a minor road. I was at her side again before she'd noticed I'd left it.

'Shall we go inside, Richard?'

'By all means,' I agreed equably.

Though I'd already had one dose of the impact, nevertheless I was again caught up in the atmosphere Caine had created. You could feel the relaxed calm of the place, the clocks pacing out the beats of a patient heart, restful and hypnotic.

Marie was there once more, as a presence only, like a ghost that had travelled with the clocks through the ages of their existence. This time I did not ignore her. Once our eyes had become used to the suppressed lighting, I introduced the two ladies. They had never met, and I had seen Marie myself only briefly, not long enough to get a true impression of her.

This was the woman who, according to Caine, had left him because she couldn't stand living in a house full of weapons. Now it seemed that she had had perhaps more cogent reasons, if Julian had been a womanizer. Yet she'd returned to him, if she *had* actually left him (perhaps more than once) and when he'd been arrested she'd stepped in and kept the business operative, if not booming. Certainly she'd been brisk and efficient in collecting the Tompion from Emily and Juno, before they had time to give it much thought. Perhaps Marie had loved her husband dearly, too dearly. Still did. Weapons or not.

These thoughts ran through my mind as I stood quietly and watched how the two women reacted to each other. Marie was a little taller than Amelia, dark, her dress, perhaps, as I'd thought before, chosen to match the mood, plain and undemonstrative. But even I could see that it hadn't been chosen casually. It was quietly elegant, emphasizing her slim poise and not her figure, which, frankly, could look after itself very well indeed. She was not a beauty, but handsome, and whereas before I'd thought her to be somewhat stiff and formal, almost repressed, once Amelia got her talking she was bright and responsive, as though breaking from a shell of repose. Amelia is very good at this sort of thing, can shine through any shades of reserve as though they do not exist, and soften people with her own radiant warmth. I felt myself to be excluded from the conversation.

Idly, because it happened to be lying on a table beside us, I picked up one of Caine's inlaid flintlocks, weighed it in my hand, verified that the action still operated by cocking it, then pressed the trigger. I got a decidedly firm 'clock' from it, which caused Marie to jump and Amelia to flash me a quick, severe glance.

'Really, Richard! Don't play with the things, please.'

'Sorry,' I said to Marie. 'I forgot. Julian said you didn't like weapons.'

'I hate them.' The mouth suddenly became prim.

Amelia caught on at once. 'And I don't blame you. I can't understand men, really I can't. They treat the things as toys – playthings – when they were never intended for anything but killing.'

Marie grimaced. 'We've got a room full of them at home.'

'How *do* you stand it!' Amelia sympathized. 'I couldn't even sleep if I knew . . .'

'I've never been able to get used to them,' Marie told her quietly. 'Oh, I know that none of them would actually fire a shot. I'm not stupid in *that* way. It's just what they represent.'

'I know, I know.' This was not the Amelia I adored. Take her to a pistol club and she would insist on having a go. Would probably blast the bull's-eye to shreds, too. Therefore, I dared not catch her eye. I just listened, waiting for my cue.

'And of course,' went on Amelia, volubly sympathetic, 'there *were* two pistols that would fire. Or so I understand from Richard.'

82

'Oh, there were, there were. And d'you know . . .' She lowered her voice as though this might be unfit to be heard by a man . . . 'he used to come back from that terrible club of his . . . can you *imagine*, all those immature men shooting away at targets all evening! It's beyond belief. Anyway, I was saying, he'd come back with them and clean them on my kitchen table.'

'Them!' I thought. But he'd told me he always took only one. The prosecution's case had been that he'd taken out both of them that evening, leaving one at Prost's house and using the other one at his club. We'd assumed he'd abandoned one pistol on the way there. Now Marie was adding a quota of confirmation to that, talking about pistols, plural. I longed to plunge in, and had to force myself to give full attention to my flintlock.

But my wife had the matter in hand. 'How distressing for you,' she said sadly.

'I wouldn't have cared so much, but he kept up a conversation, so that I could hardly walk away. So I had to watch while he got them to bits and put them back, treating them like babies, to be handled so gently and . . . and lovingly. Yes, lovingly. It made me feel quite ill.'

She'd used babies as a comparison. They'd had no children.

'And it would take quite a while,' Amelia decided.

'Yes. Ages.'

'Two of them,' Amelia murmured. 'You'd think one would be enough for an evening's banging away.'

'Wouldn't you!' said Marie.

'I wonder you could stand it. I'm glad Richard doesn't do that. Are you listening to this, Richard?'

I'd worked out how the action worked, had located where they'd put the priming charge. I looked up. 'Yes, love?'

'I was saying, I'd never put up with having you owning pistols.'

'It's never been my ambition.'

'I should think not. I do believe I'd leave you.'

'Then perhaps I'll give it some thought.'

'You dare! See,' she told Marie. 'Put an idea into their heads . . . it didn't drive you to that, I hope. Leaving him.'

'What! And let him drive me out of my kitchen! I'd shoot him first, with one of his own pistols.'

83

'Would you?' I asked with interest, trying to make it sound vague.

She bit her lip. 'Silly of me. As though I could touch one of the things.' There was a faint blush on her cheeks.

'Of course not,' said Amelia. 'But do you mind . . . would you show me the clocks. Now clocks are a different thing altogether, aren't they! One can grow to love a clock . . .'

And gently, casually, Amelia drew her away. I put down the flintlock quietly, not intending to tell Amelia that handling it had stirred an interest somewhere deep inside me, and went to find Julian Caine.

There he was, bent over his lathe with his gear-cutting attachment fitted, delicately fashioning a steel pinion. At first he didn't notice me, his head low, and I was content to stand and watch. Further along his bench, in a cleared space, were the stripped entrails of a clock, which I recognized as a bracket clock because of the bob pendulum.

He looked up, seeming unsurprised to see me. 'You'd think,' he said, 'it'd be the brass gears that'd wear first. But no, it's always the steel pinions. It's brass working on to steel, you know. Always.' He stretched, easing his back. 'And how are you progressing?'

He made it sound like a foreman on his rounds. I was just an operator. I dispelled that idea.

'I've been showing my wife round the shops. She's outside there, now, admiring the clocks.'

'Oh yes? Marie looking after her, is she?'

'Splendidly.'

A shadow crossed his eyes. For one moment his face stiffened, then he smiled. 'They'll no doubt get along very well.'

'So it seemed.'

I poked around nosily along his bench, waiting for him to change the subject. He managed it. He was no doubt wondering what Marie might say to my wife.

'You'd think the softer metal would wear first.' He showed me the brass gear on which the pinion would mesh.

'Oh, I don't know. They use a softer metal for big-end bearings.'

'For what?'

'In motor vehicle engines.'

He smiled. 'I know nothing about cars.'

'Well . . . in the same way as softer bullets wear the steel bore of one of your pistols.'

We were now in his territory. 'No. No, no. It's the deposit left from the charge in the cartridge. Get at 'em quickly enough and clean the barrel . . .' He shrugged.

'I see,' I said, nodding my understanding. 'That'd explain it.'

'Explain what? You *do* wander around with your remarks.'

'Why you'd hurry to clean your target-pistols. No further than the kitchen table. I'd have thought the extra minute or so to get to your weapons room . . .'

'*She* told you that!'

'Marie? Yes. She told my wife, in fact, and I just happened to be there.'

I saw, then, from the sudden twist of his lips, that Caine could be vicious. A man of extremes, perhaps, as nothing could have been more friendly and unself-seeking than the way he'd tried to help Eric Prost over the Tompion long-case clock, when they were virtually fighting whenever they met. But it was there, then gone in a flash, and he gave me a soft and almost conspiratorial smile.

'Women can be very silly, I've found.'

'My wife,' I confided, 'is continually surprising me.'

'Yes.' He assumed I was agreeing with him. 'Fancy Marie making such a fuss. It wasn't natural, you know. It's not as though a target twenty-two is a killing weapon.'

'But it *can* kill.'

'Oh yes. It can.'

'In the hands of an expert.'

'That of course,' he said, somewhat annoyed. 'But Marie had to learn that they weren't anything but pieces of metal that slotted together. That's all they are, come right down to it. It irritated me, I'll tell you that, this foolish . . . well, kittenish, I suppose . . . yes, kittenish attitude of hers. Women aren't *like* that these days. They don't swoon any more. They don't jump on chairs at the sight of a mouse. No. So I thought she was being very silly about my Hammerlis. I really did. That's why I used to clean them on the kitchen table. So domestic, you see.

Domestic and harmless. Just pieces of metal I was cleaning, like her pots and pans.'

'But she hated it?'

He nodded. 'Ridiculous. She didn't have to watch.'

'You said it nearly drove her into leaving you.'

'Did I? I don't remember that.'

'But of course, it'd take something more than that.'

He was silent. I hadn't been watching his face; this wasn't an interrogation. Now I glanced at him, attracted by the silence.

'Nearly came to it,' he admitted.

'But she *did* leave you?'

'Well . . . yes.'

'But not because, every Monday evening, you cleaned two pistols on the kitchen table?'

'Of course not.'

'Then why?'

'It doesn't matter. It's not your business.' His anger suddenly flared. 'Drop the subject.'

I eyed him steadily, waiting for the anger to die, waiting until I saw his minimal shrug. Then I said, 'I'd love to drop the whole affair. You asked me to prove your innocence, and I'm finding it more and more difficult. It's mounting up against you, Caine, for God's sake. Tell me to pack it in, and I'll do that. Willingly.'

'No . . . don't do that.'

'Then why,' I repeated, 'did she leave you?'

'What d'you think? Another woman.'

'Woman or women?'

'Woman, damn you. On and off.'

'Are you willing to give me her name?'

'Most certainly not.'

'Because all that's finished?'

'I've not seen her for . . .' He stopped.

'Ten years? I know. Ten years, during which your wife, who'd left you *before* the shooting . . .' I stopped, raising my eyebrows.

'Yes.'

'All right. Left you before the shooting, but came back when you were in trouble and rescued your business here, kept it ticking over . . . Here, that's good. Clocks. Ticking over. Don't you think that's good?'

'For God's sake, finish it.'

'Yes. Marie. Came back, as I say, and took over, and waited for you, and is still with you. Me, I'd have treasured her. I'd have recognized her for what she is.'

'Yes,' he said, and damn him he was so lacking in grace that he dared to criticize her to me. 'Dull and uninspiring, that's what she is. There when you look around – but for what? For inspiration? For excitement? Don't make me laugh, Patton, and don't interfere in my private life. If you please.'

I turned away because I wanted to hit him. Turned back. 'So she's turned up again.'

'What?'

'This other woman. So sparkling and exciting . . .'

'No! I told you no. I've not seen her since . . . since the shooting. I swear to you . . .'

'Don't. Please. I couldn't stand it. But perhaps I can see why Marie's stayed with you and is still with you.'

'We've worked things out.'

I smiled. 'They've been worked out for you. You've been refused a hand-gun licence, so that now she doesn't have to watch you cleaning them on her kitchen table.'

'You possibly have a point,' he conceded, his face stiff, his eyes cold. 'If it wasn't intended as a joke.'

'And that's twice I've said it. Pistols – plural. Marie said it too. Both pistols, every Monday evening. You told me you took only one each week, alternating.'

'It's not . . .'

'I'm not interested in what it's not,' I cut in. 'What *was* it, one or two?'

'It was', he said distantly, 'usually two. I'm sure I've told you this. One had started jamming. I was intending to do some work on it, get it right. *That* night I took only one, and left the other behind.'

'To which you wife, you are as good as telling me, had access?'

'I didn't say that.'

'I'm sorry. My mistake. She'd left you . . .'

'A fortnight before.'

'. . . and if she was going to return to you it's hardly likely she would do so on a Monday evening, which was pistol-cleaning Monday. And surely she wouldn't return specifically to steal one of your pistols, which she couldn't bear touching anyway, unless it was either in order to shoot you or to shoot your fancy female. Certainly not Eric Prost. So do you imagine I believe you, Caine, when you tell me you took along only one pistol that particular Monday? You've lied to me once, already. Now you're saying you *usually* took both pistols. What a coincidence, then, that you took only one on *that* particular Monday.'

'I . . . I . . .' He couldn't find an adequate answer.

'And if,' I continued without any change of tone, 'you have not seen your mistress – is that how you think of her? – your mistress, then, since you've been released, why are there fresh curtains at the windows upstairs?'

'What! How *dare* you! Marie put those curtains up. There's a sitting-room up there. If I'm working late, she stays and gets something to eat for us, and we go home late. Blast you and your impertinence! I see no reason to tell you . . .'

'But you have. You have a tendency to say too much, Caine, too often, and not always truthfully. Do you *want* me to walk out on you? If not, why do you have to toss at me all the wrong things?'

'No! No, no.'

'So you didn't bring her here?' I jerked a thumb upwards.

'Who?'

I sighed. 'You've told me there *was* a woman. Did you bring her here, or take her to your home when your wife was elsewhere?'

The air gasped out of him as though I'd punched him. 'No,' he gasped.

'No . . . what? Not here, or not at your home?'

'Not to Markham View, for God's sake. Not to Marie's home!'

I smiled at him. He was visibly fighting for self-control. By some miracle he managed finally to speak in an almost normal tone.

'If I'd known you intended to pry into my private life . . .' He raised his shoulders and stared past me.

'What?'

'I'd never have asked you to help me.'

'Then ask yourself whether, in view of the fact that I'm getting deeper and deeper into this, you really want me to go on with it now.'

He stared at me a long while. I could see his fists clenching and unclenching. Eventually, he whispered, 'Yes.'

'I'd have thought, in the circumstances, that you ought to add the little word, please.'

'Please.' It was no more than an exhalation of breath.

I turned and left him, making no promises.

7

Following the murmuring sound I eventually came across them, chatting quietly in front of the Tompion. Amelia turned to me at once, with a light I recognized in her eyes.

'Here you are, Richard. Isn't this simply magnificent?'

'It certainly is.'

'I've always thought there was something missing in the hall. That space at the foot of the stairs, you know. This would fit it perfectly, and just *make* the hall, completely transform it.'

I glanced at Marie. There was a hint of amusement in the quirk of her lips. 'Shall we take it with us?' I asked. 'I've got an idea it'd have to be stripped down and reassembled the other end. But there's a snag, love.'

'And what's that?' Amelia pouted at me.

'In order to pay for it you'd have to sell the house, and then you wouldn't have a hall to stand it in.'

There was a pert angle I always like to see in the tilt of Amelia's head. She knew this only too well, as she must have guessed this was *the* Tompion, but she cares to tease me. I go along with it. I tried to look shocked.

'I was joking, Richard.'

'Were you?'

Then I heard Julian chuckle from behind me, which was a little surprising. I'd had the impression that at this time he would prefer the company of a partly-worked pinion to that of an overworked Patton. But no. He was his old self again, relaxed and affable.

'I don't think I could bear to part with it now,' he told us.

'But surely', I said, 'it's a very valuable item for a dealer to keep.'

'Ah yes. Consider it as a capital investment. My fall-back if I fail to maintain the business.'

Marie stirred. She smiled at him. The expression was something deeper than a gentle tease, but her voice was light. 'It didn't fail when you were away, Julian. It can hardly do so now you're back.'

'Of course not,' I said for him, because there was very little he could say to that himself.

Julian dragged his eyes away from her and back to me. 'You'll have noticed the repair, of course.'

'What repair?'

'The glass naturally, but I really meant the dial.' He reached up and opened the clock-face door. 'There, you see, that's where the bullet struck.' He was indicating a spot just outside the inner ring of the dial. 'As I told you, a twenty-two bullet wouldn't penetrate the face-plate. I filled it in and smoothed it off. You can barely see it now.'

In this he was quite correct. I could barely detect it. 'You've done a good job on it.'

'A paltry little repair,' he said, his flapping hand rejecting it.

'But you've made your point.'

'How so?'

'That the bullet didn't stop the clock. So . . . how *was* it stopped?'

'There's only one way.' He opened the trunk door, exposing the pendulum and weights. 'You put a finger to the pendulum and stop it.'

I knew all this very well, but it's a good idea to have it from an expert. Besides, experts love to air their knowledge. It softens them, relaxes them.

'And to start it?' I asked.

'The opposite. Set the pendulum swinging again.' He was looking at me strangely. It'd been such a stupid question, as I'd watched him do it at his house.

'That applies to all pendulum-clocks, does it?' I went on, without any emphasis in my voice.

'What had you in mind?'

91

'The other clocks in Eric Prost's place. I'm no expert, but aren't they all pendulum-clocks?'

'I see what you mean.' He saw, certainly, but was suspicious about the direction of my thoughts. Giving himself time to sort it out, he hurried on, 'There are two lantern clocks, one of them without its side boxes, four bracket clocks, one of those a Tompion, three wall-clocks, and a rare skeleton clock by Woolley.'

'All pendulum-clocks?'

'Yes. I did say that.' He looked puzzled. 'Why does it matter?'

'Well, you see, if you're going to insist that this Tompion here wasn't stopped by the bullet, it nevertheless did stop at eighten, which need not have been the time of the two shots. Eric Prost may not have died at once, and could have been unconscious for quite a while. Yet the clock *did* stop. Perhaps it stopped when he died.' I raised an eyebrow at him, not looking at Marie, though aware that her hand had fluttered up to her face. 'In sympathy,' I murmured.

He opened his mouth, but no sound emerged. Then he cleared his throat. 'That's ridiculous. I thought we'd heard the last of that. Fantasy.'

'Yes. Certainly it is. But – you see – the other ten also stopped, and at the same time. Eight-ten.'

'Here now!' he gasped. 'Don't let's go all . . . all . . .'

'What? You're a clock-man, probably a member of some clock society.'

'It's called . . .'

'So you'll have heard if there've been any similar instances of clocks stopping at the time of their owner's death.'

'It's quite ridiculous!' he protested.

'No stories going the rounds?'

He waved one hand with a degree of agitation. 'I've never believed a word . . . yes, of course there're stories. Sheer superstition, every bit of it. Like poltergeists and . . . and ghosts and hauntings. And there was that old song, about the very old grandfather and his clock – that's why they're called grandfather clocks, by the way. But it's just a song. Look here, if you're basing all your ideas on that sort of evidence, you're heading up a blind alley. How could . . .'

'But I'm not arguing. Don't go on so. It's just that it's rather strange. Especially as they all started up again, at exactly the same and correct time, too. That's what really gets me.'

'Started up?'

'Yes. At the same time. Perhaps a ghostly finger nudged the pendulums when the body was taken from the house. I don't know. I wasn't there.'

His mouth opened and shut. He said nothing. I smiled at him.

'I just thought you might have ideas on it, that's all. Well, we'd better be getting along, I suppose, and it must be close to your closing time.' I glanced at my watch. 'Heavens, look at the time. We don't want to upset Mary, do we, love?'

'We do not,' Amelia said, her face expressionless.

So we said our goodbyes and left. When we were well clear, Amelia tugged at my arm. 'Mischief, Richard? Is that what it was?'

'I don't know, frankly. I just wondered whether he knew anything about those clocks stopping and starting again. But he didn't.'

'Does it matter, though? Does it?'

'I don't know. I feel it does, because it's so strange. But I can't see *how* it matters.'

The car-park was now nearly empty, our cars standing out in isolation. It was dark. We stood silently together for a few moments beside her Granada, then she unlocked it and slid in behind the wheel, reached over and unlocked the other door, which I opened. I slid in and sat beside her. There was more to say, and for Amelia it wouldn't wait.

'You're not getting anywhere, are you?'

'Nowhere that isn't a dead end,' I agreed.

'So why go on with it?'

'You know why.'

'Because you just hate anything to beat you.' She nodded to herself.

'That too.'

'What else is there?'

I took a deep breath. 'I think the whole thing's deeper than I imagined. We're just skirting the edges so far.'

'We? Are you including me, Richard?'

'Don't I always?'

She was silent. I waited, allowing the silence to become companionable. In the end, she went off on an entirely different tack.

'She's a very pleasant woman, don't you think?'

'Who?' When I knew damn well. 'Marie Caine?'

'Yes. I think she's been hurt very deeply. Wouldn't you agree? A quiet woman, not showing it, but I think she's still hurt and hasn't sorted herself out yet. Am I making sense, Richard?'

'I thought much the same. Not perhaps in those words, but the general idea's the same. It always surprises me, the number of men who seem to get better wives than they deserve. Take . . .'

'Like you?' she asked demurely.

'Take me,' I said, 'as I was just about to say. But it doesn't make me a villain.'

'Or me an angel.'

'True.'

She punched my arm as I reached into a pocket for my pipe. It didn't stop me from getting it out. 'I just can't make up my mind about Caine,' I admitted. 'Sometimes he can be deliberately cruel, sometimes he's just as cruel but hides it, or tries to, but he's got great strength of character. Look how he's bounced back, straight into the business as though he's never been away.'

'It *is* as though he's never been away. She's seen to that. Couldn't you feel the tension in her? Oh, you're so unobservant!'

'I thought her a very placid woman.'

'I could just sense her, every second, sort of looking over her shoulder, waiting for trouble.'

'As though whatever it is – or was, rather – is still there?'

'Yes. It's a kind of deep, hidden terror inside her. She's afraid that it hasn't finished yet. Whatever it is.'

'Just my own impression,' I assured her.

'Your impression of her . . .'

'No. I meant my impression of the situation. I don't think it's over. Maybe, now Caine's back, it'll all start again.' Silence. I waited. She said nothing. 'Which is why I feel I've got to go on with it.'

'I wish you wouldn't.'

'Then I won't.'

She sighed. 'And have you miserable and silent and mooning around the house! Oh . . . lovely.'

On cue, I became silent, waiting for her to work it out.

'But what d'you think you can *do*?' she asked at last.

'Hang around. Hope something crops up. I just don't know.'

'Then I suppose you'll have to do that.' Her voice was toneless, then it became enlivened. 'Come along, Richard. Get in your car, and we'll get moving. You lead, and not at your usual speed, mind.'

'Promise.'

I led the way out of the park. As the headlights swung in an arc they swept over the only other vehicle still there, in a far corner. Leaning against its bonnet, negligently and apparently composed, was Chief Superintendent Wainwright. I didn't stop, but simply ignored him.

It was an easy run, my only duty to see that her headlights didn't fall too far behind. She hates night-driving. I have a theory that her pupils are over-sensitive to light, closing down very small for daylight and opening up too wide for darkness. This latter effect naturally reduces the depth of field of her vision, and although she may not realize it her nervousness could relate directly to the fact that she doesn't see clearly in the dark. Perhaps she needs spectacles for driving at night. Someday, when I've worked up the nerve, I'll suggest it.

In the morning, over breakfast, Amelia was making gentle hints about all the little jobs that needed doing round the house. It was to inform me that she wasn't keen on my dashing straight off for more futile investigations. She needn't have worried; I hadn't thought of anything I could investigate.

But shortly afterwards, CS Wainwright turned up, and altered all that. I had to introduce them, my wife and the Chief Superintendent. All she knew of him was what I'd told her about our original talk, but she'd clearly accepted that as a personal insult. Nevertheless, she took him politely into the living-room and sat him down, then seated herself facing him and contemplated him coolly and silently. He recognized this for what it was. I saw his lips twitch. I sat on the arm of Amelia's chair and laid one arm along its back.

'Nice to see you again, Mr Wainwright,' I said, but not with noticeable sincerity.

'And you . . . and your charming wife.'

She said nothing. She hates that sort of thing, he expecting to ingratiate himself so obviously.

'You no doubt have a reason for this visit,' I suggested. 'Something new turned up, has it?'

His teeth appeared, then he clamped his mouth shut on them, cleared his throat, and said, 'It will not do, you know. It just will not. We can't have an ex-police officer reinvestigating his former cases.'

'If they need further work doing on them . . .'

'In no circumstances,' he said briskly and with finality. 'Don't you see the impression it creates! It could seem that the police can't accept that a conviction can be overturned, and that we're still trying to justify ourselves.'

'Or, conversely, that we're belatedly trying to put right a past wrong?' I suggested.

'It's as good as an admission of . . . something or other.'

'Nonsense.'

His eyebrows shot up. I'd made my point, that I was no longer under his authority and instructions, and with brief clarity.

'And we do not,' he continued, his voice now like cold steel, 'want publicity levelled at the integrity of a fine officer.'

'Thank you. I didn't know my integrity was at stake.'

'Not you, damn it.'

'I feared not.'

'Will you please try to take me seriously, Mr Patton!' It was not a question, not a request. A demand. 'I am very serious indeed. These days . . . hell, man, don't you read the papers? These days we're sitting targets. What with convictions being overturned right and left, and the like. Can you just imagine what they'd do with a deathbed statement, if it hit the news media. So far, we've kept the lid on it. But can't you see what the newspapers would inflate it into! Chief Superintendent's dying confession! Oh, splendid, that'd be. And if we stood up – if *I* had to stand up in front of television cameras and tell them it was no more than a replaced dustbin lid . . . oh lovely! D'you think that'd hold 'em? D'you imagine they wouldn't shout out: what else is there? A deathbed confession has to be *the lot*. They'd expect . . . imagine . . . Lord knows what. Anything.'

'And was there', I asked quietly, 'anything?'

'You see! As bad as them.'

'Was there?'

'Not in his statement,' he said distantly, seeming prepared to leap to his feet and rush out, held back only by the fact that he hadn't yet extracted what he'd come for, my promise.

'Didn't you', Amelia asked quietly, 'just call him a fine officer?'

'I did.'

'Then how could there be any more?' She turned and looked up at me, frowning, a decidedly demure light in her eye.

'But Mr Wainwright said "in the statement", love,' I explained. 'In there, I'm sure there was no more. But further enquiries have been made . . . Chief Super, am I guessing correctly?'

He flicked a hand in apparent submission. 'You are. Discreet enquiries. But you know what that sort of thing provokes. The more discreet, the more suspicion it arouses. The deeper you probe into the hole, the further down the fox hides himself.'

I'd have made a bet he'd worked that out in advance. 'Discreet and official enquiries?' I probed.

'At this stage, yes. Now do you get my point? We don't want any publicity until we're ready.' Still he manoeuvred round it, reluctant to reveal his hand.

'So . . .' I said. 'Not perhaps such a fine officer?'

'We've barely scratched . . .'

'Mr Wainwright, I have a man I convicted, if not in fact but in my reports, whom I believe to be innocent. He needs to be shown as innocent. You talk about publicity, but it's publicity he needs. Already there're threats. He's not believed to be innocent. I think I've got to go on with it.'

'And raise such a stink . . .'

'If the stink's there, you won't be able to make it smell sweet.'

'Time. Time to prepare . . .'

'To camouflage it as something else?' I asked equably, still determined not to lose my temper. But in fact it was there, rumbling away, and I was having difficulty in controlling it.

'The scandal, far and wide . . . involving so many others . . .'

'What do I care for the reputation of an officer you've as good as told me was rotten?'

'Your own friends could be . . .'

'No. I know my friends.'

He was silent, his eyes dark, head lowered like a bull. I tried to lure him into a response by forcing a smile. 'Or they're no friends of mine,' I added.

He lifted his head, and when he spoke his voice was bitter, crisply angry. But the anger was not levelled at me.

'Yes. You're probably right there. No friends of yours, and hopefully none of mine. But we have here two men, Mr Patton. Two distinct characters in one person. One as known to those below him in grade, one to those above. Except, of course, that those who were above more often than not became below later, and then it was too late to discover their mistake. A paragon of all the virtues, Pierce was, to his seniors. To those he controlled and ordered and manoeuvred, he was a complete swine. There was nothing he wouldn't do to anyone who crossed him, no trick or trap he wouldn't try, and he scattered hatred behind him like confetti at a wedding. Discarded. And no voice was ever raised against him because he was too powerful and had too many ears he could whisper into. And so many of them knew it, because theirs had been the ears he whispered into in the past. He'd climbed over shoulders, using ears to grab hold of.'

'But this was internal,' I protested. 'Inside the force.'

'Just laying the background, that's all I'm doing. His record was immaculate. He brought crooks into the dock and got them sent down. The ones who failed to please him, that is.'

Amelia interrupted. 'Please him? You mean bribe?'

'Oh no. Nothing as unsubtle as that. He wasn't offered anything, apparently, it would be closer to a demand. Failure to please him could lead to so many sins being heaped on your shoulders that you just went under. God knows how many of his cases were riddled with rigged evidence and corrupt statements. Or how many witnesses he cajoled or bullied or terrified. His response, if he met a refusal, could land you with ten years, even if you were blameless as a child. It was like a house of cards built on a firm basis of corruption. His brand of interrogation sent people scuttling down sewers rather than meet him face to face.' Then he seemed to collect himself. 'I'm speaking, you realize, from what is emerging, at this time no more than hints and shades of meaning. But by God, Patton, it's there. I know it's there.'

He was speaking, I had to remind myself, about the husband of Veronica Pierce, who'd said he would not permit himself one mistake. Had he hidden the dark side of himself from her? Or did she know of it and was afraid, not about the scratching of his polished reputation, but of the effect if the scratching of the surface of the mirror completely destroyed her reflected image of herself?

'And this is the man, you're saying, Mr Wainwright,' put in Amelia meekly, 'who made a deathbed statement about a dustbin lid! I just don't believe it. Never.'

I allowed the tips of my fingers to touch her shoulder. 'It's well-known in the force, my love. Admit to a small offence in order to hide a larger one.'

'All the same . . .' She shook her head.

'Subterfuge,' said Wainwright flatly. 'He'd probably done the same sort of thing all his life, scattering distractions all over the place to confuse the issue. How else could he have kept it all hidden, except behind some sort of a curtain of deceit? As I told you: two men. One he presented to the world, and a very tortuous one hiding behind it.'

'And how far have you got with this?' I asked.

'You're assuming I'm in charge of it.'

'Of course you are.'

He sighed. 'I'll need a year. I've got a team I'd trust anywhere, and we'll dig it out. Every rotten, dirty last shadow of it. But I need time. Time, Patton. That's what I'm asking for. From you. Publicity would blow it all apart, and you know what would happen then. I'm sure you do. A few specimen examples would be chosen – a few convictions would be quashed. But the complete picture would be distorted and stories would be prepared, and we'd lose a lot that ought to be exposed. Perhaps a lot of it would never be rectified. Perhaps.'

I got up abruptly and went to look out of the window. I hadn't cared for his tone nor the look in his eyes. I'd have preferred aggression. What I couldn't face was appeal. I turned.

'Is this one case so very important to you? Such a small thing!'

'Yes. You are. Put it like that.'

I dismissed this as a ploy too obvious to consider. 'And I'm to abandon a man to rumour and public hatred, watch his business destroyed, and his whole life . . . oh yes, that's what it would be. An innocent man, who's already done ten years in prison, and he's to be discarded now, when we ought to be supporting him . . .'

'Innocent? The evidence against him is tight. He was released on a technicality.'

'He's innocent.'

'Can you prove that?'

'No.' I shook my head. 'But I intend to.'

He sat very still for a few moments, then, with an ease that surprised me, he rose to his feet, smiled briefly at Amelia, and turned to leave, hesitated, then said, 'Let me know if you change your mind.'

'I'll let you know when I have my proof.'

He grunted. We walked out together to his car. Half on the seat, with the door still open, he said flatly, 'I could stop you, Patton. You know that. Stop you dead.'

'Yes. But would you dare?'

I closed the door for him. He backed round and drove away without a glance.

Inside, Amelia was waiting for me in the hall. 'And are you so sure?' she asked.

'About what?'

'The innocence of that man Caine?'

100

It was 'that man' now. 'No, I'm not. Far from sure. Otherwise it would make the job so much easier.'

She reached out and touched my arm. 'Come and sit down again, and we'll work out what to do next.'

I grimaced at the back of her head. Everybody seemed to want to make life difficult for me.

When we were settled comfortably she said, 'What we'll have to do, tomorrow, is find out where that wife of his lives. Widow. Mrs Pierce.'

'And then?'

'Question her, of course. For the truth. She'd *have* to know about her husband.'

'The truth?' I wondered.

'You surely didn't believe all that claptrap from the great Chief Superintendent Wainwright, did you?'

I said nothing. I guessed he'd only skimmed the surface and I didn't really want to plunge into the murky depths.

'I must certainly see her again,' I agreed.

'*We* must.'

'Of course, my love. If you say so.'

8

In the morning, after breakfast, when Amelia began to fidget at my inaction, I had to admit the difficulty.

'This Veronica Pierce you mentioned, I don't see how we can contact her, you know. All the information I have about her dead husband is that he was stationed somewhere up north. I can enquire. Ken would find out if I asked him, but now . . . I don't know. I'd prefer to keep my friends right out of it, things being as they are.'

'You're still worrying about that Wainwright person?'

I'd been thinking of little else. 'Yes. He's the sort of man to do anything, just anything, to stop me. I don't want any of it to rub off . . .'

'Don't say things like that, Richard, please.'

'He wouldn't do anything to us, Amelia. Nothing so blatantly obvious. But he'll put up barriers.'

'Then *what* do we do?'

'As far as Mrs Pierce is concerned, I've got an idea she'll come to us.'

'To you, you mean.'

'To me, then. Her attitude was of an employer. As though she could command and I'd obey. She'll want a progress report, you'll see.'

'How very dictatorial!'

'Too true. I'll have to go along with it, though.'

'I,' she said firmly. 'You keep saying that. Do you want to shut me out, Richard? Is that it?'

'Of course not. But I think she'll approach me only when I'm alone.'

'How cosy for you!'

Already it was working in Wainwright's favour, as I'd known it would. If it'd not been for his visit and his information, I'd have needed nothing from Veronica Pierce. Now I simply had to meet her again. And that necessity was erecting a barrier between Amelia and myself.

'It's not', I said, 'something to be looked forward to with pleasure. She didn't appear to me to be quite sane.'

'If she wishes to see you alone, Richard, I'd say she knew exactly what she was about. Insanity doesn't come into it.'

'Shall we', I suggested, inspiration hitting me, 'go and see them again at Winter Haven?'

'I don't see the point in that.'

I couldn't, either. 'A few friendly faces.'

'Very well. Your car or mine?'

'The Stag, I think.' Because I love driving it.

'I'll go and tell Mary, then.'

While I was waiting beside the car, Sheba came lolloping from around the house, apparently believing she was going with us. But with a female Rottweiler probably running loose – oh no, certainly not. I tried to explain this to Sheba, who wasn't afraid of anything in the dog line, but she wouldn't listen.

When she returned, Amelia asked, 'Can't she come, Richard?'

'Not with Daisy there, I thought.'

'No. I suppose not.'

So we had to leave Sheba sitting disconsolately on the drive.

The weather was still being kind, and, as I was beginning to know the journey quite well, we made good time. 'No need to rush, Richard.' Which in fact was correct. But I'd been trying to shake off the large dark car that'd been following us all the way. It had been waiting at the blank end of our approach-lane to the house. Amelia hadn't noticed so I'd said nothing, there being no point in alarming her.

It wasn't Veronica Pierce's car, I was certain of that. I hadn't seen much of it, that evening, but it had been a small car, and I'd thought blue.

We were not followed actually on to the fairground winter site. That would have been too obvious. It seemed simply to disappear, which was an optimistic thought because I was

103

certain it would reappear later, that one or a substitute. There was no doubt in my mind that it was there on Wainwright's instructions.

There was no sign of anybody at the house when I parked in front of it. The Range Rover was missing, so I assumed such matters as shopping were on the agenda. Normal life had to go on. Perhaps Juno was out and around the site, chatting to his friends. Patch? Probably with her mother.

We separated, Amelia and I, almost by mutual agreement. What interested her was different from what interested me. And vice versa. My immediate interest was the Fowler steam-tractor, which I could see parked over by the side fence. There was no need for us to discuss our intentions; we were each going to nose around, for anything, any detail that might have relevance to Eric Prost's death.

But of course, they'd all been out on the road at that time, as the whole conglomerate had arrived back here a few days after we'd sealed the empty house. Similarly, I supposed, in the case of Eric Prost's wife's death in the car incident. If Cara had died about fifteen months before Eric, yes, they'd have all been in the middle of their touring season at that time.

Nobody was guarding the Fowler. It stood proud and mag-nificent in the sunlight, gleaming with polish, smelling even now of steam and smoke and hot oil. I stood and contemplated it.

'Interested, mate?'

The voice came from behind me. I turned. He was a small, thin man with a nut-brown face, and completely bald, wearing tatty old slacks, an old-fashioned flannel shirt that needed two studs and a collar to complete it, and a waistcoat hanging loose.

'I certainly am.'

'It's not for sale.'

'Pity.'

I could just imagine myself buying it on the spot and driving it home. Amelia, following in the fumes and steam, wouldn't need to worry about my exceeding the speed limits. Or would I need her to do the stoking?

'What's funny?' he asked.

104

'A thought. Wondering what my wife would say if I bought it.'

'Proud, mate. She'd be proud.'

And maybe he was correct, I reflected.

'Here,' he said, 'you ain't an inspector or something, are y'? 'Cause if so, you're wastin' y'r time.'

'Not an inspector,' I assured him. 'Ex, you might say, but that was the police.'

'Police!' Something stirred behind his eyes.

'Ex, was what I said. I was the one who came here when Eric Prost died.'

'Well now.'

'Were you with the Ritters then, Mr Hobbs?'

'Know my name, too. I *said* you're an inspector.'

'No. Emily Ritter mentioned you. Eustace Hobbs, isn't it?'

"Sright. Got her eyes on my wagon, she has.'

I smiled at him. 'I gathered that. Were you, Mr Hobbs? With the Ritters at the time? I mean, when Eric Prost died.'

'Been with 'em as long as I can remember. A good crowd. No trouble. Here . . . you ain't come to pick up Juno, have you?'

'Not my intention.'

"Cause if that was it, you'd better do it somewhere else, matey. You'd never get him off this site, I'm promisin' you that. Not with all of us here, you wouldn't.'

I couldn't help grinning. This little periwinkle of a man, smoke-dried and smelling of hot oil, was actually threatening me. 'No such intentions, I assure you. I was simply interested in the Fowler. Solid tyres, I see. I bet you get trouble replacing those.'

'Well yeah. But I've only had to do it once. Just you try working it out. The whole summer tour, it ain't more'n five hundred mile. Couldn't be. Last a few years, this lot will.'

'And no other replacements?'

'Time to time. Bits an' pieces. If y' know where, there's always somebody who can make 'em.'

And so we chatted amicably, until I became gradually aware that there was something strangely quiet about this site. Then I realized.

'No children,' I said. 'There're no children around.'

'Course not. They're at school.'

'D'you know, that's something that never occurred to me. They'd have to go to school. But . . . a bit unsettling for them, isn't it? I mean, what do they do on tour, and are they all now at some local school?'

'You *do* ask a lot of blamed questions,' he complained.

'Sorry. A police habit.'

'Y' want to break it then, mate. It could get you a bloody nose.'

'I'll watch it. Are they? All at some local school?'

'*Now* they are, some of 'em. Rest'f the year, April to September, they're livin' with aunts and uncles and grannies, just comin' to us durin' the school holidays. Love it, they do. Just love it.'

'I reckon they would.' I walked once round the Fowler. He watched me, head tilted, a merry light in his eyes. 'Some of them, you said?' I cocked an eyebrow at him.

'You *are* a bloody inspector. Schools, I reckon.'

'Not a bit of it. Just nosy. Interested.'

'You was right first time. Nosy it is. Can't see why it matters.'

'It doesn't matter. I'm just filling in time, and you don't seem to be overbusy. My wife can't keep away from all this.'

'Yeah . . . well . . . if it matters, the rest of the kids go to private schools.'

'Well now. A bit pricey that, isn't it? You make a bit at this lark, do you?'

'Not schools,' he decided. 'Income tax. That's what y'are.'

'You're wrong again,' I assured him. 'It's just – six months on the road – it doesn't seem enough to pay for a whole year's living . . .'

'Then you're wrong. We get the kids a good education. It pays in the end. Harry Weeks has got a son who's an accountant – does all our accounts. Daley's eldest girl's a solicitor – she looks after us. Oh, we keep it in the family, we do.'

I smiled at him, produced my tobacco pouch, and began to fill my pipe. He nodded. 'Don't mind if I do.' And he produced a huge curved briar, into which half of my tobacco disappeared. It was as I'd thought. They were a tight little community, operating carefully inside the law on the principle that this

106

would form a solid background to separate them from the surrounding population. But would they keep a murder within their own confines, closely guarding its secrets? Would they leave a sudden death to the mercy of the police force, or deal with it within the family? It was something I had to bear in mind, the possibility that there could be tiny particles of evidence floating around, which they would not willingly reveal.

'It's an interesting life,' I told him. 'What do you all do when you retire?'

'Retire? What's that? We don't retire, we die on the job.'

'Now *that's* how I'd like to go,' I declared. 'The cortège led by a Fowler steam-tractor.'

He winked. 'Ah no, mate, that's for me. Reserved, it is.'

'Emily will drive it for you.' I grinned at him and strolled on. So many of them, I found, had time for a chat, proud of their equipment. I tested out what I'd deduced from my conversation with Eustace Hobbs, here and there slipping in references to Eric Prost's death, and to the death in a blazing car of Cara Prost. At that point they quietly withdrew. I was shut out. They were theirs, these deaths, to be dealt with by them when and if the culprits became known. No mention of Caine in this context, I noted, and no details as to how this dealing with was to be done, but I didn't like the sound of it.

I tested out this uneasy feeling on one or two of them, slipping in Caine's name casually, linking it with Prost's death. To my surprise, they all seemed to know Caine. But, of course, he would still have visited his friend Eric at the time all these people were wintering here. They all seemed to think well of Caine, too.

Daley, the one with the huge Dennis diesel tractor, and who, I discovered, had a dodgems set-up, put it into words.

'When poor Cara died,' he said, 'Eric near went crazy, he did. If it hadn'ta been for Caine, they'd have had him in the loony-bin, I reckon. Emily an' Juno couldn't be here all the time, 'cause we were on the road, so it was Caine who got him through it. Here every day, I heard. A damned shame they put him inside.'

'You don't think Caine shot him?'

107

'Never. They was friends.'

I got much the same response everywhere, but at one of the side-shows (a rifle-range, I understood, though the only evidence of this was a young man sitting on his caravan steps and stripping rifles) I actually obtained a clue. A genuine, down-to-earth clue!

He had half a dozen of these rifles, small calibre pump-action target-guns. Considering that they must have had plenty of wear, they seemed in good condition to me, though I'm no expert.

'They're Rossis,' he said as I crouched down beside him. 'Twenty-two calibre.'

'Dangerous things to wave around,' I suggested. 'And you, presumably, on the wrong side of the counter.'

He was a ginger-haired lad of around twenty with big ears and a big mouth, his voice strangely high. He winked at me. 'When I get tired of the missus I'm going to give her the job.'

'I heard that, Lobo!' a woman shouted from inside the caravan. She stuck her head out of the doorway, a dark, almost gypsyish girl with wondrous luminous eyes. 'The damn things scare the pants off me,' she told me.

'Don't give me ideas, girl,' said Lobo, nodding at me straight-faced. 'The trick is,' he explained, 'to remember how many you've loaded in each gun, and how many've been fired. And not cross the line of fire until the gun's been put down.'

'All the same, they're killing weapons.'

He shrugged. 'A rat, perhaps. They're special low-charge cartridges.'

'Tried it?'

'What? You mean . . . a rat? Not me. You won't get me shootin' at something alive.'

'Except the missus?'

'Ah well, fair game, y' know.'

Then he ducked, timing it splendidly, and a wet cloth just missed his head. Mine too.

I straightened to my full height, crouching down being no good at all for my leg muscles. We'd worked round neatly to what I'd wanted, the topic of shooting to kill, and from there it

108

was no effort to edge it round to the shooting of Eric Prost, and from that to the name of Julian Caine.

'Nah!' he said decisively. 'He couldna' done it.'

'Oh? Are you so sure of that?' My eyes were scanning the distance, searching for a sighting of Amelia.

'Sure I'm sure. How tall is he? Five-six at the best, I'd reckon.'

I turned my eyes on him. 'So?'

'That'd make his eye-level about five-one. That hole in the glass was five-six from the ground.'

I said coolly, 'You're very certain of yourself.' But my heart had jumped a beat.

'Yeah. Well, I done it, see, put that hole in the glass. Foolin' around with one of these rifles. I was only a kid. Lor', but pa didn't half pale into me for that. I wasn't supposed to *touch* the guns. Dad paid for the new glass, but Eric never got a new pane put in. Five-six, it was. My dad looked through it, an' he was near as damn it six feet. Like you. So how could Caine 'ave done it? Standin' on tippy-toes? You try it. All wobbly, he'd be. Stood on somethin'? Such as what? Brung it with him, did he? Summat six inches deep and big enough to stand on? Gerraway! If y'ask me, the copper as put him away didn't know what he was doin'.'

'I was the copper who put him away,' I said distantly, feeling winded and slightly nauseous.

'There y'are then,' he said agreeably.

I said good day to him and marched quickly to the house. Still no one was home. I walked round to the window. The glass was now repaired, but I thought I remembered which pane had been holed. They were eight inch by six inch panes, so that the one below the latch would've been too low, less than five feet from the ground. Not that one. The hole had been above the latch. That would put it on my own eye-level, which meant that an eye-level shot, as those two shots must have been, had to have been fired by someone at least five-eleven.

I stood and looked around me, attempting to re-establish in my mind the scene as I'd encountered it on that Tuesday, ten years before. I recalled nothing but a naked expanse of ground, with no discarded boxes six inches deep hanging around usefully. And surely it was too much to suppose that Caine had

109

been carrying something like that in his car. As Lobo had said, gerraway! The possibility of careful premeditation presented itself, but I was unable to accept that he had previously measured the height of the hole from the ground and thus prepared himself with a correctly sized support. Absurd!

There was also the point that, had such a support been used, it would have made some impression in that muddy ground. We could not have missed such an obvious sign, and the footprints of the milkman would not have disguised a regular shape. Other footprints, yes. He'd ruined those. But not a box-shaped impression!

Oh hell! I thought. Bloody hell!

This was the danger of investigating past cases, especially your own. It's so easy to find yourself facing a complete destruction of your self-esteem. It is quite shattering.

So I went to find Amelia. She is very good in this kind of crisis.

I found her sitting out in front of one of the decorated caravans on a stool. There were four people thus seated round a low table, one of them Juno. They were playing poker. Amelia never plays card games. Not to my knowledge.

There was about £17 laid out in the centre of the table. Some of it was hers. I cleared my throat.

She glanced over her shoulder. 'Not now, Richard. Let me finish this hand.'

'What've you got?'

She held them up to me. Two deuces and three other low cards, not matching in suit or in value. Not knowing much about poker, I nevertheless realized it was a hand not worth holding, unless you knew what the others held. They were watching me with suspicion, cards against their chests.

I raised my eyebrows and whistled softly. 'Hang in there, love,' I said. It's a game of bluff, I believe.

One by one, for some reason looking a little miffed, they threw in their hands. Amelia scooped up the pool, thanked them politely, and told me, 'They've been teaching me poker, Richard.'

'Too deep for me,' I admitted.

Then I took her to look at the window. I explained the difficulty, and she gave me a long, considering look.

'Isn't this what you've been looking for?' she asked, tilting her head.

'I suppose it is,' I replied, and was unable to make it sound anything but miserable.

'Well then.' She turned and surveyed the ground behind her, glanced at me, puckered her lips, and frowned heavily. 'But you didn't want to find it was your own error, did you?'

'Well . . .'

'Oh, you *do* annoy me sometimes! You're as bad as that Pierce person, all self-criticism.'

'Not quite as bad, surely.'

She stared at my rueful expression, then gave a short laugh. 'It's not the end of the world, you know! And Richard, haven't you noticed that the ground slopes upwards slightly?'

'What?'

'Slopes upwards from the house. See?'

I saw. I realized, too, why it had been so muddy on that Tuesday, beneath the window. The rainwater would run down towards the house. 'Lord yes!' I said. 'How far d'you think . . . hold on a sec'. Wait here, love, I need help.'

Not waiting for an answer, I walked rapidly back to where I'd left Lobo, and there he still was, cleaning his rifles.

'Can you spare a minute?' I asked.

'Sure thing. What's the trouble?'

'D'you mind standing up?'

'Not a bit.' He did. I eyed him.

'Five-six?' I asked. He nodded. 'About as tall as Julian Caine?'

'I reckon. What *is* all this?'

'I want to check what you said. It looks like you were right, but I need to be sure.'

He grinned at me. 'Got y' worried, ain't it!' Then he shouted to his wife that he'd be round and about.

'Bring a rifle,' I said. 'Not loaded.'

'Sure.' He slung one in his hand, and we marched back to Amelia, who, I saw, had now been joined by Patch and Daisy, and a dark young man with a stubbly chin, who was hovering around Patch possessively. He'd have been in his mid-twenties,

111

so was most likely her boy-friend. Certainly, he barely took his eyes from her, dark and thoughtful eyes beneath heavy brows. He was hefty, probably one of the roustabouts, and essential when it came to the heavy work of erecting and breaking down. He seemed amused, even slightly contemptuous of what was going on. When his eyes met mine he held the gaze for a few moments, no doubt measuring me, making up his mind about me.

Amelia, I found, had already explained the problem. Daisy seemed to agree that it was great fun.

First, I had Lobo confirm that I'd chosen the correct pane of glass, and we agreed exactly where the hole had been. I checked with Patch that Daisy would allow me to enter the house.

'Yes,' she said. 'She's with me and Pauli. But why?'

'I'm going in to sit at that desk and on that seat, and bend my head as though I'm writing. Then you, Lobo, I want you to back up and away from the window, with the rifle, until you've got a line on the back of my head, here look, where the backbone ends, and in line with where the hole was in the glass. OK?'

'Got it.'

'You're sure it's not loaded?'

'Yeah.' He was solemn. 'Wouldn't make more'n a dent in you, anyway.'

'Right. I'll get in there, then.'

I went in and round into the rear hallway, and into the room. Nothing had changed, apart from the absence of the Tompion long-case clock. I sat at the desk and bent my head in contemplation of the surface, as though writing. Two minutes, and there was a shout. 'Got it!' I went out quickly. 'Here,' said Lobo, digging a heel into the ground.

He was standing six or seven yards away from the window. I had no intention of measuring it exactly.

'What does it all mean?' asked Patch.

'It means,' I explained, 'that if Julian Caine shot your uncle Eric, then he'd have had to do it from here, which would've meant a shot through the hole in the window at a target the size of the ace of spades, and in the light of no more than a desk lamp, which would throw your uncle's head into shadow.'

112

'Oh!' She was looking miserable at the memory of that time.

'And then,' I went on, 'in order to hit the clock-face with a bullet, he'd have had to walk a bit closer – I suppose.'

'Everybody says it,' she told me, nodding, lower lip between her teeth. 'That he didn't do it,' she explained kindly.

'So I understand.'

'Not everybody,' said Pauli quietly.

It was the first time I'd heard his voice, deep, and with a tone of authority older than you'd expect. A young man with decided views, and uncompromising, I thought.

I turned to him. 'I gather you don't agree.'

His eyes seemed to smile, but not his lips. 'I think he done it.'

'Even after what you've just seen?'

He shrugged. 'There's ways.' Then he turned his shoulder to me and touched Patch's arm, nodding his head, urging her away. She bit her lip and said to him, 'I don't know what you've got against him. That I don't.'

'You know damn well,' said Pauli.

But Patch, not willing to argue about it there, went away with him quietly, Daisy loping at their side.

I watched them go, wondering about Pauli, wondering whether he had anything positive on which to base his dogmatic judgements. I could've warned him of the danger in jumping to conclusions.

Amelia and I went round to the front of the house and got into my car.

'So that's it,' she said, with a certain amount of relief in her voice.

'Is it?'

She dragged at my sleeve. 'Surely it must be. Now . . . all you've got to do is tell Wainwright, and explain it to Mr Caine so that he can tell his solicitor – or whatever the procedure is – and you'll be free of it, Richard.'

I didn't look at her, but stared straight forward through the windscreen. 'That'd be just great,' I said, trying to keep the annoyance out of my voice. 'Tell Wainwright, eh? And what d'you think he'd do with it? Would he slap me on the shoulder and say, "Hard luck old chap, but we always make one mistake in our lives," d'you think? Not a bit of it. This is just what he didn't want. In fact, he'd go haywire if he thought I was going to say one public word about it.'

'Now Richard . . .'

'Probably slap me in irons to keep me quiet.'

'Such a fuss! It's yourself you're annoyed with. Admit it. For missing it in the first place.'

'That, yes, but . . . I don't know. Something else.'

'Such as?'

'I don't know.'

'You're in one of your moods, Richard. Give it time. You'll see.'

But niggling at me, and refusing to take shape, was Pauli's remark, and its implication that even now I was missing something. I grimaced, and squeezed her hand.

'Time, yes. I suppose. I only wish I could be sure there *is* time. Just consider . . . Wainwright. He's got a man who's been released because of unsafe evidence, and he's trying to keep it all low-key. Well, of course. He wants time to dig out all the horrors Pierce might have committed, so that he'll know what to expect and how to face it. But *this* . . . if I made this public . . . oho . . . "Ex-police officer confesses to wrongful conviction." That would really blow it sky-high. Wainwright wouldn't want that. He wouldn't permit it. He'd do anything to suppress it. To start with, he'd do his best to rubbish the whole idea. You can bet on that.'

'Now how could he do that?' she demanded. 'You're just trying to wriggle out of it, and you know it. How could he, anyway?'

'Oh, I don't know. He'd think up all sorts of ways Caine could've done it, and from close up to the window.'

'Tell me one.'

'Oh . . . used his spare wheel. Rolled it up to the window and stood on it. Fantastic ideas like that.'

She laughed me out of that one. 'Oh, I'm sure he would. But don't forget, he'd have to be making a fool of himself by doing that publicly, if you'd claimed publicly what you've just found out. And Richard – you are not giving yourself time to think, my pet – *whatever* objections Mr Wainwright might throw at

114

you, he'll never be able to get round the one simple and basic fact, which you haven't really considered. Have you?'

'As my mind is a complete blank, perhaps you'd better explain that.'

'It's quite simple. Whatever tricks Julian might have got up to in order to shoot Eric Prost – even hanging upside-down with a trapeze from the roof – he *would* have had to do *something*, because we now know he couldn't have shot him simply by standing outside the window.'

I turned and stared at her blankly for a moment, before I got it. 'Yes, yes.' My brain sparked into life. 'I see what you're getting at. The shell cases! They'd have been ejected where he did fire the shots. He'd have had to hunt for them (and it would've been dark, otherwise Eric Prost wouldn't have had his desk lamp on) and then throw them down beneath the window.'

'And all of that,'she told me, patting my knee for emphasis, 'would not have been done unless he intended to claim he was too short to fire through that hole in the glass. But there was nothing – and I'm assuming this, or you'd have said – absolutely nothing said at his trial in his defence about the hole being too high for him to fire through. It means, purely and simply, that he didn't know it was too high. He'd probably never had reason to stand outside that window and notice the height of the hole.'

She had been speaking directly to the windscreen, no doubt sparing herself the sight of my expression. Now she turned and grinned at me. I reached over and kissed her cheek, then lifted my head and laughed out loud, then reached for her again, and blast that gear-lever, it always gets in the way.

'And so,' she said, fussing with her hair, 'you can tell Caine the facts, and he's got his own way out of it. Simple.'

Sobered a little, I said, 'But no. It's not enough. Now we've got to find out who really did it.'

She sighed.

9

It's all very well making these snap decisions, but very soon it became clear to me that I was right bang slap in the middle of a dilemma.

On the drive home, Amelia was silent, well aware that I would be mulling things over. Which I was. My initial idea had been that I could keep silent for now about the proof of Caine's innocence, while I plodded along hoping for evidence of someone else's guilt. This, I'd assumed, would be necessary in order to lift the last shade of guilt from Caine's public image. But now . . . would it be correct to keep this new discovery secret from Caine himself?

Wainwright would undoubtedly be most displeased if I did tell Caine, who wouldn't himself be prepared to remain silent. Could you blame him? He'd have it on the front page of all the Sunday papers: CAINE NOW ABEL TO PROVE HIS INNOCENCE. Or something corny like that. True, this evidence in no way involved Pierce and the dustbin lid, but that little bit of nonsense, which had drifted unnoticed by the press through the Appeal Court, would then inevitably be linked with it, and Wainwright's discreet background investigation into the depths of Pierce's other depredations would be prejudiced.

Yet how *could* I keep this new evidence from Caine? It was true that the Ritters might not welcome him on the site, and understandably, but it was also true that Caine had many other friends there. Thus, the story would probably, by now, have been spread around by Lobo, and Caine need only set foot inside the entrance-way to find himself being congratulated, and told why. Indeed, well-wishers would conceivably take the trouble to visit Caine Antiques in order to do just that.

I was all the rest of the day thinking about it, mooning around the house, taking Sheba for a walk even though it had begun to rain, sitting staring sightlessly at a television screen with the sound off. I couldn't find any way round it.

At around five o'clock – I think I was drinking a cup of tea – the phone rang. As I was sitting only a couple of yards from it, I got it on the third ring. Why do some rings sound more ominous than others? Expectations, I suppose.

'Patton? It's Caine.' His voice was strained.

'Yes?'

'Can you come? Please.'

'Now? What is it?'

He drew a breath, trying to steady his voice. 'My wife's been threatened. Here, in the shop. A man came in. He'd got something heavy in his hand, she can't say what. Oh God . . .'

'Take it slowly.'

'He . . . he just sort of looked around, she says, just looked around, and then smashed one of the clocks.'

'The clocks,' I repeated, my mind scrambling around.

'A bracket clock. She says . . . said . . . he grabbed her and put his face right up to hers . . . right up to hers . . . and told her she'd be next if we didn't get out of town.'

'The . . .' I cleared my throat. 'The police?' I asked. 'Did you get the police?'

'What d'you think! After a while. She was hysterical.'

'I'm sure she was.'

'They've taken her round to the station. Identification. Some rubbish like that. As though she could . . .'

'Perhaps when she's calmer,' I said, trying to sound calm myself, trying to suppress the waver of hysteria in his voice. 'She'll feel safe there.'

'They said they'd run her home, and put a guard on the house, and there's a police car just down the street from here.'

'There you are then.'

'It's all very well to say . . .'

'Sorry. I'm still trying to take it in. And you? Are you all right?' You sound a bit rough.'

117

'I'm . . . I'm scared of leaving the shop. Scared.'

'The police are there, you said. You're safe enough.'

'They're to guard the shop,' he jabbered, trying to get the words out too quickly. 'Me . . . I'm scared of going out into the street. Scared of going for my car. I tell you, Mr Patton, I'm terrified.'

There was silence. He'd asked me to go to him. He'd said please. Now he was waiting, as he'd waited for the jury foreman to pronounce the decision. It was all out of his hands, and way beyond his grasp.

'I'll come,' I promised. 'An hour. Give me an hour.'

I hung up and turned. Amelia was standing in the open doorway. She'd heard most of my end of it.

'That was Caine,' I told her.

'I realized. Why should he expect you to rush away for him? What about your dinner?'

I told her why he expected it. Caine hadn't known, but Richard Patton was in a position to gallop to his defence, both physically and verbally. Which was what he wanted, and what he now desperately needed. It seemed that Wainwright's needs were going to be jettisoned.

'Then I suppose you'll have to go,' she said without enthusiasm.

In an obscure way I was pleased to have my hand forced in this way. 'I'll have to.'

She made sure I'd got my raincoat and my hat, and told me in one sentence not to drive too fast but to hurry back. 'He'll wait for you but your dinner won't.'

'Yes love,' I said. 'I'll be right back.' But really, all desire for food seemed to have deserted me.

It was a rotten evening for driving, a terrible time to choose, and a lousy mood in which I was undertaking it. Is there a limit to self-deprecation? Would there come a point where I could say to myself, 'So what! I've ballsed up the whole thing, now let's get on with clearing it up.' And with equanimity? I doubted that. Always, rumbling away and undermining me, would be the memory of this.

The clouds had chased us home all the way from Markham Prior, and now they were settled firmly above, lashing down rain that was almost more than the windscreen wipers could cope with. Visibility was way down, and the tarmac was greasy. It was the time for the homecomers to clog the roads, and at first the journey stretched my nerves even tighter, the traffic stream slowing me to not much more than walking pace until we were over the Severn. There, most of them filtered away to right and left, allowing me a little more speed, and the roads became quieter, though winding through heavy and dripping countryside, my headlights catching the lances of rain in a curtain I seemed to be thrusting through with close to a physical effort. This, I realized, arose from my own tension and the savage pressure to get there . . . to get there.

I was much later reaching Markham Rise than I'd anticipated. Along the rise, with the first signs of the town below me, I hesitated whether to deviate to the house. But Caine had been at his shop, and he would wait for me there.

I came down to the old bridge, expecting to see the High Street as a necklace of lighted windows, as it might have been in a larger town, the shops left for the night with window-displays illuminated and dimmer lights way back in the interiors. This is partly a precaution against break-ins. But Markham Prior was too quiet for this necessity, being a discreet and reasonably civilized community, which could close down completely and present a dark, flat face to the streets, along which no villains lurked. Apart, of course, from lunatics with heavy objects in their hands and nothing much in their heads.

The Stag sighed over the humpback of the old bridge, and I was confronted by an almost deserted street, poorly lit, modestly crouching in the rain-storm. A man with an umbrella hurried along a pavement, a car crossed an intersection, a silent police car was parked just the other side of Caine Antiques. There, the windows were still dimly lit, with enough light from them for me to see he had his metal guard-grids fitted.

There was no traffic behind me, nothing in front. I drew nearly to a halt, making a decision. If I drove along and parked behind the police car I'd be inviting attention, probably intervention, and possibly a protracted discussion. In the mood in which I found myself, it would most likely be a heated one. No – perhaps the car-park, and walk from there.

Easing forward in bottom gear, keeping one wary eye on the shop and another for the car-park entrance, I put on my right-hand indicator at the exact moment that Caine's shop lights went off. I stopped with the Stag at an angle, nose almost inside the nearest of the two entrances.

Now my view of the High Street was angled, and therefore distorted by the portion of windscreen over on the passenger's side, where it was not completely swept by the wipers. The shop door opened and closed. I saw a shadow standing in the doorway recess. Then he came out into the rain, with no umbrella but wearing a hat and a raincoat. He had despaired of me, given me up as a bad job. There was no movement from the police car. No doubt their instructions had been to guard the shop, not the man. That was my duty. If Wainwright was in charge of this end of the affair, he would no doubt have delegated the duty of Caine's protector to me.

I hesitated long enough to confirm that Caine had turned towards the car-park. Then I finished my turn inside, my view now cut off by the four foot wall along the frontage.

There were two empty cars only, one probably Caine's, a Rover. The other was parked nose out, silent and dark, to one side. There was a possibility it was Wainwright sitting inside, waiting. If so, he'd have a long wait before I approached. Wainwright, just at that time, would have been more than I could handle. I parked alongside the Rover, got out, reached inside for mac and hat, and was shrugging into it when he entered the car-park. Caine it was, walking head down in the shambling and exhausted gait of a shattered man. He made his way towards the Rover, not seeing me waiting, plodding close to the side wall as though it offered protection.

I took a couple of paces forward. 'Caine!' He lifted his head. 'It's Patton,' I said, as an engine burst into life behind me and lights flooded over him. He threw up a hand to protect his eyes. I heard the squealing of tyres, scrambling for grip, and the light danced as the car slewed, then it was past me so close that the wing-mirror brushed my sleeve, and in a straight line as though on rails with Caine pinned within the beams, arms flung up, face distorted by a scream I couldn't hear.

At the last possible moment, when it seemed the bonnet must

plunge into the wall as well as into Caine, the wheel was thrown over and the brakes were clamped on, and with a lurching slide the car scrabbled and recovered and stabilized itself, nose out now towards the entrance but with the tail still sliding sideways.

I was running then, shouting uselessly. The tail of the car flicked Caine sideways, as it would a puddle of water, and crushed him against the wall. Then, still recovering direction, the car shot out of the entrance. I saw a rear wheel leave the ground as it swerved sharply left, and it was away and gone over the bridge with tyres and engine whining and a clanking, grinding sound of buckled metal against one of the tyres.

I ran to Caine.

The light was very poor here, as he was lying against the enclosing wall. One of the orange street-lights angled across, and he was deep down in the shadow it threw, like a purple blanket thrown across him. I crouched down until my eyes were in the shadow, but I couldn't see enough to make any sort of examination. His head was angled against the wall, his eyes, I thought, catching an orange spark, so they were open. So was his mouth. My gentle, questing fingers to his face came away smeared. I lifted my hand into the orange light, but blood in such light looks lighter, greyer. I couldn't be sure, but he seemed to be bleeding from the mouth. His one leg was angled strangely. I put a hand to the wet tarmac just beyond his leg in order to lean closer, and thought I heard a rattle of breath. Then my fingers discovered his jugular, and there was a faint, irregular beat.

Clambering to my feet, I knew I had to get help. The police car! I stumbled towards the entrance, aware that they must have heard the sound of impact and screaming tyres because there was blue light sparking into the orange and a hand hit the siren. For heaven's sake, why? Then I realized they were intending to go past in pursuit of the car.

With a blind effort I plunged myself through the entrance gap on to the roadway, and nearly beneath their wheels. It at least attracted their attention, the car braking into a snaking skid that nearly ended against a lamp-post. I ran across the road. A door was flung open. 'What the bloody hell . . .'

I clutched at his arm. 'An accident. We'll need an ambulance. Get on your radio.'

The officer gave me one startled glance, then he ran into the car-park. 'By the wall,' I shouted after him, no running ability left in me. Then, after only a few seconds, he raised his head and shouted to his driver mate, who turned out to be a woman, to get an ambulance and report in.

Then, abruptly, all the energy seemed to drain from my legs, and it was all I could do to remain standing. I had become a useless nothing, a witness who could be left until later, and from then on I was swept into the stream of events, caught like a twig in the river, spinning and turning at the will of the current.

I managed to get to the Stag, flop down in the seat, and put on the interior light. Then I fumbled tobacco into my pipe, lit it, and sat back. Waiting. It would come to me.

The ambulance arrived, parking with its lights blazing into the shadows of the wall. I watched through the windscreen. It had ceased raining, and two quick flips of the wiper cleared the glass for me. You get to know their actions, to recognize the methods of treatment, as related to the delicacy of the patient's condition. He was alive. It was a living man they slid into the ambulance. It pulled away. I sat on. They would come to me next.

It was the WPC who opened the passenger's door and slid in beside me. 'I'll have to take down some details, sir. You were here – a witness. Could I have your name and address to start with, please?'

Oh, very polite! She was dealing with a civilian, who would no doubt be distressed. And so I had been, but it was working off now, gradually being replaced by a deep and rumbling fury, which I hoped I could contain a little longer.

'I can save you time and effort, young lady. I'm an ex-police officer myself. I was meeting him here . . .' And so on. Experience helps. I knew what she wanted and in what form, and I could rattle it out. The expression on her face told me that I was not succeeding in hiding the bitter anger, but she said nothing. Her shorthand was good; I didn't have to slow down for her. In fact, towards the end I was talking faster, having noticed that two plain cars had drawn in, and a group of men was busy around the scene. One of them was Wainwright.

'Well . . . thank you,' she said at the end. 'As you'll know, we may need a statement. We'll be in touch.'

'I've got an idea I'll be around,' I told her.

I watched her walk away, to be intercepted by a senior officer in uniform and Wainwright. She was answering questions. I saw them glance towards the Stag. Then, eventually, Wainwright walked across to me. Alone. I sat facing forward as he got in the car. He slammed the door. We were silent, each waiting for the other. I blew smoke at the windscreen.

'Any ideas?' he asked at last. His voice was strangely smooth, uninflected by any emotion.

'The obvious one.' I tried to match him, but I could hear the biting attack in my voice. There was acid in my throat. 'You said it yourself, Wainwright. You'd stop me, you said. Dead. Is this supposed to do that?'

'He's not dead.' He was deliberately pretending to be obtuse.

'And it's not going to stop me.'

'It wasn't me.'

I turned to him. There was just a little smile on his face, just a hint of teeth. 'I'm not a complete fool. Of course it wasn't you. You wouldn't do anything like that yourself. One of your blasted undercover team, that's who it might have been. Get Caine out of the picture, you'd say. Just do it. And it was done.'

'Christ, you *are* a fool, Patton. I know you're upset . . .' It seemed for one moment that he would pat my knee.

'Upset!'

'When you can think – later – you'll realize it would gain me nothing. Caine out of the way? Tcha! It's you I want out of the way.'

'And this . . .'

He bit on the words. 'This, you damned idiot, does just the opposite, and I know that.' He reached over and tapped my knee with his hard finger, not quite so insulting as a pat would have been. 'D'you think I don't understand that? I know you. Know you better than you know yourself, and I know what I'd do in your shoes. And God help us all, I'm quite aware that this is going to dig you in all the deeper.'

There was a silence. In the end, he went on more quietly. 'We've already found the car, abandoned two miles out of town. Stolen yesterday in Worcester.'

'Worcester?'

'Mean anything?'

'No. Just . . . it's quite a distance from here.'

'Yes.'

More silence. Again it was he who broke it. I had the feeling he was deciding how much he would tell me, and whether it would influence me in any way in respect to my future actions.

'It's going to be a long, hard haul, you know, this thing I'm landed with. Already . . . what d'you think about false arrests in order to bully your man into giving false evidence? There's that. What d'you think about charging a man with a minor offence in order to hide a greater one, because a friend – you might call him – might become involved? There's that too. And that friend knowing too much to be trusted and dying in a house fire? And the man who set that fire being mysteriously tipped off, and disappearing to Cuba or Brazil or somewhere? Little items like that . . . they're peeping through, Patton.'

'Nasty.'

'That's just the tip of a bloody cold iceberg. I'm getting glimpses. No more. The cover-ups have been complicated, but everywhere I look I keep coming across the name of Pierce.'

By the end, his voice had assumed a growling rasp, with something behind it that I couldn't quite understand. Was it that he was already beginning to realize it was too big for him, that his efforts would produce too little for too much labour, so that he would lose it, have it taken out of his hands before he'd got a firm enough grip on it. He was nervous. He'd be afraid to face side-issues and distractions.

'I don't envy you.'

I must have used the wrong tone. Perhaps I'd sounded insincere, not caring as much as he'd have liked for his predicament.

'I'm sure you don't,' he said harshly. 'You couldn't care less, and you sodding well know it. But I'm not going to have it blow up in my face. You get me?'

'Of course not.' I left him to decide to what aspect of it I was

124

alluding. But I could see what he was getting at, sense it coming, and all I could do in defence was to withdraw from him, my tone cold and unencouraging. I wasn't going to let him coerce me into going home and forgetting all I knew. 'For your information, I can tell you I'm now in a position to prove Caine's innocence. His innocence, not just a paltry bit of unsafe evidence, this time, but a positive fact that'll show he couldn't have done it.'

He sighed. 'Tell me.' It was a straightforward demand.

'So that you can bury it?' I asked with scorn.

'So that I can bear it in mind.' His voice was heavy, his patience stretched.

So I told him. In detail. He was silent for so long that I thought he was having difficulty controlling his anger. But no. He was still quite calm when he spoke, perhaps even relieved.

'You know I could knock holes in that. Impossible shot or not, from that distance, I could produce a police marksman who'd demonstrate it.'

'What the hell would that mean? Nothing. It wouldn't prove Caine could've done it like that. Don't you see! He's already had his conviction quashed, and it's done nothing for him. Any newspaper would jump on this evidence of positive innocence, and make a birthday out of it. Then he'd be known to be innocent, and it'd stop this ridiculous persecution of him. It's what he wants – what he desperately needs to have. What I can give him. Tell me why I shouldn't give it to him. No . . . tell me why I should go to extreme lengths, and that's what they'd have to be, to persuade him not to publicize it himself. If he lives, that is.'

He spoke in a voice choked with disgust. 'And there'd be calls for a public investigation. I'll be dumped off it, and they'll take a year to set it up, like a film, to go out as mass entertainment. Entertainment! Christ! And all the worst bits'll get lost, all the worst crooks go free, all the bent coppers will destroy the worst files – and the whole thing'll go to nowt. Nowt, Patton. Would that be the sort of justice you want to see?'

At the end it seemed that all his disgust was levelled at me, but I'd been correct in my assessment of him. I'd suspected it;

125

now it shone clear. In spite of his claims, behind it all there was himself, his reputation, his future in the force. He wanted – was desperately scrabbling for – success. Self! Though it may not have occurred to him, it stood there mockingly, taunting him. Was there never a plain and unscarred desire for truth and justice?

I could now deal with him without a spark of conscience. 'The kind of justice I want to see is justice for Caine.'

'One minnow in a shoal of sharks!' he said cynically.

'Yes. But he's my minnow now.'

His teeth bit down on his words. 'You're a stubborn bastard. D'you know that?'

'So I've been told.' It was all I had left to cling to, a determination to see it through.

He opened the door beside him and stepped out, raised his head and looked at the sky. 'Clouds're clearing. I can see the moon.' He turned, his hand ready to slam the door. 'They've taken him to St Asaph's.' He slammed it. I didn't get time to ask him the location of St Asaph's Hospital.

But in the end there'd been a touch of magnanimity.

10

Think of something else and it comes to you. I thought of something else, of Amelia and her concern if I didn't phone her soon, and it came. St Asaph's! It'd been one of those Victorian cottage hospitals, somewhere beyond Much Wenlock, with a dozen beds and one theatre for small operations such as ingrowing toe-nails, and a consulting room tucked in a corner. Small, cosy and informal. Surely, in the modern climate of NHS rationality, it would have been closed down, used perhaps now as a community-hall. But apparently not.

I had difficulty remembering its exact location, never actually having been inside it, and for about ten miles I was driving by instinct, sniffing it out as though the smell of iodoform might be in the air. But eventually I ran through a small township whose name I didn't catch, and caught a glimpse of a signpost in the headlights. Hospital. I swung left, and suddenly there it was, spread behind a row of trees, which were still dripping from the rain.

There was much extension work attached to the old red-brick buiding, a certain modern practicality about it, not exactly a joy to behold unless you were the one lying in pain in the ambulance, but plainly functional. The car-park seemed very much larger than they would need, and very empty with only a scattering of cars, but then I recalled that this couldn't be very far from the motorway, and it was possibly an emergency unit in case of multiple pile-ups. If so, it would present a readily available and special expertise in cases such as Julian Caine's. If, of course, this was indeed St Asaph's.

It was. I locked the car and walked over to the public

127

entrance, located in the general darkness by a single dim globe above the steps. The words 'Saint Asaph's Hospital' were worked into the stone arch above. All was quiet. No one around. I walked through swing-doors into a small reception hall, with corridors running off in both directions. At nine-twenty in the evening the reception desk was unstaffed. A bell-push was labelled 'Ring For Attention'. I didn't do so – why disturb them? – but explored the double swing-doors ahead. A corridor faced me, to each side more swing-doors with round porthole windows, a peep through them being enough to confirm that they were wards, most of the beds empty and the lights dim. There was strangely no activity visible. I wandered onwards to where the corridor opened out sideways on both sides, to become a waiting-room or area. There were small tables, a few chairs, but the seating accommodation was mainly green-upholstered and rather tiring, even to look at, bench seats. Ancient magazines, a few of them recent enough to be printed in colour, were scattered around.

One such magazine lay open and disregarded on the lap of Marie Caine. She did not at once see me. I felt she saw nothing. Her eyes had the glazed look of shock and her face was pinched and grey, with deep lines around her mouth, which seemed now to be lipless. I went and stood over her until I saw movement in her eyes, a partial awareness.

'Marie,' I said gently. 'It's Richard Patton.'

Recognition came. She tried, oh she tried very hard, but the smile didn't quite fight its way through. 'Oh . . . yes. Hello.' She seemed confused by my presence, wondering perhaps whom I might be visiting.

I reached back and swung forward a chair, tubular metal with the same padding, but the bench seat was not for me, especially when my intention was to face her.

'Any news?' I asked. I had to prompt. 'Julian.'

She suddenly burst out, 'Why? Why do this to him . . .'

'I don't know.'

'. . . to us? They know he didn't do it. He's been released. It isn't right. It's not right.'

'No.' I kept it short. She had to have her say or she'd explode.

'Not fair! I've done nothing – nothing. But that . . . creature put his nasty sneering face right up to mine. Oh God!' She clamped her spread fingers over her face. Through them I could see her cheeks hot with colour. To such a woman as Marie, quiet and inoffensive herself, a gentlewoman in its old and honourable meaning, it would have been a terrible experience, such a face thrust at hers, she to whom the merest hint of violence, as demonstrated by Julian's stripped target-pistols, was something from which to withdraw with a shudder.

Gently, I took her through it while the image still controlled her mind. 'He wore no mask, then?'

'No, no.' The fingers were lowered. 'Mask? No. His face was enough.'

'You were able to describe him to the police?'

She not so much shook her head as waved it from side to side, searching for release from the memory.

'And he smashed one of the clocks, I understand.'

'Yes.' The air woofed out of her in a huge sigh. 'A vicious, mindless assault.' It seemed she felt this the greater evil than the hands laid on her. But of course, the clocks were beautiful and harmless, gently performing their duties and offending nobody. Marie was the kind of woman to search her conscience for past imperfections of character, in case she had perhaps deserved punishment. The clocks certainly didn't.

'But . . . but,' she went on, 'to do *that* to Julian! To do that! What sort of person could that be? Oh, Mr Patton, what've we done to deserve this?'

So I'd guessed correctly. 'It wouldn't have been one person, I think. Persons. Two of them.'

'Did it take two, for one woman and such an inoffensive man as Julian?' That was said with contempt.

'No. I meant that the two attacks were probably unconnected. Except of course, in so far as the attack on you kept Julian late at the shop, waiting for me. *His* attacker merely waited in the car-park for the chance to arise. The later Julian came, the fewer parked vehicles there'd be, thus making it easier.'

'I don't know what happened there.' She looked round her. For news, perhaps.

'No. I suppose you wouldn't. Just say he was run down by a car.'

129

I was leaning forward with hands on my knees, using an unemotional voice such as I would have adopted when giving evidence in court. This sometimes helps with people in shock, for whom the incident fills their minds to overflowing and excludes all reasonable extraneous thought. It impresses on them that it is an incident set in the surroundings of normal life. It reminds them that there is such a thing as normality.

'But the person who came to the shop', I went on, 'was an entirely different personality from the one in the car. What you got was one of these self-appointed guardians of the law, who're not satisfied with courts and decisions and the laws of society. They know best, and if the law acts like a fool, then he, this big hero, has got to put it right. This . . . the attack on you and the clock, and the warning . . . this would be something he'd be proud to do, on behalf of society.'

She was staring at me. Now she whispered. 'Are you quite mad?'

I smiled. 'Sometimes I wonder. Seriously, there are people like that. Think how it simplifies their lives, this wonderful self-conceit, that only they can be right. One could envy such simplification.'

'Could you?'

'If I made a bit of an effort.'

'You're a strange man, Mr Patton.'

'Please . . . Richard. I suppose I am.' You see, it sometimes works. Allow me my own small self-conceit. Her thoughts were now centred outside herself. 'But we're not talking about me. Julian. What about him? What news have you got?'

Had I switched the image too abruptly? Her face darkened, her gaze flitted past me. 'Alive. Yes, he's alive. I'm waiting to hear. So long . . . it seems so long. They always say the longer it is, the less chance.'

'Quite untrue. I'd have said the opposite.'

Her lips flexed. A smile. She saw right through me. 'And I'm sure they won't wait for ever.'

'Who?'

'They brought me here. A police car.'

'They'll wait.'

'Oh, they've been so good to me. So kind and so sympathetic.

130

At least . . .' She put a hand to her lips and her eyes came alight above it. 'At least, I suppose that was what it was, their remarks in the car. Positively obscene, they were. I suppose they assumed I wasn't listening. But I was.'

I tried not to smile. 'Yes. They don't care for people like that, either the one who frightened you or the one who drove that car into Julian. You can see why it couldn't have been the same man. This with Julian, it was a planned and worked-out deliberate attempt to kill him. The car was stolen in Worcester for the purpose.'

'Worcester?' It's strange that people seize on the insignificant. 'Why there?'

'It doesn't really matter. It's somewhere to steal a car from. But Marie – you must see that the important thing *is* that the attempt was on his life. Somebody wanted him dead. It was imperative. Now . . . who would want that? Can you help me there?'

'To do with his release from prison,' she suggested weakly.

'No. Oh no. His release has probably brought it all into the light, but it can't be *because* of it. It means that Julian is a threat to somebody, and his presence has provoked an old hatred.'

'Oh – how could that be?'

'Or an old love,' I tried gently.

'You can't kill somebody for love!' she protested, as though I'd defiled a basic truth.

'Oh Marie . . . surely you're not that naïve! There're more deaths caused by love than by anything else, love and its derivatives: jealousy, sex, distorted passion.'

'You must have led a very strange life,' was all she could suggest.

'But think,' I asked her, as though tutoring a pupil for an exam. 'Julian came out of prison and asked me to prove his innocence. In fact, I can now do that, but I'm not certain that fact can be the reason for the attack on *him*. On me, I could understand. But killing him doesn't affect my findings. It wouldn't stop me saying it out loud, shouting it if necessary.'

'What're you saying!' she flung out a hand in emphasis. I held it for a few moments as she went on. 'You can really do this? *Prove* he's innocent?'

131

'Yes, I can', I assured her, more confidently perhaps than the facts dictated. 'I can prove it. But this attempt on Julian's life can be connected with that proof only in a marginal sense. Someone is becoming desperate because I'm getting too close to him. Or to her. If Julian didn't shoot Eric Prost, who did? Does Julian know something he hasn't revealed? Does he perhaps suspect something, or is believed to? You can see my point. It centres around Julian, but not specifically around Prost's killing.'

'It's too complicated for me.'

'No it isn't. It's logic, Marie,' I said softly. 'You left him. More than once, I believe. There was a woman – or more than one.'

'Yes,' she breathed, her eyes dark, massaging the hand I'd gripped.

'He's admitted to me there was one.'

'I know of one,' she admitted cautiously.

'And where there is a woman, there could well be a husband.'

'I don't know what you mean.'

'If the . . . um . . . relationship has been resumed.'

She was staring at me with large, shocked eyes, hard lines from the corners of her mouth because she was gritting her teeth. But she said nothing, unwilling to accept such a thing could have happened. Since he'd come back to her? She said nothing.

'Do you know a name?' I asked gently.

'No.' Her lips barely moved. She was shutting me out. I was discussing his infidelity, when he could be dying. He had all her fidelity, and she had to cling to that.

'But you're certain there was only one?' I persisted.

'Only one I know about.' She bit off the words, staring around, trying not to meet my eyes.

'Know about? In what way? Did he tell you?'

'A woman doesn't need to be told.' Evasive action, now.

'So I've heard. Did he take her to the house? When you were away, say. At a time when you'd left him.' I was insisting, drawing her into it, making her respond.

'Yes,' she whispered. 'And . . . and to the rooms above the shop.' This seemed to upset her more than the thought of the house. '*Our* room, that was.' She almost choked. 'It was – well,

132

so insulting. It's set up as a kind of bed-sitter. We did actually live there, before we bought the house. We did . . . did our courting there.'

'Naturally.'

'And he took her *there*!'

'You could tell?'

'Yes.' She bit it off.

'How?'

'The usual. Scent. The same as at the house. The odd hair I came across . . . oh, a hundred little details.'

'So you left him?'

'Yes.'

'But came back?'

'I couldn't', she said simply, 'live without him.'

'Lucky man. Did you know anything about her at all? No name, you say, but . . . background?'

There was a small flash of opposition. 'Why do you wish to know this?'

Because I was groping around, fumbling for some connection. Eric Prost's death had to be involved, if only peripherally, but I hadn't any leads, no clues, no ideas.

'Because I wish to know.' I shrugged.

She flexed her lips. It could have been a smile. 'She was, I think, something to do with antiques. I only suspect this. But how else could he meet another woman, except through his profession?'

'Yes. I see your point.' In a hundred ways, that was how, but she would be going by what women call intuition, and which I've always thought to be an ability to put dozens of tiny fragments together and make a whole. 'And when Eric Prost died and Julian was arrested . . . you weren't there.' I had been to the house that Tuesday evening, and seen no wife. 'Was that one of the times you'd left him?'

'Before that, yes. But I went back on the Monday.'

'The Monday Prost died?'

'Yes. I didn't know, of course, then. But on Tuesday – there were rumours going around.'

'I didn't see you at the house,' I said quietly.

133

'No. Julian told me to keep out of the way. I was upstairs in the bedroom.'

'So he knew?'

'Only that his friend was dead. We didn't know . . . how it had happened.'

Perhaps Julian had, I thought. Perhaps he'd known more than he'd told Marie, otherwise he wouldn't have asked her to keep out of the way. He'd been preparing himself for a visitor, who turned out to be me.

'It was convenient, as it turned out, though,' I suggested. At her blank stare I amplified, 'You were there to take over the shop.'

'Yes,' she agreed dully. She was losing interest, her mind wandering to the outer reaches, where Julian now lay. 'Somebody had to. I'd worked there anyway. I know as much as Julian does about clocks.'

'But not pistols?'

That got me a thin smile. 'No. Not those. And I couldn't do the clock renovation. You'll understand that.'

'Not really. It needs knowledge and a good eye and a pair of hands. You've got all those.'

'But I'd be scared of doing some terrible harm.'

'Yes. I suppose I would, too.'

'And it's not really a woman's work, lathes and files and tools and things.'

I smiled. I could produce whole regiments of women who would contest that statement forcefully. 'But in any event, you didn't attempt it.'

'No.'

'Yet you'd have to do the buying, attending auction sales, that sort of thing.'

'Oh yes. But I could do that.'

Yes, she wasn't short of competence. Looking round, I said, 'You get the impression they've all gone home. Quiet. I'll go and sniff out the situation, shall I?'

'Oh yes, please. I didn't like to.'

I got to my feet, patting my pockets, knowing I couldn't smoke in there but checking I still had my pipe. Yes, I had that, but I was low on tobacco. I was thus not attending to where I was going, and nearly walked into a man who'd entered from one of the rear doors. He wore a green smock, a face-mask loose around his neck.

'Mrs Caine?'

'Oh yes.' She fumbled to her feet, almost stumbling. 'How is . . . what is . . .'

He smiled. He'd done this a vast number of times. 'He's going to live, Mrs Caine. We were afraid a rib had punctured his lung, but no, though it was a close thing. Some concussion, a broken leg and a broken arm. From what I've heard happened, you could say he's been lucky.'

'Can I see him?'

'We'll tuck him into a bed, then you can see him. But he's still asleep, and will be for hours, so there's really no point. In the morning, perhaps he'll be able to talk.'

'Oh . . . yes. Thank you. I . . . I think I'll stay, though.'

'Really, you know, you'd do no good. And we've no facilities for food and drink. Far better to go home and get some rest.'

'Home!'

I was watching her face, seeing the emotions surging across it. The empty house and no Julian there. The attacker – would he try again? The agonizing yearning for sleep, now that the immediate fear had been swept away.

I moved forward, catching the doctor's eye. 'I'll look after her. There's a police car waiting outside to take her home, and . . .' I caught her eye and nodded. '. . . another guarding the house. She'll be all right.'

'Fine.' He smiled at us, the one smile sweeping economically from one to the other. 'I'll leave it in good hands, then.' At that, he nodded and went away. I didn't know whether he was finished for the day, but he looked and moved like someone in urgent need of rest himself.

We went outside. The air smelt fresh and damp. The only light was the globe above the entrance.

'Where's your police car? Ah, I see it. Over there. Come along, Marie.'

'I'd much rather stay, you know,' she pleaded, hanging back.

'Now, you mustn't be selfish. When he opens his eyes in the

135

morning he'll want to see a fresh and smiling Marie, not one who dozes off as soon as he wakes.'

'What a tortuous mind you have, Richard.'

'Here we are.'

I opened the rear door, and the two police officers jerked awake. 'You may take her home gentlemen,' I told them. 'And as a favour, just check that there's a guard on the house. If not, contact your HQ and see it's laid on. Then, if you'd be so good, you might collect the Rover from the car-park in Markham Prior. You've got your keys, Marie?'

'Yes. But really . . . the trouble.'

'No trouble, is it officer?' I asked the driver, who still seemed to be half asleep. 'If it is, ask Chief Superintendent Wainwright for instructions. She'll need the car in the morning. Good night to you. And sleep well, Marie.'

She said something, but the car was already moving away, the two men already asking her about Caine. I felt good. It'd been just like old times, working out the routine and issuing the instructions, though these days it was necessary to be more polite. Then I went back inside the entrance-lobby, where I'd noticed a public phone on the wall. It was ten-seventeen, and I knew I hadn't finished with that day.

I had only a little loose cash in my pockets, so that the first thing I did when Amelia answered was to give her my number, so that she could call me back if we hadn't finished. I had an idea it might be an extended conversation.

'I'm sorry, love,' I said, 'but I got caught.'

'You always get caught,' she told me severely, but there was a hint of resignation in her voice. 'Where are you?'

'I'm at a hospital called Saint Asaph's.'

'Hospital!'

So I had to explain that. She always expects me to get myself into the sort of trouble that will land me in a hospital bed.

Rather predictably, when I'd finished, she said, 'Oh, that poor woman!'

'She'll be all right. There'll be a police guard on the house.'

'But she'll be alone.'

'Now . . . Amelia . . .'

'Has she got anybody to sit with her?'

'I told her to go to bed.'

'How very unfeeling of you, Richard.'

'It seemed a good idea.'

A slight pause, then, 'I can be there in an hour.'

'It's not necessary. You don't like night-driving.'

'The roads will be fairly clear of traffic at this time of night.'

When she makes this kind of decision, my wife is normally beyond persuasion. It would be no good to tell her that she'd be on the road at the time the pubs would be emptying, and that most of the customers would be a hazard more dangerous than her depleted night-sight. But I had to try, and in the end we compromised. She would do exactly as she wished, and I would contact her at Markham View.

'When, Richard? You'll surely get there first.'

I was silent.

'Richard, surely you will.'

'I'm not certain, love.'

'Now . . . what does *that* mean?'

'Strike while the iron's hot.'

'What', she asked distinctly, 'is hot about the situation?'

'I'm not certain.'

'Your wretched instincts, I suppose. Have you eaten?'

'No.'

'But surely there must be somewhere . . .'

'I haven't seen anywhere, but I'll certainly keep an eye open.'

After an extended list of instructions as to my welfare, she hung up, no doubt expecting me to be gaunt and hungry-looking when we next met. Ruefully, I had to admit to an emptiness, and I could have murdered a couple of pints of best bitter. It seemed that I'd have to find a pub before closing time. They might have a curling sandwich left. But I knew, before I walked out again into the dark and silent night, that the odds were against my going anywhere for a little while.

I stood on the steps outside and slowly filled my pipe. Very low on tobacco now. I had little to sustain me, one way and another. I got it going, wafted a cloud of smoke at the moon, which had decided to pay us a visit, and slowly walked towards the Stag.

She was there, as I'd known she would be, having noted a

small blue car as I'd driven in. It was still there, or rather its shadow was. She was sitting half perched on my bonnet. Veronica Pierce.

My stomach rumbled.

11

With only the globe above the entrance to offer any light, it was very dim out there where my car was, but I could detect that she was in slacks and a tailored jacket, the white flash of a blouse catching a hint of the glow. There was not much of her face to be seen, but I didn't need an expression to reveal that she was under stress. Her voice told me all, though she made an attempt at attack, as though it was I who'd kept her waiting outside there in the cold, when she might well have ventured inside.

'They've got him inside here, haven't they?' she demanded.

'Him? To whom are you referring?' All very formal, that was, so that she'd be in no doubt that my sympathies were not with her. Cool. Detached.

'Julian Caine. You know who we're talking about, so don't try to be clever.'

'Yes, they brought him here. Why didn't you come inside and find out?'

She threw back her head. The eyes caught a gleam of reflected light. '*She* was in there.'

'She?'

'His wife.'

'Ah. We must be absolutely sure, mustn't we!'

She made an angry gesture. 'Is he . . . alive? All right. Is he going to live? Put it like that.'

'I'm sorry. I have to tell you he'll live.'

'Sorry! What the hell does that mean?'

'I assumed you'd prefer him dead.'

With one compact movement she rose from the bonnet and

turned away, even took two paces before she swung back. 'You're a fool, Patton. A damned fool. I couldn't bear him to die. I don't think I could live through that.'

I left it for a few seconds, giving her time to make up her mind, whether to walk away or to remain. But of course, she had first to plunder my mind for information. As far as I was concerned, she could have the lot, but I was going to make her work for it. Tit for tat.

'Let me get this straight,' I said fumbling with my tobacco pouch then realising my pipe was still going. 'Straight,' I repeated. 'Your wish . . . no, your demand . . . was that I should produce evidence, positive evidence, of Caine's guilt regarding Eric Prost's killing, and now you tell me you couldn't bear it if he were to die. There's something contradictory there, or I'm going insane. Go on, encourage me. Tell me how straightforward and sensible it is.' I grinned at her, but I doubt she got the full benefit of it.

She threw her head back, hair dancing. Just as Vera had done. But now there was no jerk to my heart. She had very little in common with my first wife.

'Well, you *are* insane,' she pointed out. 'Or at least, none too bright. Just as well for you that my husband didn't have you in his squad. He'd have got rid of you, you can bet your life on that.'

'I'm sure he would. Your so-admirable husband, who couldn't bear to consider the smallest of errors . . .'

'And don't you dare sneer at him, Patton,' she cut in. 'You're not fit to be mentioned in the same sentence.'

She was doing her best to annoy me, to distract me. But I had let it go on long enough. 'Suppose we get back to the anomaly. You know what I mean? Anomaly. Wanting Caine proved guilty but not dead. Will you kindly explain that.'

'I doubt you'd have the intelligence to understand.'

'Try me.'

'I will not have my husband's name sullied because of a paltry error with . . .'

'Oh, I can assure you that such a thing isn't on the cards. But if you loved your husband so much . . .'

'I didn't say that.'

'Admired then. Venerated. Looked up to, if you want it simpler.'

'He was a fine and upright man.'

'If you believe that.'

'Of course I believe it. I know it. I lived with him, shared his life with him, understood him, knew exactly how precious his reputation was to him . . .' She paused for breath. I moved round slightly, so that the poor light from that globe had a fair chance of betraying her expression. She still wasn't telling the truth.

'And while all this admiration was being heaped on your husband . . . Arthur, I believe his name was . . . you were able to spare your real affection for Julian Caine?'

She stared at me for a few moments as though she did indeed believe me to be mad, then with a shrug she turned and began to move away from me. All right, if she wanted to walk, I was quite prepared to go along with her. She had realized I had the advantage of the globe's light, and the moon, in its first quarter, wasn't helping much. So we would walk side by side, faces averted. Now I realized how tall she was for a woman.

'And did he know?' I asked after a few yards.

She tossed me a glance. 'Who know what?'

'Did Arthur know your affections were elsewhere? Did he know you were in love with Julian Caine?'

'Of course not.'

'So definite. Could you be so certain?'

'He was completely absorbed in his career.'

'But Veronica,' I said gently, 'we're talking about ten years ago. His career had barely started when Caine was arrested. When Caine supposedly shot Eric Prost – if you remember – your husband was a plain DC. This undercover affair of yours with Caine must've been going on at that time. Not recently. Not since Caine came out of prison, because Arthur was dead at that time. Remember? It was because of a deathbed statement that Caine was released.'

I was saying this with a measured patience. We were, apparently, talking about a love-affair with Caine that'd carried over for the whole ten years of his imprisonment. After all, she

141

had said she could *now* not bear that he should die. I still couldn't understand her. Or maybe I could. The hint of an idea crept into a corner of my mind. I shook myself free of it, and returned to my main point. 'Will you please explain.'

She turned to face me again for a moment. 'I knew Julian before I met Arthur. He was married, of course. Julian, that is. Arthur wasn't. Somehow, he excited me. Arthur did. He had such plans, such splendid possibilities for the future. There couldn't be any future for me with Julian. We understood each other, Julian and I. There'd be no shaking him free from Marie. Oh, I knew that. So I married Arthur. I had to think of *my* future. And . . . and it all came to nothing.'

I knew what she meant. They'd had no family.

'The future didn't?' I asked. 'But Arthur's future *did*, and so splendidly. Chief Superintendent. That was really moving.'

'My future didn't.' It was said quietly, almost to herself.

'Ah. I see. Your career, you mean. What were you doing at that time?'

'You must know that, or you're quite stupid. I was an antiques dealer. Free-lance. I'd scout out choice pieces for other dealers, working on a commission.'

I smiled to myself into the night. Give her a chance to fight back at me and she would tell me anything. Anything at all. I had rather vaguely guessed this, as it linked with Caine having had an affair with Veronica. Once that was confirmed, the career of antiques dealer fitted her background perfectly. But it did not explain her apparent ambivalent attitude to Caine.

She stopped abruptly. We'd done one complete circuit of the car-park. 'I don't see why we should continue with this. You've told me what I wanted to know.'

'Which is that Julian is alive and will continue to be so. Having lost Arthur, you'll now be able to devote all your time and attention to Julian. Things are working out very conveniently for you.'

She made a sound of disgust and tried to thrust past me. I moved sideways and laid a hand on her arm to restrain her. Furiously, she shook herself free.

'Though I suppose', I conceded, 'that if I proved his guilt,

142

and he found out you'd wished for that, he'd hardly welcome you with open arms.'

'I can't help that, can I!'

'Or you must suffer the pain of having your husband's name sullied?' I watched her face, as much as was visible. She compressed her lips and averted her head. 'Or am I a little wrong there?' I asked. No response. 'Your beautiful and clandestine love-affair, is it to founder over a dustbin lid?'

'Will you please get out of my way!'

'No. You wanted to speak to me. That's what we're doing. So now – you can do a bit of listening. You see, Veronica, I just don't believe you. Your husband's reputation! Rubbish. You said how close you were, and how much you were in his confidence. No, don't shake your head. It's not his deathbed statement that's worrying you, is it? Not that one paltry error with a dustbin lid. You know as well as I do . . . damn sight better . . . that this fine and noble husband of yours has had a career absolutely riddled with deception and corruption. And what you're afraid of – what's terrifying you – is that any deep investigation will discover that *you* had a part in it, that *you* went along with everything he did, that *you* actually helped him, when your presence was required in a clandestine manner. He'd find dozens of roles for you to play. That would explain why you can't let Julian rest . . .'

'No!' she shouted, having held it in too long.

'Hush now. People are asleep inside. Veronica . . . I do sympathize. Really I do. Loving the man, yet knowing how his very presence is a threat to you . . .'

'That's a damned lie!'

'Listen to me . . .' I put a hand on her arm again, and she tried once more to shake herself free. This time I didn't let her go, and held her firmly. 'Listen. This is for your own good. You ought to know that your husband's fellow-officers are already delving into his career. They'll surely uncover the lot. No stopping them now. It's no longer anything related at all to Julian – it's only that his release has sparked it off.' I stared into the shadowed planes of her numbed face. 'Don't you *see!*' I said softly. 'Julian will live. You can continue to love him, or whatever you felt for him. It's no longer necessary to hide it.'

'Hide . . . what?' It came deep down from her throat.

'Arthur's rotten and twisted career. Did you imagine I meant your love-affair? You can't hide that, either, because I'll have a few things to say to Julian when he's well enough to take them in. And to Marie.'

'Take your hand off me, blast you.'

'Not until you understand it's finished. It's been finished a long while, but you won't let it lie. The death of Eric Prost put an end to it.'

'I don't know what you mean,' she breathed distantly.

'Eric Prost recognized you, leaving the alley-way beside Caine Antiques.'

'What the hell d'you mean by that?' she demanded forcefully. 'If you're saying Julian shot him because of our affair . . .'

'No.' She'd completely surprised me. I'd not had such a thought. 'Of course not. I wondered *how* Eric Prost recognized you. I'd like to know when he'd seen you previously. In other words, recognized you as what?'

She seemed to relax. I felt the tension slip from her arm. 'Of *course* he would know me, you fool. It was I who went to him about the Tompion long-case clock. He'd remember me from then.'

It was the mental image that'd tripped me up. The Mercedes car and the smart young woman from London. Veronica had never featured in that situation. Now I realized that she slipped quite neatly into the pattern. I would have liked more time to consider this and its implications, but she was impatient, and I felt not a little worried. If she decided she wanted to leave now, I wouldn't be able to stop her. Veronica was a forceful woman, not easily to be restrained. I had to be patient with her, express my ignorance so that she would not abandon the interview when an opportunity remained to belittle me.

'Well of course!' I said. 'I ought to have realized Julian would have told you about Eric and his collection of clocks. You could not have resisted the opportunity to go there and cheat Eric Prost into parting with one of them – cheap – and give you a good profit at auction. I wonder whether your upright husband knew about this. Did he approve? I'm told you turned up with a van and a man to help you. Here . . .' I touched her arm,

144

allowing myself to pursue the subject as something of a joke, making my voice light. 'That man wasn't your Arthur by any chance! Now *that* would be a really splendid twist to the drama.'

'You make me sick, Patton. D'you know that! Of *course* Arthur didn't know. Of *course* I didn't go to the house with the intention of buying one of Eric Prost's clocks for myself.' So pleased was she to be able to elaborate on my lack of understanding that she actually stopped beneath the globe, its light eerily throwing the planes of her face into deep shadows. And she was laughing at me, her expression wide open with the pleasure of it.

'Perhaps you'd explain,' I suggested.

'We rigged it between us, Julian and me. It's an age-old scam, this one. Julian knew the value of every one of the clocks in that place, but he'd got his eye on the Tompion long-case clock. What we'd do was that I'd go along first and make an offer, and leave Prost to think about it. Julian knew his so-called friend was short of cash at the time. So he'd go along a day or two later, pretend to be shocked at my offer, and make a slightly better one, just to stop me getting it. It's a well-used trick. Always works, because it's based on psychology. The poor mug thinks the second offer's a bargain, and jumps at it. You want to learn something about life, Patton. It's a wonder you've lived to your age.'

It was very like Julian's own version, slanted only by the question of his intentions and motivations.

'So what went wrong?' I asked.

'The rotten sod . . .'

'This is Julian you're talking about?'

'Yes.' She snapped it like a shot into the night. 'He cheated me. Bought the Tompion as we'd planned, then left it in Prost's house, for some damned reason of his own. I was mad at him – you can guess. We'd have made nearly twenty thousand out of it. Each. And the bastard left it there.'

'Definitely a rift in the loot,' I observed. 'How very annoying of him. And then Prost died. Now . . . I wonder if there's any . . .'

'Of course there's a damned connection, you idiot,' she told me. 'With Prost dead Julian could claim it as his, and shut me right out of it.'

Then she turned on her heel and marched towards her car, so incensed by the memory that she was quite prepared to drive away from me, as fast as possible. But I wasn't prepared to let her go. We hadn't finished. I caught up with her as her hand fell on the door handle. Laid my hand on hers. She didn't turn, but her shoulders stiffened.

'But that is not so,' I said quietly into the back of her ear. 'He'd acquired it, you say, from Prost's death. Nothing in your scheme was altered by that. You could still have shared the plunder.'

'You know what happened.' Her voice was terse. She still had not turned to face me. 'He was arrested, and *she*, that wife of his, she collected it. Then I was shut right out of it.'

'Shame!' I said.

That turned her, her eyes sparking, catching what light there was. 'Don't try to be too clever, Patton.'

'It's hardly likely, is it, that he would plan his own arrest so that you'd lose out on the clock? Or that he'd kill Prost with that object in mind. That's just damned stupid.'

'I'm tired of this. Will you please stand away and let me get into my car.'

Instead, I took both shoulders into my hands so that she couldn't turn away again. 'But you still love him? When, you say, he cheated you.'

'It was a long while ago.' Then the defiance seemed to sigh from her, and she went on softly. 'Things . . .kind of change. And it wasn't really his fault that his wife got hold of the clock. Yes, I find I still love him. Does that satisfy you, Patton? What he thinks of me . . .' I felt the shoulders shrug beneath my fingers, '. . . I no longer know. And now,' she continued in the same quiet and emotionless tone, 'will you please take your filthy hands off me, or by God I'll cripple you.'

I released her, laughed, playfully patted her cheeks, and stepped back. Smartly. There was no denying that she'd have done just that.

'A bit of advice,' I suggested. 'You go home, wherever it is,

146

and try to forget him. I've got an idea you'll never be able to get between Marie and Julian again.'

For a moment I thought she was going to hit me, but then the firm line of her lips softened, the muscle-line easing so that Vera peeped through at me again, then she gave me a wide, open smile. 'You want to bet?'

Perhaps she was capable of warmth, and it was only the present situation that tensed her. But she was a fighter, this woman. To the bitter end.

'I'm not going to bet on anything,' I assured her. 'But . . . a little bit of information for you. They won't renew the licence for his pistols.'

'What's that mean?'

'They will not be available to Marie. If she felt she needed them, I mean. To be rid of you.'

Her face played around with expressions before she managed to laugh easily, swinging the car door open behind her. 'What! Her! She'd be scared of touching the things. Haven't you met her?' It was said with contempt, and she turned away, so that I couldn't see the expression materialize.

I stood and watched her drive away. I didn't think she'd take my advice and go home, but it was still unclear what she might intend to accomplish if she didn't. Then I realized I'd omitted to inform her that I could now prove Julian's innocence. Not that it made any difference. She'd wanted me to prove his guilt in order to nullify the effect of her husband's deathbed statement, and thus spark off a deeper investigation. It had seemed, even when she'd first approached me, a very paltry reason for such a drastic treatment. Now that I knew she'd been his mistress, it seemed even more unacceptable. She would surely want him out, not inside prison. There had to be a stronger motivation for her attitude.

If I could believe her about their joint operation over the Tompion clock, that might still rankle. It might well be that with this in mind she'd wanted further proof of his guilt. Certainly, armed with such proof, she would have been in a position to force his hand, make him put the clock up for auction, and thus achieve her original aim. Not, now, for the money, but simply because it had been a bargain between them and right was right.

This was perhaps not the sentiment expected from the admiring wife of Arthur Pierce.

Not satisfied, far from pleased with where all this was leading me, I went to my car and drove away. The dashboard clock indicated twenty minutes past midnight. Heavens, I'd wasted so much time! Amelia would already be at Markham View, and wondering where the hell I'd got to.

12

It was a clear night now, the moon no more than a thin slice, exactly the circumstances in which I like to find myself with twenty miles of winding country roads ahead. The Stag is a sheer delight to drive at these times. With the roads nearly empty, and headlights visible a mile ahead, it's possible to press the adhesion to the limit, driving into the corners and powering out of them. In that distance I met not one other driver. Overtook a couple, but met none coming the other way. It was the sort of concentrated pleasure that I needed, in order to take my mind from the case for a while.

Markham Prior was ahead almost before I expected it. I had to go past the turn-off to Winter Haven, and all that was left was to negotiate the two bridges and the town, and I'd be there. Judging by the glow in the sky to my left, it seemed that there was still activity over there, but I supposed that fairground people were used to retiring late.

Amelia's Granada was parked out on the drive in front of Caine's place. So was a dark and silent police car. No lights were on in the house that I could see, but it didn't mean they'd both retired. Marie maybe, but Amelia would be impatient to reach her own bed.

She must have been sitting quietly with her ears cocked. As I drew to a halt the hall lights went on; as I slammed the car door the house door opened. And as I walked up the three steps into the porch Amelia said, 'Richard! Whatever's happened? I've been half out of my mind . . .'

I put an arm round her shoulders and kissed her where it

would conveniently stop the flow. 'Sorry love, but I got caught. I'll tell you later. How is she?'

'Quiet. Repressed. As you'd expect.'

'Gone to bed?'

'No. She says she doesn't want to.'

'Hmm! Think she's up to a bit of questioning, do you?'

We'd been moving along the hall. She stopped, a hand on my arm. 'Must you? She's quiet now. It'd be a pity to upset her.'

'I don't think I'll do that. Unless she takes exception to talking about Julian's mistress – as we'll call her.'

She smiled up at me, her hand on the knob of the living-room door. 'So you know who that is?'

'Oh yes. It's the Veronica Pierce I told you about. That's what's kept me, talking to her, or being talked to, put it how you like. But she revealed a lot, and perhaps Marie could confirm some of it – or deny it. Shall we go in?'

'Then be careful, Richard, please.'

I smiled at her. We went into what they called the sitting-room.

This was a room into which I'd not previously been invited. Four days or so before, Marie had served me tea in the kitchen. I had not then been a visitor, but simply Julian's tame detective, under his employment one might say, but unpaid. I'd seen the gun-room, which had had its own atmosphere of brutal practicality. This was different. The room we were entering was indeed a room for living in, spacious, with a high and decorated ceiling, but its proportions in no way giving an impression of furniture scattered around to fill up the space. No. Think about it, work it out, and you would be unable to add one piece or take one away, without upsetting the balance. The rear wall was hung with a spread of curtains, now drawn together. I guessed that these hid wide french windows, which probably opened on to a terrace.

It was obvious that Caine dabbled in antiques other than clocks and pistols. Clocks there were. Would he care to enter a room with none? But it was the furniture that blended it all together with such quiet and dignified taste. I'm not qualified to name pieces at a glance, but I guessed that Hepplewhite wouldn't have been ashamed to admit to creating one or two items, and Sheraton could have had more than one hand in it. And on a beautiful settee, looking, herself, very decorative in a casual dress – did she shun slacks or jeans? – was Marie.

'Hello,' I said. 'And how are you feeling now?'

'More myself,' she admitted with the hint of a rueful smile. 'Did you get any more news? I suppose that was what you waited for.'

'No,' I admitted, watching Amelia returning to the Queen-Anne chair she'd obviously been using. 'Not news of Julian. I was delayed.'

'And how was that?' asked Marie, without any enthusiasm and just keeping it going, and disappointed that my complete attention should not have been concentrated on Julian.

'She was waiting for me in the car-park,' I explained. 'Apparently she didn't want to go inside for news, because you were there. That's natural enough. So she sat quietly in her car until the police had taken you away, and then she expected to get up-to-date news from me.'

'She?' Marie said, raising her eyebrows and attempting to look baffled, though I could feel she was abruptly more tense. She swung her feet down to the floor, then reached up and fussed her hair back into position. 'Who is this you're talking about? I don't understand.'

'It was Veronica Pierce.'

She blinked, but her expression remained blank. She had guessed whom I meant, but perhaps the name hadn't been known to her.

'I don't know . . .'

'Julian's woman,' I explained. 'His mistress. Whatever you wish to call her.'

'I do not wish to call her anything.'

'You didn't know her name?'

'No. No, I certainly did not. Would you expect me to ask Julian about her? Do you imagine we would chat casually about *her*? He pretended she didn't exist. Do you know, I actually believe he thought I didn't guess a thing. How very stupid of him. Of course I knew she existed. Why else would I have left him? Exists, I suppose, if she's cropped up again.'

151

Now there was a distinct bite to her voice. There had been a ten-year gap. Marie would assume that the affair was over, dead and gone, so that it would now be a difficult thought to handle, the possibility that for Veronica the passion – if that was the word Marie would use to herself – had survived. The thought had to arise, too, that perhaps Julian's feelings had also survived the period of separation.

'Cropped up?' I asked. 'Well, I suppose you could call it that. She's certainly on the scene again, though there's no evidence that she's set eyes on Julian.' I thought Marie deserved a little encouragement in that direction.

Her right fist thumped down hard on the chair-arm. 'Then why was she at the hospital?' she demanded.

'For news of him.'

'How did she know he was there?'

'I don't know. I didn't ask.'

'But I'm sure you told her what she wanted to hear. That he's got a good chance of living through it. You'd tell her that.'

'There was no point in lying.'

'I didn't mean that. I hope you made her feel happy!' she said sourly, darting a quick glance at Amelia, who nodded, apparently not pleased with the way I was putting this; that I was putting it at all.

'Well . . .' I didn't want to sit, wishing to keep this all very casual, eye-to-eye contact not being the correct psychological approach. So I wandered around, making a show of being interested in the décor and the furnishings. 'Well . . . I can't be sure it made her happy. Frankly, I can't be sure exactly what it made her. She'd told me she wanted me to find proof that Julian had killed Eric Prost. Proof. And now . . .'

'What!' She jerked herself upright.

'Don't ask me to explain it,' I went on casually. 'Apparently it's something to do with protecting the good name of her husband, who's now dead. But certainly she didn't want Julian dead. At least, that's her present attitude.'

There was a bitter tang to her voice. 'Oh no, she wouldn't want him dead.'

'In fact, she said she couldn't bear it if he died,' I amplified, one eye on Amelia, who at once whispered a protest and raised a hand to silence me.

At that time I was across at the far side of the room, so that Marie had to turn her head to face me. As our eyes met, she jerked back away from me, not willing to allow me to see her emotion. But for a second she'd put a hand to her face, just touched her forehead, then controlled herself at once.

'So it's all to start again!' she whispered.

'Doesn't that rather depend on Julian's attitude?' I asked. 'He may not be willing . . .'

'He's a fool. Always has been.'

'*You* may not be willing to let it start again.' It was a suggestion. She'd always, apparently, been weak and helpless in the face of Julian's affairs. I wondered whether she was still of the same mind.

'I'd kill her first!' she snapped, suddenly glaring at me as though I might intend to get in the way of that.

I was so surprised at this from Marie that I barely knew how to handle it. 'Oh, that'd be fine, that would. Another killing, another prison-sentence. What a pity Julian hasn't got his target-pistols any more. You could have gone out hunting for her and gunned her down.'

'If you care to be facetious . . .' She shrugged. Then she decided I'd been insulting. 'Who are you to imply I could do nothing? I will not be treated as a weak little thing, expected to stand back and let people walk all over me.'

'I'm sorry if I . . .'

'And so you should be, Richard,' put in my wife, not aware of what I was groping for.

I wasn't sure myself, some potential perhaps in this gentle Marie, some tendency towards vigorous defence. But Marie herself rescued me.

'And I *would* shoot her,' she claimed, nodding. 'Without a qualm.'

'There're still the antique pistols. Too heavy for you, perhaps.' I laughed, at myself mainly. 'Why are we talking about shootings, when everybody knows you couldn't even touch a pistol!'

153

'But that is not true.' She raised her chin, a tiny smile touching her lips.

'You couldn't even bear to watch Julian cleaning them.'

'That, too, is untrue.' A suggestion of satisfaction entered her voice. 'Julian made that up. He said it was to protect me, though I couldn't see why I needed protecting. But – and I know he told you a lie about this – he knew one of his pistols was missing when he got home that evening. The evening Eric Prost died, that is. When he'd finished cleaning the one he'd taken with him, and was putting it away, he opened the other gun-case. Something about doing some work on that pistol because it'd been jamming. And it wasn't there. So he knew. And it wouldn't have been missing unless something unpleasant was involved. We couldn't guess what. But – whatever it was – he was determined to keep me out of it. So he invented that story, all about me not being able to bear to watch him cleaning them. Just in case, he told me, anybody ever said I might have used the missing one. Because, of course, I was about the only one who knew how to get at the pistols, once he'd locked up. I wonder', she mused, 'whether he had his Veronica in mind . . .' She looked at me with sudden mischief in her eyes.

'I know all about the pendulum and the key,' I told her quietly, my minding racing away in the background.

I had expected to prod her into some sort of revelation, as there were missing pieces in the overall picture, but I'd not expected this. I reached for a chair and sat where I could now face her. Not close, not too overpoweringly close, though it began to seem that she was not, after all, the sort of woman to be overborne easily. I'd heard Amelia make a small, surprised sound, but I didn't dare to look at her.

'Are you telling me', I asked, 'that you've actually handled Julian's target-pistols?'

'Of course I have. The handgrip was a little large for my hand – with twenty-two target-pistols you fire one-handed, arm fully extended. Maybe you didn't know that. And they were rather heavy for me. He wanted me to apply for my own licence and buy my own target-pistol, but I didn't find it sufficiently interesting.' She turned and smiled at Amelia. 'I'm sure you'll understand that.'

'Oh, I do. It's not exactly an exciting pastime.'

'Sport. It's a sport,' Marie corrected.

'Oh. I see.' Amelia didn't know how to continue with it. I did.

'Marie. Let me get this straight. You're implying that you'd fired Julian's pistols. Do you mean at the club?'

This seemed to annoy her. Her mouth took on a stern line and she made a small and dismissive gesture with one hand. 'An unsuitable occupation for a woman, Richard? Is that it? But women do shoot. They enter competitions. Julian used to take me along to his club as a guest, and I'd use one of his pistols. That was the *real* reason he bought two, I believe. It was a kind of suggestion, an invitation, perhaps, for me to make use of one of them. Perhaps I should have gone along with him on it. I can see that now. He did like to share his pleasures with me.'

But there'd been one pleasure for which he'd gone elsewhere.

'You're very old-fashioned, Richard,' she said, smiling now.

'I suppose I am. And were you any good at it, this shooting?'

'Reasonably good. They told me that I was as good as any of the club's regular women members. Better, even.'

'It's a pity I didn't know that.'

'Yes. Isn't it! They'd have told you at the club, if you'd asked.'

'I did enquire there, but only about the times Julian arrived and left that night, and to confirm he was one of their top marksmen.'

This was not completely true, a lie of omission. I'd been told that Julian often brought a woman guest there. Different ones. When I'd asked whether they were any good they'd said they were all hopeless, couldn't hit the far wall of the range let alone a target. All except one. *She* was good. They hadn't known this one was his wife, though now it seemed that was the case. But I didn't see any point in telling Marie this. She knew about Veronica; that was about all she could handle.

She continued, although my face had probably gone blank with concentrating on the memory.

'They were quite right about Julian, of course. And they'd have told you I was quite good myself. And also that I knew a target-pistol wasn't usually lethal. And that I knew where it *could* be, if the shot was well aimed. And then, if you'd come to

155

me, I'd have told you that if I'd taken one of Julian's pistols it would have been in order to shoot that bitch of his, if I could ever get a sight of her, and believe me, I'd have known exactly where every shot would've been most effective. But not to kill, Richard. Oh no. To cause pain. To hurt her, as she's hurt me. And I'd enjoy it. Every moment of it.' Then the almost elated tension flowed from her, and she fell back against the settee and gave me a weak little smile. 'And that answers your other question, if you think about it. No, I didn't know her name, and I've never really set eyes on her, as I've said. Otherwise, it would perhaps have ended years before the shooting of Eric Prost. You see, Julian's pistols were available then.'

'Well . . .' said Amelia, into the silence that followed. I looked across at her, my eyebrows raised. Her tone had been the one that usually preceded something like, 'I suppose we ought to be going . . .'

But I wasn't ready to leave. Amelia was, I saw, a little embarrassed to hear so suddenly these aggressive sentiments from so mild and gentle a woman as Marie. But I'd had a lot more experience than she had of violence. Every man has a point beyond which he may not be pushed, and beyond which he, however mildly sociable he might normally be, is abruptly converted into a raging killer. Fortunately, few are so far pressed. With women, the contrast between the two moods is greater. The more normally placid they are, the more violently vicious they can become. Deadlier, as they say, than the male.

What was upsetting Amelia was the calm manner in which Marie had expressed such violent sentiments. The hurt must have been very deep, the wound more painful because it had been so carefully concealed. Now Marie was watching me with bright eyes, mocking me, waiting for my reaction.

'How tall are you, Marie?' I asked blandly.

'What?' I'd surprised her, after all.

'Tall. Height.'

'Oh . . . five feet five. What on earth . . .'

'About as tall as your husband?'

'About. Give or take half an inch. Why do you ask?'

I beamed at her, and lied with my usual facility. 'To change the subject.'

But I saw she knew I'd lied. I got to my feet again, restless. This was not the woman of the hospital, lost and distraught. This was a woman who could come back to fight again, a dour and determined battler. Hadn't she left Julian a number of times, yet always returned for another go at it? Veronica couldn't know the opposition she faced, if she still had her intentions settled on Julian. If. It was difficult to understand exactly what Veronica wanted. Not so with Marie. She wanted Julian, and that was it.

'You said years,' I observed from behind her, having walked round to examine the books in the glass-fronted bookcase. I might have guessed: all on antiques. 'Years that it'd been going on, this affair of your husband's.'

She didn't turn her head. 'We've been married fifteen years. It began two years later.'

'Can you be so certain of that?' asked Amelia, more interested now that we'd switched from pistols to sex. If you could call that a switch, pistols being in some way a masculine macho symbol, a phallic one even. Which was why I'd not expected women to involve themselves in the pastime. Sorry, sport.

'I *can* be so certain,' Marie claimed. 'You're fortunate if you haven't experienced it.'

'I consider myself fortunate.'

'I grinned at her. Amelia grimaced. Then she went on, 'But Marie, you must have been aware that this woman of his was in the antiques business.'

'Not at first.' I watched her head shake minimally. 'Of course, he was away from the shop a great deal, at auctions and private sales. I knew there was somebody, but he could have met anybody, anybody at all.'

'And then,' Amelia suggested gently, 'there must have been a time when you came very close to meeting her.'

'I don't know what you mean.'

She was suddenly on the defensive again. I wandered round until I could see her face, in profile, and she glanced away from me. It meant she was afraid of betraying something and knew I would recognize the moment when she did.

'I think,' I said, 'that I know what my wife means. This

Veronica must surely have become incautious and over-confident, because she continued the affair at closer range. You've already told us something of this,' I reminded her, trying to smile, trying not to bully her. 'The room above your shop premises. And even here, you said.'

She shook her head, shaking free the memory, looking down at her hands.

'I can just imagine how terrible that must have been for you,' Amelia prompted sympathetically.

'Oh yes!' Marie burst out. 'Yes. And I really had myself to blame over that. It was my fault. I shouldn't have given them the chance.'

'How was that?'

She glanced at me, and away. 'I suggested I should do some of the outside work. I mean, I knew as much as Julian about the value of clocks. I could bid as well as he did. But really, my intention was to get to know the regular dealers and ask around. Cautiously, you understand. About Julian's . . . acquaintances, shall we say, when *he* went to the sales. But it got me nowhere, and they met . . . oh, damn him, he actually brought her here, to my home, and to the shop. When I was away. *That* I couldn't forgive.'

'And that was why you left him?' Amelia nodded to herself. She understood. I understood, too. Amelia wouldn't leave me in similar circumstances, though. No. She would make me wish I'd left her, and my life would become a complete misery.

Marie was different. 'I left him, yes. And I returned. And left him, and returned again. And so on. You see, I couldn't live without him.'

As she'd said before.

'And one of these returnings,' I ventured, as she seemed not to be intending to go on with it, 'just happened to be the Monday evening when Julian was at his club, that special Monday evening when Eric Prost died?'

She was silent, staring down at her fingers, which didn't seem to want to lie still.

'Marie?' I prompted quietly.

'Well yes, so it was,' she said brightly, lifting up her head, throwing back her hair in the same gesture. 'But that was of course on purpose.'

Once more she seemed to think she could leave it all unsaid. I had to prompt again. 'In what way purposeful?'

'Partly because I knew he wouldn't be at home.' She shrugged. 'One wishes to be prepared, you see, not to arrive on the front doorstep like a waif, but to be in my own home, welcoming *him* back.'

'Of course,' Amelia murmured.

'And also,' Marie amplified, 'because I'd caught her once before like that. Alone in the house, she was. He'd left her to go and do his shooting. How very romantic, when you'd expect him to treasure every precious moment he could be with her! But a year or so before it'd been the same, and I'd caught her alone in the house.' She gave a short and bitter laugh. 'Oh dear me, she was out of the back door like a rabbit bolting down a hole. I'd known she was there. I mean, her car was out at the front, on the drive. Like a fool, I wasted time. Instead of going to stand by her car and confront her, I wasted time getting into the gun-room and loading one of the pistols. The one he'd left behind. Then I ran out to the front, and the car was just moving.'

She stopped, rocking back and forth in the chair, smiling to herself at the memory.

'You actually took a shot at her?' I asked, breathing it so as not to shatter the mood. I was unable to match the image to the woman.

'Oh yes, I did. Two shots. I can remember the side window being starred. She shot off with the gravel flying all over the place. But oh dear me, I did enjoy that, though I didn't see her face. Not at all clearly. But you can understand, I assumed it would scare her off for good. And it didn't. You can imagine my disappointment when I realized it had all started again.'

'But surely,' said Amelia, who seemed calmly to accept this undisciplined behaviour more easily than I did, 'surely you wouldn't expect her to visit the house again?'

Marie shrugged. 'No. And I don't believe she did. But the next time I left him – because I knew by that time that he'd been taking her to the rooms over the shop premises – I chose a

159

Monday again to return on. You never know your luck. As it happened, I was unlucky. The house was quiet and deserted. The Monday Eric Prost died, this was . . .'

'I understood that,' I put in.

'So I simply waited for Julian to return from his club. I knew when that would be. He always left at ten o'clock, and arrived here at twenty-five past.'

'Which he did that evening?'

'Oh yes. Right on time.'

'Which was when he discovered a pistol was missing?'

'Yes.'

'But you were sort of hiding in the bedroom when I came here, on the following evening?'

'Yes. Julian sent me out of the way as soon as he saw your car.'

'Of course. How foolish of me,' I admitted. 'He wouldn't want me to hear that you'd already used one of his pistols to take a pot-shot at his mistress.'

'You have it completely correct,' she conceded.

So I had, and I was not at all pleased with the result. No wonder Veronica had been reluctant to enter St Asaph's and confront Marie! I'd imagined that Veronica would have been the aggressive partner for Julian, offset by Marie, the quiet and reliable one. He had been able to luxuriate in both facets of character in his two females. Yet – and he couldn't have realized this – he already had both in the one woman, Marie. No wonder Veronica was afraid of her. In the shop, this evening, it must have been the smashing of the clock that had shaken Marie. A closely-thrust face wouldn't have done that. If her assailant hadn't left rapidly, he'd probably have needed to be carried out.

I eyed her with quiet admiration. Amelia, I saw, was also eyeing her, but with amusement and understanding.

'And when Julian came home that Monday evening . . .' I said. 'Can you remember, Marie . . . did he clean his pistol, as he'd always done, at the kitchen table?'

Her lips assumed a firm line. 'He did. Stubborn. To show me that his life had been in no way disturbed by my absence. Just walked in, nodded, and said something like, "You're back,

160

then," and simply carried on. It was as though I'd never been away. Does it matter?'

Yes, it did. If he'd taken out only one pistol that evening, as he'd claimed, and left it behind in the dustbin, he'd have had no pistol to clean on his return home. The prosecution case had been that he'd taken out both, intending to leave one. Perhaps we'd been correct after all. But no . . . I was forgetting . . . I was now certain he was innocent.

'Well . . .' said Amelia, 'it's quite clear you can look after yourself, so perhaps . . .' A glance at me. 'Shouldn't we be heading for home, Richard? Poor Mary will be worried out of her mind.'

'We can easily phone her.'

'It's in the hall,' said Marie. 'Please use it. And I shall be quite all right now.'

So Amelia went to phone Mary, while I tried to lighten the atmosphere with a pleasantry or two.

'Isn't it a good job', I said, 'that you've got no motive for killing Eric Prost, Marie.'

'Why do you say that?'

'Access to the pistol, a faked alibi, which would be intended to assist Julian . . .'

'But I do have a motive,' she cut in, almost as though proud of it. 'The same as Julian's. Eric Prost was intent on ruining Julian's reputation. Don't you think that would concern me? After what I've told you.'

'Of course. But Julian asked me to prove his innocence. He wouldn't be pleased if I did that by proving your guilt.'

She took that as a joke. It had been intended so, but it wasn't too far from being a distinct possibility. She laughed lightly.

'I do honestly believe he wouldn't be at all pleased.'

'So it's just as well you're not tall enough,' I commented.

'What? I don't understand.'

'And just as well you don't understand.'

Then Amelia returned to tell us that Mary had been worried, but mainly because she had something hot in the oven waiting for me. 'You haven't eaten anything, Richard, I'm sure. I know you.'

I admitted I hadn't. Marie sprang to her feet, complaining of

161

her own selfishness and lack of hospitality, and insisting she should prepare something. But I wanted to get moving, and to stand in the open air so that I could light my pipe. We therefore managed to get out on to the drive eventually, me patting my pockets and groaning.

'Now what?' Amelia asked.

'I'm starving . . . and now I've just realized I'm out of tobacco.'

'Don't worry. I guessed you would be, so I've brought you a packet. It's in the car.'

As I think I've said before, I count myself a lucky man.

13

If it had not been because of that, which led me to stand beside the Stag getting my pipe going and gazing beyond it into the distance, I might possibly not have reached the truth. Amelia was already in her Granada and had started the engine. I was savouring the calm night.

From there, the spectacular daytime view was now, at two in the morning, nothing more than the dimly-lit streets of Markham Prior. If the sky had been light enough, perhaps the grey loops of the river would have been visible. But beyond, the other side of the far bridge, there was a splash of light. I had assumed the fairground people to be late retirers, but this was taking it a bit far. Not simply that – the splash of light seemed to be concentrated and not as a general spread, as one would expect from the disposition of the caravans. Brighter, too. For one moment I suspected a fire, but this light was steady, though in some way scattered with colour.

I went over to the Granada and said, 'Come out for a minute and take a look at this, love. It puzzles me a bit.'

She cut the engine and put off her lights. It improved the definition, but as I've said, her night-sight isn't good.

'I can't make it out,' she admitted.

'Something's going on. Shall we go and have a look?'

'Must we?'

'I shan't be happy to drive away from it.'

'But you must be starving!'

'And you tired. I know. But I don't like the look of it.'

'You *do* annoy me sometimes.'

'Sorry. But it shouldn't take long.'

'Haven't I heard that before?'

'If they're up and about,' I said, 'they might take pity on us and find us a sandwich.'

'Or a bag of popcorn, or a candy-floss?'

'Either of those would be very welcome.'

So we climbed into our respective cars and she followed me out of the drive into Prior Close, along to the main road where we turned right, and drove down the hill into Markham Prior, through it and over the next bridge, and all the while the glow in the sky was becoming stronger.

As we swung right into the winding lane I caught a brief glimpse of a vehicle parked well back into a farm entrance. It could have been a farm vehicle, of course, but it looked very like the Range Rover from Winter Haven. I had the distinct impression that it had been deliberately placed there, its driver quietly observing who might approach. Our cars would by that time be known and recognized, so there now seemed to be no point in doing what I'd intended; to leave the two cars out in the lane and proceed craftily on foot into the site.

Therefore, I openly drove on with dipped heads and indicated a right turn through the gap in the thorn hedge, and into the grounds of Winter Haven.

The splash of light came instantly into view. At the far end of the site, beyond the house and almost behind it, one of the shows was in full and brilliant display. There was no time to observe more than that. Two men stepped into my path, each carrying a torch. They waved them up and down. I was to stop. As the alternative would have been to run them down, I stopped, switched the engine off, and got out.

One of them was Lobo, from the shooting-range. The other I hadn't seen before, a great and lumpy lout. Lobo was carrying one of his rifles in the crook of his right arm.

I stood and waited. They strolled up to me, the bigger one with a surly slouch. 'What's this?' I asked, trying to keep things friendly.

'Oh, it's you, Mr Patton,' said Lobo. 'And your wife. Hello there. What brings you here at this time?'

I pointed past his shoulder. 'That. You can see the light from miles away.'

164

'I know,' Lobo agreed. His mate grunted. 'That's why we're here, in case it attracts attention. To stop outsiders getting in.'

'Very clever,' I said, and I'm afraid weariness allowed a snap to creep into my voice. 'What a really bright idea! And suppose I'd been the police, and my car a police car. How d'you think it would've looked, being greeted by an idiot toting a rifle and trying to look like a second-hand and shrunk John Wayne!'

'It's all right . . .'

'All right be damned. Is the thing loaded?'

'Not your affair, Mr Patton.'

'Is it not, then? You think it's not my affair. I'll just tell you something. I'm going to walk past you, or through you, or over you – I don't care how you have it. I don't like being threatened with guns . . .'

'It's only a twenty-two.'

'What the hell does it matter what calibre it is! It's a criminal offence to threaten anybody with a weapon, loaded or not. So you will please stand aside. I intend to see what's going on, and you're not going to stop me. Understood?'

There was a threatening grunt from Lobo's mate, but I ignored it. 'You're trespassing,' muttered Lobo. A note of desperation forced that out. It was a pitiful retreat.

'It's not your property,' I reminded him. 'Now stand aside. I'm coming through. My wife will stay in her car . . .'

'Your wife will do nothing of the sort,' she said at my elbow.

That didn't make it any easier for me, but I was not going to degrade my position by starting a domestic dispute at that time, particularly as she inevitably gets the better of me. She had made up her mind; she would come with me. To Lobo, therefore, everything had to be made crystal clear.

'We are going through,' I told him softly. 'And if I hear that rifle fired, even if it's only into the air, I shall come back and break it over your head.' I heard another grunt from his mate, and glanced at him. 'And stuff the remains down your friend's throat for afters. Is that understood, Lobo? You need only nod – while you still can.'

He nodded. The two men stood apart. We marched through. Amelia took my arm.

'You can be very frightening, Richard,' she whispered. 'When you try.'

I snorted. 'He's just a stupid lad, but a rifle in a man's hands can make him very arrogant. Besides, if they're putting guards around the place, there's something happening that we've got to see.'

Now we needed only to keep walking in a direct line towards the source of light. It was increasingly obvious that it came from one of the rides, because the impression was of a round stage, lit brightly internally, and with its multi-coloured lights surrounding the edges of the canopy. In contrast, to both sides of us the caravans and their towing vehicles were silent and dark. Occasionally I caught a dim reflection of light in a caravan window or in the dead headlights of the tractor vehicles, which were all parked nose inwards. Very little light fell at our feet. I could feel the surface to be soft, but was unable to see where each successive foot fell. Our steps made no sound. Neither of us felt like speaking. I could tell from the grip on my arm that Amelia was feeling as I did. Unease was progressing towards shocked disbelief.

It became apparent that the blocked shadows around the ride were people. The whole population was gathered there, but they made no sound. It was the lack of sound that was so frightening, tingling at my nerves. Not a concerted groan, not a murmur of approval or disapproval. Silence. Grim, patient and destructive silence.

Then a single voice was raised. It seemed to fly away into the night. 'Are we all agreed that Pauli Stewart is guilty?'

At last they made a sound, a sibilant sigh, a whisper of agreement, chill as a night breeze.

'Then it only remains to pass sentence.'

There was no mention of what that sentence might be. The hollow throb of urgent hatred would have been sufficient punishment for me, had I been the accused. The indrawn breath of anticipation caught at my heart.

It was a kangaroo court. These people kept themselves to themselves, a tight community within the greater authority of the surrounding legal structure, but they were nevertheless

166

outside it. They would not surrender Pauli to regular forces of law and order. The sentence was theirs.

We were a couple of hundred yards short of the closest of the throbbing shadows. I stopped, detached Amelia's hand, and said quickly, 'Stay here, love. Please. I can't let this go on. God knows . . .'

'It's not your affair.'

'Now it is.'

Then, not waiting for any more discussion, I broke into a run.

The outer grouping was random, and consisted mostly of women. The general philosophy was chauvinistic in its real sense, their tight patriotic fervour still confining their women-folk to a back place. Because of this I was at first able to make good progress. 'Excuse me. Sorry. Can I get through, please?' Very polite, but I had no time to pause and observe the response. Closer in, I encountered the men. They were by no means so tractable, were in fact disgruntled and obstructive. Now, words became useless, and I simply thrust through, having a weight advantage in most cases. There were curses, some threats. I didn't stop to discuss it, my angry and impatient passage creating sufficient ripples and noise at least to halt the proceedings on the stage.

They must have rigged it especially for this purpose, choosing a stage that was round in which to enact their gruesome rites. Its base was two feet high from the ground, but without any of the equipment to obstruct the surface. It was a deliberately contrived theatre-in-the-round. One of their heathen rites was now in progress, the trial and punishment of Pauli Stewart.

I reached this inner circle, panting a little but still in good voice. I could see Juno Ritter in the centre there, with Pauli. Just the two of them, Juno staring out at the disruption. Was Juno judge, jury and prosecuting counsel? But there, at that spot, I was forced to a halt. There was a circle of carefully chosen men around the foot of the stage, a disciplined circle standing solidly with a space of a yard between their adjacent shoulders. They were each large and solid men, their bodies and muscles hardened by heavy physical labour. They faced inwards, at that moment standing firmly on the surrounding ground. There were three steps up to the inner surface. It was clear that this was the un-decked base of a roundabout.

There I came to a halt. My first attempt simply to walk between them was baulked by two arms raised as a barrier. My eyes hunted round for a face I knew, these near faces weirdly caught into differing colours, according to which colour light bulb was closest. Where was Emily Ritter? Where was Patch? I would have expected Emmie to be close to Juno. They were, after all, joint bosses of this lot, in fact Emily might be said to exercise the greater authority, because it was she who organized their movements, their lives. But I couldn't see her. Perhaps, in this gruesome masculine ritual, the women were excluded, and those on the outer edges had sneaked along to get a look at the excitement.

But not all were excluded. There, ten feet away to my right, was Patch, the only female here amongst the heavy mass of masculinity. She had Daisy with her on a short lead, the dog uneasy, her ears flicking, her eyes raising every second or two to Patch's face, seeking guidance. I began to edge sideways towards Patch as Juno Ritter called out, 'Who's out there? What's goin' on?'

Then, from all round me, there was a mutter of, 'Stranger! Stranger!'

I thrust onwards. Patch saw me coming, and made some effort to reach me half way. The men around her gave way. They followed her progress with strange, lacklustre eyes, the coloured lights catching flares in them.

I reached her, caught her arm. 'What the devil's going on, Patch?'

I couldn't tell the cast of her features in that light, but her voice was low and fearful, a halt in it, close to tearful. 'They're trying Pauli.'

'What for?'

'Assault at Mr Caine's shop.'

Pauli? Had it been Pauli who'd terrified Marie and smashed the clock?

'They can't do this,' I said, knowing that they could do what the hell they liked. 'Has this been anything like a proper trial?'

'I don't know what a proper trial's like,' she whispered, her face close to my bent head. 'Pauli just won't say anything, Mr Patton. Just stands there.'

'You out there!' shouted Juno, unable to see anything beyond his pool of light. 'Who's that?'

'It's Richard Patton, Juno,' I called.

'Go away. There ain't anythin' for you here.'

The groan of agreement from around me was like the shudder of a distant earthquake. They seemed to sway against me, threatening to topple in and stifle me.

'I'm coming up there to talk to you, Juno,' I shouted, for everybody to hear. 'Tell your people to let me through.'

'Go away.'

I'd been shouting between two burly shoulders. One of the men turned his head. 'Get lost.'

I moved to force my way between them. They threw out an arm each, muscles rippling beneath their T-shirts, heavy and firm as a five-barred gate. I grabbed an arm, and because he was pressing backwards I was able to whip it round and into the small of his back. In the same movement I hooked my spare arm under his chin. You learn useful moves in the force. He choked on a cry of pain.

'Let me through or I'll dislocate your arm,' I whispered into his ear.

Pain must have blanketed his brain, or perhaps he didn't have one. Another two seconds, and half a dozen of them would've picked me from him and stamped me into the ground. But he moved sideways and I was through, had run quickly up the steps and on to the open stage.

Juno stood straight and proud to face me, stern as a judge. He threw up a hand to restrain his men, who had done no more than make a sullen sound. For a few moments we faced each other, six yards apart. I said nothing, hesitating, as Juno raised his chin, not willing to discard one iota of his authority in front of his people.

Pauli Stewart stood beside him, his eyes defiantly ahead. His T-shirt was torn, his face bruised. Blood had run from the corner of his mouth. But his stance was equally authoritative as Juno's.

I said, 'If this is what I think it is, Juno, you can't do it. The whole thing's a mockery of the law. It's archaic. It's obscene, man, can't you see that!'

'We deal with our own.'

'That's legally assault.'

'He's admitted to what he's done. It was outside our group, in the town, so that makes it worse.'

'It makes it a police matter.'

'He's gone an' made a confession.'

'For God's sake . . .' I looked round me at the circle of faces, beyond which there was nothing but a simmering blackness. These faces, the guards, although differently coloured in relationship to the coloured lights, were shaped uniformly, remorseless, vicious, eagerly anticipant. 'Anybody would confess to anything in these circumstances.'

'No,' said Juno flatly. 'He done it. Ask him.'

I glanced at Pauli. For one second his eyes met mine, in them a naked terror.

His fear suddenly caught at me as I realized what the sentence would be. They would advance on him inwards, Juno abandoning the stage to them. Pauli could try to fight his way free, try, but they would converge on him until he was a beaten wreck at their feet. Then, no doubt, he'd be dumped outside in the lane, expelled. And me with him, perhaps, as I didn't have Juno's option of abandoning him.

'And what the hell d'you call yourself, Juno!' I shouted, this being the only way I could disguise the fear in my voice. 'Judge, is it? Prosecuting counsel? Jury? Who in God's name d'you think you are! You can't cut yourselves off like this. You've got no damned right, legal or moral, to pass judgement on anybody. Anybody! You say he's confessed. All right. So who's spoken for him? Anybody out there?' I flung my arm out wildly. It didn't matter where I pointed. Everywhere there was one of them. But not one who would speak for Pauli!

'Who's spoken for him?' I demanded, finding myself almost raging now at the silent, the too-silent, mass out there. I whirled round, including every one of them. 'Nobody?' I demanded into the darkness. 'Because he's admitted to it? Oh, very useful that is. Try it in a real court! Terrify the poor sod enough . . .'

'He admitted it,' cut in Juno, gruff and impatient. 'Nobody was pushin' him.'

'No? Then he's got a right to have somebody speak for him in mitigation. You know what that is, Juno? Mitigation. In any legal system in the world, the accused person's got a right to be heard on the whys and wherefores. Is this some special court, higher than any other? What're you, Juno, God himself? The man's got a right to be spoken for.'

'He ain't doin' no speakin' for hisself,' said Juno, his dialect tripping him up the more he became annoyed.

'Then I'll speak for him.'

Juno laughed hectically, sardonically. 'How the hell d'you know his whys an' his bleedin' wherefores, Patton?'

'I don't know. So I'll have to ask him. As you ought to have done, Juno.'

'Not my job.'

'Then I'm volunteering. You hear that, Pauli?' I turned to him, walked round him until I could look him fully in the face. It was not the face I'd expected to see. I had imagined a mindless lout, all muscle and no brain. This wasn't what I saw. I'd met him before, with Patch, but hadn't at that time paid much attention to him. Now I did. I studied him intently, because this was critically important. Six feet tall, an inch taller than myself, good shoulders, a certain grace in the way he carried his head. His face was wide at the brows, tapering to a narrow chin, his hair all tight dark curls, his eyes a clear grey and shining with intelligence. This man had done what he'd done knowing full well his reasons, driven by them. All I had to do was prise those reasons from him, and hope they'd do something to soften the sentence against him.

'You'll speak to me, won't you, Pauli?'

He stared at me in stony silence. It was going to be difficult.

'You don't look like a man who would terrorize women, especially an older woman, six inches shorter than you and probably half your weight. Took a lot of guts that did, I bet,' I sneered at him.

It provoked him into a response. 'It hadda be done.'

'Had it? Can you explain that?'

'Why should I?'

'To save your own neck, you damned fool.'

He considered that. Then, 'It weren't for me.'

'You didn't do it for fun, then? Not for the thrill of it?'

'It hadda . . .'

'I know. Be done. But why?'

'It was for Patch.'

He'd lowered his voice for that one sentence. But out there in the darkness the silence was so tense that I could taste it, a bitter and sharp silence, so acute that his words must have reached the far boundaries. There was a sigh like a soft breeze through aspens.

I raised my voice. 'Patch! You still out there, are you? Come on up.'

'Heh!' said Juno. 'Hold on a minute.'

'You heard him. For your daughter, he said. So don't you want to hear what it is? It might be something *you* could have done for her.'

'No,' said Patch tonelessly from behind me. 'Dad doesn't know.'

She must have been waiting for this opportunity, aching for it. The possibility that a female should be allowed up on the stage would have been inconceivable. She'd now snatched at the chance to stand beside her man.

'No,' she said again. 'Dad didn't know.' At which Juno made a grunting sound, perhaps in relief that his deficiencies were not to be exposed.

She still had Daisy on a short lead, Daisy looking baffled and worried, and poised. One word of command and she'd be there in a flash, doing something, anything, in this strange situation, in order to relieve the tension. They stood together. Pauli managed a small flicker of a smile at Patch.

'What was it your father didn't know?' I asked, being careful to keep any tone from my voice. A fine court this was, no oaths taken, just the truth as it was, naked and unprotected.

Patch shrugged. 'Well . . . he knew, I suppose. Must have done. But he's kind of forgotten.'

'Me?' said Juno, as though abruptly he was the accused.

'Yes, you Dad,' she said fondly. 'I was only nine, so I suppose

172

you thought I'd forgotten too. But I haven't, you know. How *could* I! Ask yourself.'

Juno spread his hands, hunched his shoulders. 'What the hell is this?'

'We'll find out,' I assured him quickly. 'Pauli – why did you go to Caine Antiques and threaten Marie Caine and smash a clock, and all because of something Patch hasn't forgotten?'

I smiled at him, having deliberately phrased it to sound unbelievable and unacceptable. To jolt him into a response.

'I didn't mean to do the clock in,' he muttered.

'No? A blow with a heavy object – that seems to have quite a bit of meaning to me.'

'It was kind of . . . well, impulse. Is that the word? Yeah. It was sorta emphasis.'

'What did you wish to emphasize?'

'The warning. Didn't seem to me it was gettin' through.' He smiled shyly. 'I was never much good at frightenin' people.'

'For your information, you as near as dammit scared her into hysterics. And for why? What possible reason . . .'

'Patch was frightened.'

I turned to her. A sturdy girl, she was, standing now in what was a quite aggressive stance, as one might well adopt with a Rottweiler at one's side. But dog or not, Patch wouldn't be easy to scare.

'You were frightened, Patch, of a quiet and inoffensive woman?'

No need to mention Marie's hidden depths, I thought. I looked round at what I could see of our audience, wondering whether I might draw a disclaimer to my remark. But no. They were silent and intent, caught in it.

'Not of her,' said Pauli quickly. 'But she was Caine's woman. Patch was scared of Caine's woman, and scared of Caine.'

'But she's probably not even met Caine's woman, as you call her. Never even entered the shop, I bet.' I didn't understand his distinction.

'I saw her once,' Patch whispered. 'Only once. I didn't know who she was, of course, but Uncle Eric called her Caine's woman. I was only nine, but I never forgot. And I *did* see her that once, after that happened. Not in the shop but coming

173

away from it. And I remembered. She wouldn't have known me, of course, not by sight. Not now I'm all grown up. But she could find out, and it scared me, being so close and all through the winter, and Pauli said . . . Pauli said . . .'

It had tripped out, all jumbled up, as though it was lined up in her mind, tripped out until it came to the stumbling block of Pauli. There she stopped, not certain whether or not she was helping him.

I looked at Pauli. 'And what was it you said?'

'Me? I said she'd be happier if they was both outa town. He's come back, see. Ten years he's been away, and Patch'd pretty near forgot. Now he's back. So it's all here again.'

'What's all here?'

'Her Uncle Eric got himself shot to death over it.'

Were we talking about that Tompion clock? No, we were not.

'All right,' I said. 'We're getting somewhere, but I wish to God I could see where. Patch's Uncle Eric got himself shot over it, you say. Over what? Why do you think Eric Prost was shot, Pauli? The reason for it.' I wanted no misunderstanding now.

He allowed a small measure of contempt to enter his voice, which was a bit of cheek, considering that I was trying to help him. 'It was in his letter. Patch told me you'd read it, so you don't have to look like you never heard. Her Uncle Eric said he'd recognized her in town. Then just after that – 'cause she'd seen she'd been recognized – he was shot. Eric's wife, Cara, was killed in that car. It was another stupid woman's fault, but Eric saw her later, and that was as good as a death warrant. Now it's Patch. Patch was in that car . . .'

'What!'

'Damn it all – you stoopid or something?' Pauli demanded.

'Is this true, Juno?' I asked, just to give myself time.

'Yes,' he said harshly. 'We don't speak about it. Little Patch – only nine then – she was stayin' with her uncle and aunt. Goin' to school in the town, she was, so they couldn't 'ave left her in the house all day, all on her own. So they took her with 'em that day. Patch was in the back . . . we don't like to talk about it . . .' He looked uneasily at Patch, who continued with it in a dead and neutral tone.

174

'They don't talk about it, Ma and Pa. They think I've forgotten, but I never did. Even now, I get these horrible nightmares. Never mind about that. I was in the car. In the back. I could get my door open, but Auntie Cara was stuck somehow. And I saw that woman. Caine's woman, Uncle Eric said in his letter. Saw her clear as daylight. And the car that crashed into us, almost, if Auntie Cara hadn't swerved, that car came from where Mr Caine lives. And I never forgot her face, and now it's all going to start again . . .'

Her voice faded away into nothing more than the weak acceptance that her life would be haunted for ever by that incident, as though she was almost resigned to the loss of her own life, because she'd seen that face.

But this must surely be fantasy. Nobody was going to commit a murder in order to cover up a possible charge of dangerous driving, even one of manslaughter – which would be stretching it a little. There had to be more to it than that, even if we could accept that Eric Prost's killing was motivated by a fear of being recognized. Which I found I could not.

'Now let's get this straight,' I said, trying to do just that in my mind so that I could lay it out in words. 'You're saying that Eric Prost was killed because of the car crash that killed his wife. Is that it, Pauli?' He gave a nod at Patch. It was she who had fed him this idea. 'And you're claiming that Patch hadn't got anything to be afraid of while Julian Caine was in prison. In other words, you're not suggesting that Marie Caine could have shot Eric Prost?'

'That'd be daft,' he admitted. 'That woman couldn't . . .'

Could she not? I cut in quickly before he developed that idea. 'So . . . you believe that it was Julian Caine protecting his woman from being recognized by Eric, and now, because he's out of prison, he'll go on protecting her because Patch also saw her?'

'Summat like that,' Pauli said, though with a shade of doubt. His tone was that of a person who sees it much more clearly in his own mind, and resents the naked words that strip it of romance, laying it out in cold basic logic.

'And this woman, you're saying, did no more than drive dangerously from a side road, causing a fatal accident . . .'

'Nothing *more!*' put in Juno forcefully. Though he didn't seem to realize it, he was suddenly on Pauli's side. Or was it Patch's he was on? To me, they seemed to be the same. 'Nothing more! She bloody well drove away, leaving it, drove away when Cara was struggling to get out and the stench of petrol was enough to choke you. An' you talk about nothin' more! Christ!'

'All right. Legally then. Leaving the scene of an accident – an offence. Driving dangerously – another offence. But it's not killing material, Juno, and you know it.'

'All the same . . .' said Pauli weakly.

I stared at him. He believed *something*, but that was not it. So why was he skating all round it? I was having to drag every blasted word out like drawing teeth.

'But don't you *see* . . .' I appealed. 'Heavens, you can't be accusing Marie Caine of shooting Patch's uncle!'

'Of course not,' Patch put in severely. 'Pauli's said that.'

'Then who? Julian Caine? On her behalf. But damn it all . . . Pauli, you were there, when we did that test with the gun. It proved Caine couldn't have shot him. The shot required a marksman, and he's the only one around. Admitted. But he's not tall enough to have done it. Are you saying he did it on stilts? Or did he have his shoes built-up by six inches? I'm trying to speak for you in justification, you idiot. I'm trying to show that you had a valid and reasonably possible cause for threatening Marie Caine and adding your bloody emphasis by smashing a clock. And now you – and Patch by the sound of it – say you base all her fears on the assumption that Caine killed Prost! When that couldn't have been . . .'

My voice had been rising somewhat towards the end of that, and sweat was trickling down my back. I was beginning to realize that I'd jumped into this situation blind, with some sort of vestigial confidence that I could carry it through. Now here I was, trying to justify behaviour that seemed to have no sensible base to stand on. That crowd out there could feel it. There was that sort of impatient tension. All I'd done was delay the inevitable end, it seemed. Groans and mutters scattered themselves into the night. Above me, the canvas thumped as a sudden breeze caught it.

Then Pauli – blast and bless him – came to my rescue, and yes, abruptly it was he rescuing me.

'O' course he did,' he said confidently. 'I wasn't here then. Only joined the fair a coupla' years ago. So I suppose when I heard about it, I saw it all different. No distractions.' This he said in a condescending tone, Pauli wishing not to be too hard on me.

'Distractions,' I repeated. 'Such as?'

'That hole in the glass, for one thing. They told me all about that, but o' course the glass'd been changed when I saw the window, so there was no hole, and so it didn't mean anythin' to me. There was none of them pre-whatsits.'

'Preconceptions,' I suggested.

'Yeah. Them.'

He was talking well, now, confidently, head up and throwing his voice to the far reaches. But showmen would naturally acquire that art.

'Not till I saw you playin' around,' he went on. 'You and Lobo. And I thought to myself, at that time, it was just daft. I mean, all that blah about where the hole was an' where Caine would've hadda stand. Well . . . I mean . . . I coulda laughed out loud, but you was so serious about it, when it was all as obvious as hell. A kid coulda told you. It weren't nothing to do with how tall Caine was. Nothin'.'

At this stage I could see that I dared not dispute this claim too fiercely, because I was there to justify his actions. That was how it had started out, anyway. All the same, I did feel I had to defend myself.

'What was so obvious about it?'

'You just made a wrong assumption, that's all. It's easy to do. He wasn't shot from out there.'

'The cartridge cases were there, under the window.'

'O' course they were. They was picked up and left there. That's all it was. One of 'em was, anyway.'

'You think you know everything, don't you . . .'

'Eric Prost', he declared, taking the lead now that his confidence was flowing free, 'musta been shot from inside the room, and the cartridge case picked up . . .'

'What about the clock?'

He dismissed that. 'Obvious. It was stopped, and left so as it showed ten past eight – cause that give him an alibi, see – then a shot was put in its face. Made a lovely alibi, that did, an' I bet you all fell for it.'

'The glass on the floor,' I tried. I had to make an effort, because he was making a fool of me, and so easily, too. But he wouldn't let me say my bit, doing his own talking now, but too late for me to back out and leave him to it. I was caught in it, trapped in that lake of light, drowning in it. He went on with it, his voice harsh with scorn.

'Oh yes,' he conceded, '*that* shot would've been from outside, but it wouldn't've been so difficult, a whole clock-face to aim at. It was to make it look like it was all done from outside, both shots, when it weren't. Just one shot at the clock-face. Killed two birds with one shot, that did. It faked the alibi an' it made it look like both shots was from outside. Clever, that. Not clever enough, though.'

'Not clever enough to fool you, anyway,' I said, my voice a little sour.

'Y're dead right,' he agreed with sickening complacency. 'An' when y' come to think about it, wasn't Caine supposed to be a friend! Some friend, that. But who else but somebody who called himself a friend could stand behind Patch's Uncle Eric, when he was writin' at his desk? Obvious, it all was. Yah! You pigs ain't got a clue.'

I took exception to being called a pig. But I could remind myself that I had, in reserve, a whole bundle of things Caine had told me at that time, and more recently, that would ruin Pauli's bright idea. Oh yes, it was certainly a bit of crafty thinking, I thought, but it all fell down when you came to consider that Caine had never even suggested that the hole was too high for him to have shot through from outside. Which he would've done if he'd gone to all that trouble to fake it. By that time, I was somewhat annoyed that I was being made a fool of, and publicly, but I had to play it carefully.

Then, along with the annoyance, there flooded over me the realization that Pauli's idea had to be basically correct in its method. I felt my neck grow hot, and a sudden trickle of sweat ran down my back. Damn it all, he *was* correct. And I'd missed

178

it. I had sailed through the case, had equally sailed through the present review of it, and always with the fixed belief in my mind that the shots had come from outside the window. Everything had indicated that. Both of them. But . . . if the first one had not . . . then the whole thing was turned on its head, and in a few hot seconds, as it raced through my mind, I saw the complete truth, like a photograph taking life in a developing dish, the truth that had so painfully eluded me. All of it.

I was aware that Pauli was staring at me with one eyebrow raised, that Juno was worried, head on one side, waiting for me to say something. In spite of the fact that Pauli was the one who'd said it all, it was I, the ex-policeman, whose decision seemed to count.

'We pigs', I conceded, just to play for time, 'can sometimes have second thoughts.'

'There y'are, then,' said Pauli.

But my mind was frantically taking it on. There was another consideration. Possibly out there that very second . . . listening to this . . . oh dear Lord! Hearing this, which would mean an end to it for someone. Hearing the revelation that carried the stain of guilt. Knowing that I – standing there like a petrified idiot – had finally reached the truth, had been presented with it. Out there, where I couldn't see, could be somebody. Out there on the periphery of the silent accusers, knowing that now there could be no way of hiding it . . .

And now I was in the unique position of having to support Pauli's idea, and publicly, if I was to do anything for him. Thus, I would be demonstrating my own inadequacy by accepting the new truth. I felt exposed and naked, almost found myself cringing from the light that bathed me. With a great effort I managed to produce a grin, hoping that it would hide my true emotional reaction, and stepped forward to slap Pauli on the shoulder.

'But that's just great!' I cried. 'Damned good thinking. So you knew that Caine had killed Prost, and you were scared Patch would be the victim of another killing. That's all very logical. Don't you think that's logical, Juno? Damn it, man, don't just stand there gaping. Say something. As judge and jury and general panjandrum, don't you think he was justified in what he did? What's your verdict now? Say something, man.'

Juno rubbed a hand all over his face, then he held it up for silence. There'd been nothing else but silence, a horrible and threatening silence, for too long. But it seemed actually to become more so. Perhaps they stopped breathing.

'How say you?' he demanded, using his fairground bellow and a phrase from genuine court procedure. 'Is he not guilty? All in favour say aye.'

There was a sudden barked howl of 'aye'.

'Case dismissed,' shouted Juno.

It was farcical. Everybody knew Pauli had done the threatening and the breaking, but in their reckoning it was 'not guilty'. I said nothing, half expecting floods of well-wishers to swamp us, all slapping Pauli's back and thus inflicting nearly as much damage as his punishment would have done. But no. All was quiet satisfaction, after that shout of 'aye'. It had been done to protect their precious Patch, one of their own. It was therefore good. It would be savoured and cherished, and his rewards would come later.

I turned. Pauli and Patch were conducting their own mutual congratulations. Daisy was even more uneasy, never having got the hang of kissing. Juno prized loose a hand of Pauli's from around Patch's back and shook it, then he smiled in embarrassment at me, and off he went with the others.

It would have been a perfect fade-out for a film, the shot tracking back with the two of them clasped together in the centre of that stage, with Daisy now more relaxed and patiently waiting. But I would have spoiled it, because I was waiting, too.

They untangled themselves, assumed I'd hung around to be thanked, and they thanked me accordingly.

'And now, Pauli,' I said, 'you're coming with me.'

'What!' he said. 'Where?' he asked.

'The nearest police station. I'm taking you in for assault on one woman and one clock.'

I was desperately carrying it on, this belief in Pauli's theory of how Caine had killed Eric Prost. It was for the benefit of somebody who might – just might – be hanging around out there.

14

'Now wait a minute,' he said, and Patch added, 'You can't do that.'

I sighed. 'What d'you think's been going on here? Did you think that was a proper legal procedure? Not guilty, so that makes it all right! That's no more than a dirty laugh. No, Pauli. You committed assault in the town. The police were called in. They've probably got a dragnet out for you, with road-blocks in all directions . . .'

'Come *on*!' He tried an embarrassed grin.

'All the same, they'll want to question you, so I'm taking you in.'

'I'm going to fetch my dad,' said Patch threateningly.

'You do that, Patch. Fetch your pa. He's not going to be able to do anything, though. There's an assault to be answered for. I'm not saying . . . put it like this: if Pauli went along and apologized nicely to Mrs Caine, with say a dozen roses in his fist, then we might be able to get that part of it forgotten. But there's the clock, Pauli. The clock. What about that?'

We were standing now on the outer edge of the stage, with me squinting out into the darkness. 'You there, love?' I asked vaguely, wondering why I'd not heard from Amelia. Worrying.

'I'm here,' she told me, walking into the edge of the spread of light. 'Just recovering. Richard, you fool, you nearly got yourself into deep trouble, there.'

I scratched my neck, not willing to tell her it was not necessarily over, that the trouble could be running deeper. 'I'm taking him in.'

'Must you?'

'I don't know yet. I was just explaining . . .'

It was then that somebody threw a switch somewhere, and all the lights went out. The abrupt darkness was stunning. Pauli could have made a break for it then. He, more than I, might have been prepared for some such thing, and he needed to do no more than put his head down and run. Instead, he put a hand on my arm, as though I was a decrepit old man, and said easily, 'If you stand still, your night-sight will come back in a minute.'

And this was to somebody who'd spent hundreds – perhaps thousands – of hours on night-watch for somebody or something.

'Thank you,' I said, 'for your advice.'

Gradually the shapes reappeared, Amelia standing below patiently, beyond and behind her the blocks that were caravans and part-rigged shows and tractor vehicles, with here and there a gaslight or electric bulb coming on as they settled down to a well-earned rest. But not Patch. For her it wasn't finished. I turned. She was slowly walking away, Daisy at her side, presumably to fetch her father to sort me out.

'Let's go and sit in my wife's car,' I said to Pauli. 'We can talk there.'

'Yes,' Amelia agreed. 'I really must sit down. My legs are still all wobbly.'

'Sorry love.' Then I lifted my voice and shouted after Patch. 'We'll be in one of the cars down by the entrance, Patch.' And she flipped a hand in acknowledgement.

We headed back towards where we'd left the cars, not an easy accomplishment as we now had no lighter patch to which we could aim. All there was to guide us was the bulked masses of caravans and the rest to each side of us, and these a couple of hundred yards back. We had to march down the middle, but Pauli seemed confident of his direction. He strolled beside us, seemingly unconcerned. Even now he could have run for it – but to where? This was his home, these his people. One of those caravans would be his. And he knew I could have a car-ful of coppers on the grounds in the morning. But principally, I thought, his apparent easy compliance might have had a background of uneasiness. The clock had been mentioned. That could worry him.

'The clock . . .' he ventured, proving my guess to be correct. 'In a minute.'

With every yard of that walk across the dark and deserted centre of the site, my eyes were darting around for a shadow a little darker, a movement where one should not have been.

We'd left our cars with the keys in, mine with its door wide open, but nothing had been touched. Perhaps Lobo and his mate had guarded the cars, too. If so, they had now abandoned everything. There was no sign of either of them. I walked past my dark and silent Stag to Amelia's Granada. We'd have more room in that. She had left it parked at an angle, so perhaps my abrupt halt had caught her unprepared.

She climbed in behind the wheel and unlocked a rear door. I ushered Pauli inside and slid in beside him. Amelia turned and stared at us around the head-rest. She had put on the interior light.

'Now Pauli,' I said. 'We'd better get a few things straightened out. Mrs Caine, the last time we saw her, seemed to be very well recovered from the shock you gave her. She's much more concerned for her husband. Somebody ran him down with a car in the car-park this evening. That wasn't you, by any chance, trying to make absolutely certain of Patch's safety?'

'Me? What? Oh Christ, no.'

'I didn't really think it was. But it's not going to be easy to explain to Mrs Caine the reason you frightened her. I mean . . . she'll have to be given a good and sensible reason, or she won't be prepared to forgive you. You can see my point. Are you going to stand in front of her and explain that you wanted to frighten them into leaving town because Patch recognized her as the woman who caused her aunt's death in the car accident. And that Patch was therefore terrified of what Mr Caine would do to her. You can see that would be embarrassing at the very least. I'm sure you can.'

'I don't . . . I can't . . .' Pauli's mind scrambled for it. 'I can't tell her *that*!'

'Then how else can you explain your conduct? Of course, it's now true that you've spread that accusation far and wide.'

'Accusation?'

'That accusation about her having caused the car accident. You've stated that, out loud, to several hundred people only half an hour ago. Poor Caine, if he's now got to kill off all the people who now believe his wife caused the death of Cara Prost! Difficult, as I said, to approach her with the true story of why you frightened her.'

He glanced at Amelia, who nodded, then back to me. 'I don't see why I've gotta make something up,' he said, hurt.

'No, no. I'm not suggesting that,' I assured him. 'Because, in any event, there's something basically wrong with your theory. Don't you realize that?'

'My theory? No,' he claimed stubbornly. 'Nothing wrong with it at all.'

I shrugged. 'All right. Leave that for now. Because, you see, however you might be able to explain your behaviour to Mrs Caine, there's still the clock.'

'The clock!'

'You smashed a clock on those premises. You are legally responsible for that action, and can be expected to replace it.'

'Oh . . . that!' He relaxed, thumping back against the seat. 'I'll buy 'em a new one. Plenty of clocks about, and better than that old-fashioned thing. I could get 'em a quartz clock, a date clock. I've seen 'em with those rotating balls. Nice, they are. Yeah, I don't mind doin' that.'

'Isn't it pathetic!' I said to Amelia. 'Oh, the naïve innocence of youth! Pauli, that was an antique clock. Valuable. Are you prepared to dig into your pocket and pay for it?'

'Well sure. If that's all right. How much?'

'I don't know which of the clocks you ruined, so there'd be a big range of possible prices. Say, from five thousand to ten thousand. More or less. How does that strike you?'

'Pounds?' he whispered.

'Of course. What did you think, Japanese yen?'

'Shee . . . ee!' he hissed through his teeth.

I grinned at Amelia, who was looking very puzzled indeed. It was to her I spoke, while Pauli was recovering.

'You can see his difficulty, my love. Caine's in hospital, so

there's no immediate worry, but Pauli's made a public accusation as to Caine's guilt in respect of Eric Prost's death. Caine
isn't going to be too pleased about that, certainly not pleased
enough to shrug and say, "What's the odd clock here and
there?" No, he'll be after blood. He'll have Pauli in court and
sue the pants off him for the value of that clock, and then they'll
start in on slander charges.'

'Here,' said Pauli. 'Hold on. You don't have to flog it to
death. If I can prove he did it, he ain't goin' to be shouting
around about courts and things.'

'But that's the snag. You can't do that.'

'O' course I can. You heard . . .'

I cut him short. I'd heard enough already. 'He shot old Prost
from inside the room, you say. But it's not on, you know. It's
just not on.'

'You're only sayin' that,' he claimed shrewdly, 'because you
didn't think of it yourself.'

'There could be some truth in that, laddie. But now we've got
to consider it more closely. Just you take a look at the picture.
You may not have heard all the details. In fact, you couldn't
have done, or you wouldn't have come up with that fancy idea.'

'It's not fancy . . .'

'Just listen. Eric Prost was sitting at his desk, facing the door
to the room and facing the clock. Nobody could've entered that
room without him noticing. And if . . .' I said heavily, 'you're
going to talk another load of rubbish about somebody reaching
through the hole in the glass and opening the window, then I'll
have to tell you that the latch was rusted solid. That's quite
apart from the impossibility of doing it in absolute silence.'

'I never thought that,' he claimed miserably. 'You don't have
to go all tricky. It would've been easy enough. They was
supposed to be friends. Eric'd let in his friend. He wouldn't
even trouble if Caine went behind him and stood there and
took out his pistol.'

'Eric Prost was writing a letter, Pauli.'

'So what! Eric'd probably say, "Just a minute while I finish
this". Or summat like that. Don't seem all that complicated to
me.'

185

'It is if you consider the fact that the letter was intended for Caine himself.'

That silenced him. He shook his head. 'Was it? You sure of that?'

'I'm sure of it. A half-finished letter, Pauli. He was actually writing it when he was shot.'

'Oh hell!'

'Exactly.' I grinned at him. 'No way round that, is there?'

'I know! Caine walks in with a gun in his hand and says, "Write what I tell you." And shoots him while he's doing it.'

'In that event, he wouldn't ask him to write something that implicated himself. Think again.'

'Can't think of anythin' else,' he admitted, right down in the dumps now.

'And there's the fact that the shot at the clock-face, which you admit had to be done from outside, *didn't* stop the clock. And if he hadn't been inside the room, he couldn't have stopped it by hand.'

'Lordy! Is that so?'

I didn't mention the other clocks. I didn't want to think about the other clocks. When the old man died? There had to be a logical explanation to that, or I'd take up spiritualism.

Amelia was studying his face with a frown. She glanced at me, back again to Pauli.

'Never mind,' she said. 'It doesn't really matter. The fact is that you *thought* Caine was a threat to Patch. That's what matters. The fact that you were quite wrong isn't important.'

'All the same . . .'

'It was a good idea,' I told him. 'Very good. In fact, it's probably the correct one.'

'But you just said . . .'

'I know. I mean, the method of killing was probably correct. It's just that you picked the wrong murderer.'

'Who else is there?' he demanded.

I shrugged. 'The one most immediately affected. If the motive's as you say, that the fear was that Eric Prost – and now Patch herself – could have recognized the woman driving that car, then the obvious murderer is that woman.'

Amelia's head came up. 'You can't mean Marie!' she breathed. 'I just can't believe that.'

'The circumstances could fit,' I told her. 'That car accident was at about the same time that Marie left him, one of her times. She'd perhaps be blinded by emotion, and be driving without her mind on it. But the motive's not strong enough for murder. What that woman driver did was terrible, though mainly because she drove away from the accident without offering any assistance at all. But it's not as terrible as a deliberate murder, and certainly not one in the circumstances we've been discussing.'

'You've lost me,' admitted Pauli vaguely, staring past Amelia and out into the night. 'Something's going on at the house.'

I ignored that as a useless distraction. 'However mad she might have been at her husband – and I can assure you, Pauli, that Marie had a damn good reason for being mad at him – she wouldn't have deliberately forced Eric into writing a letter that implicated him, and faked a clock's timing to *look* like a faked alibi, and used Caine's spare pistol, and abandoned it to be found easily. No. No, I don't think so.'

'Something's going on,' Pauli insisted.

And so it was. By this time the site had settled down. Still there were a few dim lights in some of the caravan windows, probably those people who still couldn't prevent themselves from discussing the night's happenings. But over at the house itself there were lights on in most of the windows, and it seemed to me that I saw a door open.

'Just a sec',' I said. 'I'll go and have a look.'

I got out of the car and closed the door behind me, so that the latch touched and made no sound. We were already exposed by the illumination from the interior light, but I didn't want anything else to draw attention to us. I'd had an uneasy feeling that something would happen. Almost an intuition, though I didn't know what were the threads I'd woven together in order to feel it. Something *was* happening – but . . . from the house? That I hadn't expected. Slowly I moved sideways until I was lost in the darkness. My Stag, parked ahead, had been obstructing the forward view, but now I could see clearly that the front door of the house was indeed open. It seemed, from the variations in light and shade, that somebody was walking out into the darkness. There was a moving, prancing shadow blurring the outline, so I decided this had to be Patch, with Daisy at her side. She had to be heading this way, towards the Granada, as she carried no hand torch, and must therefore be guiding herself in a straight line towards the only point of light, dim though it must have appeared from there.

She was in silhouette against the house lights, so that it became evident she was moving in a strange manner. I was unable to interpret it, and moved slowly forward in concentration. Patch was walking as though on ice. I wanted to get opposite the Stag, so that if necessary I could put on the headlights and flood the scene with light. Just beyond the rear wheel I tripped over something. It felt soft to my foot, like a discarded bag of refuse. I fell to one knee and fumbled around, my fingers contacting material, then flesh, and then, more urgently now, detecting the shape of a face.

'Lights!' I called back over my shoulder. 'Amelia, put on your lights.'

They suddenly splashed on me, but half obliterated because the Granada was at an angle and the Stag threw shadows. But I could see enough. It was Lobo.

I bent close. He was alive, but breathing stertorously, deeply unconscious. I felt gently for the back of his head and detected an abrasion. My fingers came away sticky, and when I held them up to catch the light, it was blood.

Then Pauli was kneeling beside me.

'It's Lobo,' he said.

'Yes. What about his mate? He'd got a mate with him. Look around.'

Pauli scrambled away, dodging and searching, flitting from shadow to light and back again. He called out, 'No sign of anybody. That was Rae Turner. Lazy sod. Reckon he's turned in.'

Then I remembered. 'The gun, Pauli. Lobo was toting one of his rifles. Look for the gun.'

Amelia could see our difficulty. She started her engine and edged the car round until we had full light from her dipped heads. We searched. There was no gun. If it had simply fallen from his hands when he was struck, it would have been beside him. It was not. Now it was quite clear why he'd been attacked. It was for the gun.

The Granada's heads had the effect of deepening the darkness just outside their reach. That was how close the danger might be. 'It might not have been loaded,' I whispered to Pauli.

'Sure to be. I know him. Always showin' off. O' course he'd load it.'

'If you know him – how many does it take?'

'The gun . . . shots, you mean? Anythin' up to twenty,' he breathed, he too feeling the pressure of that surrounding darkness.

'Hell!'

I lifted my head, slowly got to my feet. Now, with the Granada's heads skimming the surface, Patch was becoming more plainly visible. I was even able to see why she was walking so slowly and so carefully. In both hands, she was carrying a bracket clock, delicately so as not to harm it, and, because she couldn't clearly see her footing, putting one foot in front of the other with a tentative sliding action. And it was certainly Daisy at her hip, but not on a lead because Patch had to be free of her, and moving, weirdly, in a similarly hesitant pace as Patch's, and no doubt completely puzzled.

I began to run towards her. I couldn't shout for her to drop flat, because she wouldn't be able to do that with the clock in her hands. My voice would halt her, too, and at least the target she presented was a moving one. It seemed clear that Emily and Juno had decided I should take this clock to Marie. In recompense.

But I didn't value the clock to any great degree, when balanced against a life. It was true that a twenty-two pistol wasn't lethal, but I didn't know whether this held for a rifle. Perhaps it had a higher muzzle velocity. I didn't know, and wasn't prepared to risk it. I had every intention of bowling her over, and to hell with the clock.

There was suddenly, from behind her I thought, the snap of a shot. Patch screamed and staggered, then was down on one knee, placing down the clock with ridiculous delicacy before she twisted round and sat, both hands clasped to her right thigh. Daisy was barking in delirium, aware of an assailant and unable to see one. And I was still running. I had to hope she didn't take me for the attacker, but I had no alternative now. Patch tutted something, and Daisy sat, panting, impatient. There was another crack, and I thought I saw the flash beyond her. Something plucked at my sleeve, then I dived to the ground beside Patch, thrust aside Daisy's face, and levered myself up on one knee.

I said, 'Is it bad?'

She screwed up her face at me. Blood seeped between her fingers. She looked at me with huge eyes, her lower lip suddenly caught in her teeth, and she nodded. Daisy was walking round us in circles. I raised my head and shouted. 'Lights! Let's have some lights here!'

That attracted two more shots, both of them off-target. Patch and myself and Daisy presented a tight little tableau, caught on the fringe of the heads from Amelia's Granada. But this light did not reach out as far as the sniper. Perhaps dimly, but there was certainly nothing definite that I could see. For a moment I wondered why Amelia hadn't cut the lights, then I realized she'd made the decision that we needed light more than darkness.

In the meantime, Pauli was running round the perimeter shouting to his friends for lights. Already they were stirring, attracted by the commotion. But he continued to shout, and it got him two shots, clearly missing because it didn't stop him at it.

'Lights!' he bawled. 'Come on, damn you, lights!'

I came to a decision and stood up to my full height, facing the sound of the rifle. I saw a flash, heard the crack. Nothing. I winced at the nothing. Here and there a vehicle's lights were coming on, engines were started to boost the batteries. I had to try bluff, though my thinking wasn't too clear.

'Put down that gun!' I called. 'Put it down, Veronica. It's too late now. We know who and why and how.' That was exaggerating it a little.

More lights flooded on, and she became visible, as though rising from a dark and treacherous sea. I could see that she was taking careful aim. The rifle snapped, more loudly it seemed

190

with the increased illumination. Behind me, Patch screamed. I'd thought I'd be blanking her. I turned. Her eyes were wide as the blood ran down into them from her left brow. The shot had struck an inch above her eyebrow. She realized this, and screamed again.

Then the lights were blasting inwards more quickly, building up and overlapping. There were shouts, and from one side I saw Pauli closing in on Veronica, moving quietly, menacingly. She was eighty yards away from us, standing with feet apart with the rifle-butt tucked against her chin. She was taking careful and precise aim, even though the world was breaking apart all around her.

At last Daisy had worked it out. The aggressor had become visible. The injured party was Patch. Daisy raised her head and let out an attack-howl that curdled my blood, then she was away, at once into full speed, ears flying and with a snarl of rage deep in her throat. Veronica saw her coming and again took careful aim. Me, I'd have turned and run. But she stood her ground and took aim. Yet, after all, the whole thing had taken strong, cool nerves.

She fired, then quickly again, her left hand jerking back the slide. Daisy howled and swerved to her right, taking weight from her right fore, then she had corrected and was again in full flight, baying her hatred and fury.

'Call her off, Patch!' I shouted. 'For God's sake, call her off!'

I couldn't find it in me to wish for Veronica's death with her throat torn out. Nor could I contemplate with equanimity a death sentence for Daisy in those circumstances.

'Patch!' I yelled, not daring to waste time in order to glance round, praying that she was still conscious.

Through her fingers, it sounded like, she cried out, 'Daisy! Stay. Stay, Daisy! Heel! Heel!'

She was half a second too late. Daisy had launched into her final bound, as Pauli, coming in fast from the side, dived into a tackle. He took Veronica off her feet as she threw up her arm, more in an effort to balance than in defence. That was where Daisy got her, the teeth clamping on Veronica's forearm, then they were over together, Veronica's screams mingling with the savage snarls. And Patch somehow got to her feet and limped

191

forward, blood almost blinding her, crying out, 'Daisy, Daisy . . . come. Daisy heel.' With tears in her voice.

And Daisy stood back, poised and alert, snarling but still. Patch came up and put an arm round her neck, and wept against her head, and Veronica went on screaming and screaming.

I knelt beside her. The arm poured blood, but I didn't think she would lose it. I lifted my head.

'Pauli . . . ambulance and police. Quick as you can.'

Then, as he galloped away, Amelia came running up with the first-aid kit from her car.

'No bed for us tonight, my love,' I said, tension producing these peculiar irrelevances.

'Oh heavens, look at that arm,' she replied, which was no reply at all.

Then we waited. We managed to control the flow of blood from Veronica's arm; somebody produced a pillow and a blanket. The community gathered silently around us.

I remained kneeling at Veronica's side, waiting for her to whimper down to silence and be able to understand what I was saying. And from time to time glancing at the rocking, weeping Patch, still with her arms clasped around Daisy's neck, and with the twenty-two bullet clearly visible, impressed into the flesh above her eyebrow.

She seemed unaware of it. How *could* she sit there on the ground with a bullet plainly visible in her forehead, and not pass out? But concussion is unpredictable. It could hit her at any time, along with the shock and the pain. I forced myself to look away.

15

I said gently, 'You'll go from here to a hospital, Veronica. Probably St Asaph's. That'll be nice for you, with Julian in the next ward.'

She bared her teeth. Her lips stuck to them. It need not have been intended as a sneer; possibly an ironic smile.

'And then the police will charge you with the murder of Eric Prost and the attempted murder of Julian Caine.'

She turned her head away. Amelia said in my ear, 'Are you sure of that, Richard?'

'Yes,' I said. 'From the moment Caine was released from prison, he became a threat. Isn't that so, Veronica?'

'He knew,' she whispered. 'I was certain he'd connect things up.'

'He gave me not one hint.'

She shook her head. It was beyond her comprehension. 'He must have known.'

'Veronica, think about it. He wanted me to prove his innocence. He made it a challenge, throwing more and more facts at me that all went against him. Don't you think – if he'd suspected it was you who killed Prost, he would surely have hinted.'

She stirred, and bit her lip as the pain hit her again. 'How long will they be?' she mumbled.

'Soon.'

She was silent for a moment, then she made a feeble attempt at self-justification. 'If Julian had died, you'd have stopped asking around, you damned nosy bastard.'

'Would I? I doubt it. It'd already gone too far.'

'Well . . . how was I to know!' she complained bitterly.

I could tell, from Amelia's grasp on my arm, that she was finding it difficult to understand Veronica's twisted personality. 'Can't I do anything to help?' she asked quietly.

She meant, could I find her an excuse to send her somewhere else? She didn't want to continue to watch Veronica's face, the emotions chasing across it from contempt to annoyance, that she was not correctly understood, her honourable motivations being distorted. I shook my head.

Then Juno and Emily were there, come to take Patch away, back to the house presumably, where she could await the ambulance. But Patch wasn't like Amelia. Her experience was immature. Veronica fascinated her, now that the terror had departed.

'Better leave her,' I suggested, getting a pained smile from Patch. 'Better not moved, I'd think.'

It was then that Patch gave a moan of pain, whispered, '. . . head,' and passed out, falling forward across Daisy. Juno and Emily fell to their knees, trying to get a blanket around her, weeping and crooning, with Daisy trying to stick her head in, Juno trying to force her away. 'How'll we get her into the ambulance?' he appealed, something close to panic in his voice. 'Daisy'll go wild if they try to take her away.'

Daisy was doing her own repair work, licking the three-inch furrow along her right foreleg. I could see that we had a problem there, and suggested that Daisy should be taken back to the house before the ambulance arrived. This, after a little blasphemous persuasion, Juno managed to do, and we had quiet for a few moments. Then Pauli said he would go with Patch in the ambulance, which started an argument with Emily, so I suggested he should go back to the cars and see that Lobo was all right. 'There's an anorak in my car,' I told him. 'You could put that over him.'

'I've already done that,' Amelia said.

'All right. Then – Pauli – I suggest you find Lobo's wife and show her where he is. She'll be going crackers.'

'She's already found him,' said Amelia. 'I left her crying over him.'

'All right,' I said, this time more tersely.

So Emily and Pauli were free to continue their argument, as

the local population drew closer and closer around us, casting their shadows in strange, crossed confusion. And I was free to return my attention to Veronica, who was moaning quietly to herself, and only half-conscious.

But I got no further than whispering her name, when we were interrupted again. Wainwright came stumping heavily across the site, shouldering his way through and talking before he reached us.

'What the hell's going on here, Patton?' he demanded. 'A man lying by your car with his wife weeping all over him. And somebody,' he nodded to Amelia, 'going to have her battery run flat if she leaves her lights on.'

'Oh!' she cried. 'Of course. I'll get back there now.' And off she went.

Wainwright hunched down beside me, and I explained in crisp and compact detail exactly what had been going on.

'Ye Gods!' he said. 'What century are they living in here? It'll take me an hour or two to work out how many laws have been fractured, and a week to get 'em on paper.'

'I'm making no charges,' said Pauli with dignity.

'*You* aren't?' Wainwright demanded. 'You're going to get charged yourself, my lad.'

'If you must,' Pauli grumbled. He spoke to Patch, then got to his feet.

'Oh, I must. You can be sure of that.'

'Take it easy,' I said equably. 'There are a lot of much more serious charges hanging around here. Assault on Lobo – whatever his surname is – with a heavy object. Assault with a deadly weapon on Patch Ritter here. The murder of Eric Prost, and the attempted murder of Julian Caine. This is Arthur Pierce's wife, Veronica. You must know her.'

Wainwright stared at Veronica. 'I didn't recognize her. Mrs Pierce, hello. We'll have to consider these charges most seriously.'

Strangely, he sounded very gentle and soothing. But when he turned back to me his tone changed abruptly. You'd have thought I was the villain around there.

'You're saying she was the one in that car in the car-park, Patton?'

'Yes. That's what I'm saying.'

'But why? Why would she want to kill him?'

'We can go into that later. No doubt she'll have a lot to tell you.'

'Will you stop talking about me as though I'm not here!' Veronica gasped out.

'Making the most of the opportunity,' I told her. 'Very soon you won't be.'

'Clever, clever!' she hissed, as another spasm hit her. 'How long will they be? How long?'

Wainwright got to his feet. Like me, he didn't care to crouch for too long. I joined him, and he jerked his head, indicating he wanted to talk privately. We moved a few yards away, as I heard the first distant wails of sirens, saw the lights flashing in the sky.

'Look here,' said Wainwright. 'If there's anything in what you've been saying, I'm not having you questioning her before she's had the appropriate warning and been told her rights.'

'And quite proper, too,' I said approvingly.

'We've got to talk.'

'We're talking now.'

'Not here, you fool. We'll be flooded with police and ambulances in no time at all, and I want to hide somewhere . . .'

'My wife's car,' I suggested. And, 'Hide?' I asked as we walked towards it.

'I don't want to get mixed up in what's going on here until I know how it might involve her husband. Arthur Pierce,' he added, in case I'd forgotten.

'Of course it involves him.'

'Well then. I'd better hear what you've got to say. That your car?'

It was, still with Lobo there, and his wife, with Pauli squatting down and talking comforting language. But Wainwright would have something to say later about that rifle. Pauli had obviously come ahead to welcome and direct the ambulances.

We walked round them, Lobo's wife smiling wanly at me. Amelia was waiting in the Granada, again with the interior light on. We stood for a moment as the first of the ambulances lurched through the entrance, followed by a police car. Pauli

196

waved down the ambulance, and another swerved past it. The centre of their interest would be very plain to them. Wainwright turned his back, and when the following entourage of police cars had gone past he said, 'Let's get inside.'

I held open the rear door for us, Wainwright climbing in first. Amelia turned. 'I'm going to get a crick in my neck, I know it. You two carry on, and I'll just listen.'

And say nothing? No chance of that. I smiled at her as a third ambulance bounced past, and Wainwright slumped low in the seat.

'I'd have to take control,' he explained. 'Rank. And you'd sneak away.'

'We would drive away,' I admitted, 'because we are both very tired and very hungry. But, for you Mr Wainwright, we'll spare a few minutes.'

'Let's get on with it, Richard,' said Amelia. Tired and a little brisk, that was my wife.

'Right. Let's go back to the murder of Eric Prost. I got it all wrong, I'll admit that. Wrong. The wrong method and the wrong motive, and the wrong murderer. I could claim I'd been deliberately misled, but it's no excuse. I'll have a lot of apologizing to do to Caine.'

'You're saying you can now prove, positively, that he didn't kill Prost?'

'Yes. Positively. By showing you that it was Veronica Pierce.'

'In that event, he'd get a full pardon, and adequate compensation,' he said, nodding, as though that made it all right. 'But carry on. Veronica Pierce, you said.'

'At that time, she'd recently married Arthur Pierce, who was a DC. She'd been Caine's mistress, and also his partner in antique deals and frauds – but I'm not sure about that – and was probably still seeing him even after her marriage. Perhaps our Arthur had something she admired, his drive and ambition and his intelligence. Perhaps he hadn't got all she needed – Caine's warmth and sexual skill. I don't know. I'll never understand women.'

'Listen to him!' Amelia whispered.

'Whatever it was,' said Wainwright impatiently. He wasn't

197

the type of policeman to concern himself with emotional problems.

'Right,' I said. 'However it was. Veronica, in any event, was actually caught at Caine's house by his wife, Marie, who was returning unexpectedly from one of the times she'd left him. At the house! Marie took a couple of shots at her . . .'

'What!'

'Marie did. With one of Caine's target-pistols. But Veronica was in her car by then, and you can imagine she'd be away from there like a rocket. But two things are certain, one that Veronica had her own key to the house, and the other that she therefore had access to those pistols herself. But this was over a year before Eric Prost's death. It was roughly the time of Eric's wife's death, in a car accident. Somebody drove wildly from Prior Close, where Caine lives, and caused a fatal accident, then drove away. It fits neatly with the shooting incident. Veronica *would* be driving wildly. But the result was that Veronica was terrified over being identified as the driver.'

'Not too serious,' Wainwright muttered.

'No. That's what I thought. In itself, certainly not justification for Eric Prost's murder. But don't forget, Veronica was married to Arthur Pierce, and they moved into this area when he switched into the CID. I don't know where they'd been before, but suddenly Veronica had to live with the worry of being in the district and possibly being recognized by Eric Prost. With anybody else than our Arthur as a husband, that wouldn't have been too serious. But with Arthur . . . ambitious, keen to get on, intelligent . . . he wouldn't want his wife in court, being charged with having been the cause of a death. Oh no, he wouldn't. He'd kill her first.'

'Kill her?' Wainwright raised his eyebrows at me, then nodded. 'Well yes, come to think about it, the Arthur Pierce I'm getting to know would have killed her. Done something nasty, anyway. And you're saying?'

'That when she did meet Eric Prost in the town, and she knew he'd recognized her, she knew she'd have to remove him from the scene. Or face Arthur's anger.'

Wainwright grunted. 'Get on the wrong side of our Arthur,

198

and you might as well commit suicide.' He'd been thinking a lot about Pierce.

'Good,' I said.

'Good?' Amelia asked. 'What's good about it?'

'I didn't want to think that any woman could be as aggressive and deceitful and ruthless as Veronica's been, unless she had a damn good reason.'

'You great big romantic fool,' she said.

'Perhaps. But she did have her husband driving her, even though he might not have realized it. Where was I?'

Wainwright had been watching them load Lobo into the ambulance. As it turned away, Pauli came to the door and Amelia wound down her window. He said Lobo had come round, but he was going in for X-ray. Then he hurried off back to see what they were doing with Patch. Wainwright watched him go, then turned to me.

'You'd got to the bit about Arthur Pierce terrifying his wife,' he reminded me.

'Yes. And there's a kind of contradiction there. When it came to it and she needed help, she must have gone straight to him.'

'Quite natural,' said Amelia.

'If you say so, love.'

'When she needed him?' Wainwright asked. 'What for?'

'I'm coming to that. Veronica, I said, realized that Prost had recognized her. Now . . . this is what's puzzling me. Veronica, you see, was an antiques dealer, or an agent. Scouting round, that sort of thing. It was how she'd come to meet Caine in the first place, I'd guess. And there was a clock, a valuable clock that Prost owned. I'm not sure of the truth of this, but I suspect she heard about this Tompion eight-day clock from Caine, and tried to cheat Prost with a ridiculously low offer. But Caine stepped in and outbid her, or out-thought her, and bought it himself. However it was – and Caine might not be entirely innocent there – she believed Caine had cheated her. But – and this is the point – she'd have had to come face to face with Prost over this deal when she went to his house. This would be about a year after the car incident, and a month or so before Eric Prost's death. Yet it doesn't seem that he recognized her then as the driver of the car.'

Wainwright shrugged. 'She knew who he was, the man she was going to meet, and went disguised.'

'No!' I said. 'She'd never have gone near the house if she'd known Prost had been the man in the car. I reckon she must have walked in there blind and recognized *him*, and could see he half knew her, but perhaps not from the car accident. She was, as a matter of fact, decked out as a smart London dealer, and she'd hired a flash car for effect. So that would put him off. But he did see her later, coming from the side entrance of Caine's shop. He wrote to his sister saying he'd recognized her.'

'Of course!' Amelia put in. 'That's what he meant in his letter, that he recognized her as the dealer who'd tried to cheat him, and who, he thought, had been working a fiddle with Caine.'

'They thought otherwise, the Ritters. They assumed he'd seen the woman driver who caused Eric's death. But I think they were wrong. Eric saw where she'd come from, and he'd assume she was intimate with Caine, and had cheated him together. That would explain his animosity towards Caine.'

'Can we get to the bloody murder,' Wainwright grumbled.

'Very well, the murder. Veronica had her own key to Caine's house. Having already been there several times, she would no doubt have been shown the gun-room, and he would have produced the key quite casually. As he did for me. That hiding place was to deceive crooks, not friends. So she would know. When she felt she had need of a weapon, she simply waited until Caine was clear of the house that evening, then she got in and took the pistol he'd left behind. She had to remove Prost before they met again in the street, and he remembered her for what she really was. Round at Prost's house, it wouldn't have been a simple matter of shooting him through the hole in the window. She was no markswoman. No, she'd have to get in the house openly, perhaps as the same antiques dealer, return-ing to see him again about the clock. Perhaps she simply threatened him with the pistol. In his office, I'd suggest, she could best get him to write a letter of complaint to Caine by telling him that Caine had cheated both of them. Yes, I'm sure she must have presented herself as the dealer. Prost would in that way have been more likely to write what he did. Or start

200

to. In those circumstances, he wouldn't have been suspicious or even disturbed if she stood behind him, and from a few feet away she shot him in the back of the head. Then she left. I expect she'd be in a panic by that time. It's not a small thing, taking a life. She would be shocked and distressed.'

'What!' said Amelia. 'Veronica? Hard as nails, she is.'

'Yes. But she hadn't done a murder before. That was when she took her problems to her husband, threw herself on his mercy, you can say, and he helped her out. There can be no other explanation for the way the scene was rigged. The set-up was left in a condition to mislead whoever took charge of the case. Which was me. And I was misled into the assumption intended, that both shots had been fired from outside the window. *That*, you see, was the reason for the shot at the clock-face. Not to stop it, but simply to scatter glass on the floor. It would indicate that nobody could have entered or left the room after the shots.'

'Clever,' said Wainwright sourly. 'Sounds just like our Arthur.'

'Well . . . I fell for it, clever or not. It gave me a neat case against Caine, because I was looking for a marksman. That was probably what Pierce intended. After all, Caine had been Veronica's lover. She'd have had to admit that. And he could still have been. So Pierce had no reason to like Caine, and he'd have had no scruples about framing him. He left the pistol on top of the stuff in the dustbin, and that was that.'

'But he couldn't', Wainwright pointed out, 'have expected to be on the squad you took along.'

'Sheer chance,' I agreed. 'It put him on the spot to make any bright suggestions that might be necessary to lead me where he wanted, if I didn't take the desired route. He needn't have worried, though. I fell for it, and Caine got ten years in prison for nothing.'

'Hmm!' said Wainwright.

We were all three silent as the other ambulances departed. Two ambulances, two patients. But Veronica would probably go to a different hospital from Patch. They would have a police car each.

'It makes nonsense of Pierce's deathbed statement, though,'

said Wainwright. 'That early bit of finagling was very minor compared with what's been happening since.'

'Perhaps that's the point,' I suggested. 'Perhaps that was his very first distortion of the truth. He deliberately poured rainwater on that pistol, to fit in with the time shown by the clock. Eight-ten. It was raining at that time. Bright young lad, his eyes on promotion, all eager to tread the path of law and order, in the search of truth and justice . . . and he found himself making a mockery of it.'

Wainwright made a rude noise.

'All right,' I agreed. 'But he could have been that sort of romantic in those days. And then he was literally forced into an illegal action by this beautiful young wife of his. Damn it all, he'd hate himself, and he'd hate her. She'd ruined the whole pristine perfection of it. Then, once that was gone, maybe he lost heart and threw away all his beautiful beliefs, and went hell for leather in the wrong direction. And did he, d'you think, bitterly regret it? I don't know. But for all those years he'd have possessed that wife of his, she'd have belonged to him body and soul, because she'd handed herself over to him the moment she went to him for help – and the moment he agreed.'

'A bit cynical, Richard?' Amelia asked, forgetting I was supposed to be a romantic, too.

'Maybe. But don't you see how he'd have to cling to her, partly because he'd have to have somebody to punish for it, to pay, other than himself. And, I bet, for every one of his multiple crimes from then on, she'd have had to suffer. And then, in the end, what he admitted to in his statement was that tiny first indiscretion – the dustbin lid. You see, even then he wasn't telling anything near the truth. It was just enough to obtain Caine's release. Perhaps Caine was on his conscience, because it happened at the time when Pierce still had a conscience. But it's strange he said no more in his statement. No mention of Veronica. Strange.'

'Oh, I don't think so,' said Amelia. 'All it means is that he must have gone on loving her, through it all. If he hadn't, he had it in his hands to destroy her. But he didn't. He kept her with him.'

'She'd be afraid to leave him,' I pointed out.

'Exactly. That was what he wanted.' And she nodded. There! Sort that one out.

Wainwright grumbled in his throat. 'Sounds damned inhuman to me. Obscene. Like a cat, keeping a mouse alive so that it can go on torturing it.'

'Yes,' I agreed. 'But which was the cat and which the mouse? You can see that one of them would have to break in the end. It was Veronica. She could no longer live with her Arthur, and dared not leave him, because he'd seek her out for his revenge. So she killed him.'

'Eh?' said Wainwright.

'Somebody did. Try it on her. Drop it in when she's not expecting it. After all, it wouldn't be a difficult thing to do. There's a cap in the centre of the steering-wheel. Underneath, there's a nut. All you do is remove it and throw it away. *She* told me that. The steering wheel would stay in place because it's on splines, and it'd seem firm until it worked its way off. It might take some time, but it'd be sure to happen at a moment when there was a load on it. Coming out of a bend or going into one. Easy. Almost foolproof, and you don't have to watch it happen. Ask her. Trip her up. I bet she'll admit it, be proud to.'

'Richard!' said my wife. 'How horrible! D'you think she'd have waved to him as he drove away? Waved him goodbye!'

'Certainly. And if it's true that she did that, how ironical that he should have shielded her so carefully in his statement. And he did, you know. He said only enough to get Caine his freedom.'

There was silence in the car for a short period, when Wainwright broke it by slapping his knees, making a complacent sound out of it, and said, 'Well, I'll be getting along. Plenty of work to be done. Oh, they're going to love this, the big brains in London. Love it.' He smacked his lips, said goodnight although it was now day, and got out of the car. We watched him walk away. They'd have to let him keep the Pierce case now.

'Well,' said Amelia. 'Shall we go and see if there's anybody left to say goodbye to?'

'We'll go. Bet there isn't.'

I was correct. Only Daisy was at home.

On the way back to our cars we nearly tripped over the clock. There was now enough light in the sky just to reveal its shape. It had been forgotten.

'Better take it along,' I decided. It could sit beside Amelia in the Granada. 'We'll be visiting Marie and Caine again. Sure to.'

Then, in that half-light of early dawn which casts such deceptive shadows, we drove, one behind the other, not fast but steadily, home.

16

Mary was in a fine state when we arrived, having sat up by the phone all night. We all ate heartily, after she'd recovered, and I told her the eventual outcome. Then we all retired to bed. With the curtains drawn close it was possible to exclude any sense of time. Only Sheba in the whole household wasn't suffering from jet lag, and demanded her early morning walk.

At last I could take Amelia in my arms as we lay quietly, half asleep, and attempted to make our minds slow down. Only one thing seemed still to be worrying her.

'Richard,' she whispered. 'You still haven't explained about the clocks.'

'Oh . . . the clocks!' The question could have slept with us, I'd have thought. Never mind. Get it done with.

'It was Pierce, of course,' I said. 'Just imagine how it would be. Wife comes home, carrying pistol, declaring she's shot somebody. So he'd have to go and have a look at it – the situation – to see what he could do, and of course he'd peer first through the hole in the window. It would be late on that Monday night, I'd guess. I don't know where they were living, but certainly in the district, so one could assume . . . oh, say ten o'clock that night that he got there. It doesn't really matter. He'd look through the window. Desk lamp lit. Eric Prost dead, and there was the hole in the glass, dead in line with Prost's head. So he'd go inside – easy enough, I did it myself. Go inside and look for a way to protect Veronica. You asleep, my love?'

'Nearly. But go on.'

'Yes. Well . . . he'd already have all the details from his wife.

Marie away. Caine arriving home ten-thirtyish. Say it was after that time, and Pierce could see how he could do what he wanted to, and frame Caine at the same time. He could simply pick up the empty shell case from the floor, take it outside, then fire another shot through the hole in the glass, aiming at the clock-face, and leave scattered glass to indicate that the shots . . . plural . . . had been fired from outside. That made it look like a marksman's job.'

'You said that,' she murmured sleepily.

'So I have. But I reckon he would have hoped to kill two birds with one bullet, scatter glass *and* stop the clock. It would then look as though Prost had been shot at a time when Caine didn't have an alibi. Which suited Arthur fine. Only . . . one snag . . . the shot didn't stop the clock.'

'Didn't really matter.'

'No. But say he looked in again the next morning, just to check. On his way to sign in for duty, perhaps. And found that the clock had, by that time, stopped. And showing eight-ten. In the morning, though. Caine said it was due. They were all eight-day clocks, Caine told me, and he'd last wound them on the previous Sunday. But think how annoying this would be for Pierce. He couldn't get into the room again because of the glass on the floor, so he couldn't alter the clock, and its time as shown now gave Caine an alibi. And Pierce had no way of knowing whether he'd be on the case himself, to put in the odd suggestions, nor who might be in charge. It could even have been some unimaginative clod of a DI, who wouldn't see past the end of his nose.'

'And how right he was,' she murmured.

'True. But you see the point – he had to do something to make it clear that the eight-ten time was faked.'

Her head nestled beneath my chin. 'So he went through the house and stopped the other clocks?'

I could feel her voice through my chin. 'Not quite. What we've been forgetting is that the other clocks would have stopped by then, and they'd all be showing different times. This would be infuriating for him, because it added weight to the fact that the Tompion had been stopped artificially, by the bullet. It actually strengthened Caine's alibi. So Pierce had to do

206

something, and he couldn't get at the Tompion because of the glass he'd spread on the floor himself. If he started all the other clocks, he'd make it worse – better for Caine, an even tighter alibi. So the only thing left was to leave them all stopped, but all indicating eight-ten. Then at least he'd pointed to the fact of rigging, and made it look as though Caine had simply over-done his emphasis on the time factor.'

'How very devious.'

'That's how Pierce was – devious. And what a waste of time. One of the first things he'd have heard me saying was that it was clearly a faked alibi. And at that time I hadn't even seen the rest of the clocks. I didn't walk through the other rooms until after the team had packed in and left, though Pierce wouldn't have known that. *Then* I saw them. All stopped. And the impression I got at that time wasn't anything like Pierce could have guessed. It was all weird, and that was that.'

'That . . . was . . . you . . .' She'd almost gone.

'So, as the alibi had already been accepted as false, and Caine had been arrested, Pierce thought he'd better start the clocks again, in case I decided to return for a last look round, thought it strange, and began to have second thoughts about the alibi. And guess who I sent along to put the official seal on the house?'

'Arthur Pierce, of course. Now . . . can we get some sleep, Richard?'

'Sleep?' I asked. 'Who's sleepy?' And I drew her closer.